ARCADIA

A Spicy Forbidden Romance

SAINT BRYDE

DEDICATION

For readers who enjoy their romance like their wine—French, aged, and a little scandalous.

CONTENT DISCLAIMER

This is a full-length MFM romance with a guaranteed HEA. While part of a duet, this book can be read as a complete standalone.

Contains spicy, explicit scenes and forbidden relationships with **NO sword-crossing (no MM content).**

Intended for mature readers 18+.

Please note:

This story features a significant **age gap** romance between an 18-year-old woman and two men—one in his forties, and the other in his twenties—who are **father and son.**

There is a scene involving **both men intimately sharing the same partner at the same time,** including **double vaginal penetration.** But the men aren't into each other.

Includes themes of **dubious consent, drug use,** and **neglectful parental figures.**

If age differences, taboo family dynamics, or group intimacy make you uncomfortable, this book may not be for you.

FRENCH GLOSSARY

1. "Allez, monte," **Come on.**

2. "Tout va bien? Dis-moi!" **Are you okay? Talk to me!**

3. "Ne t'inquiète pas, je te tiens." **Don't worry, I've got you.**

4. "Tiens bon, on y est presque" **Hold on, we're almost there.**

5. "Tu t'es fait mal?" **Does it hurt?**

6. "Nous sommes de retour," **We're home.**

7. "Elle a dit non, Gilles. Recule." **She said no, Gilles. Back off.**

8. "Cela ne te regarde pas, Léon" **This doesn't concern you, Leon.**

9. "Je t'ai demandé de reculer." **I said, go fuck yourself.**

10. " D'accord, d'accord. Pas besoin de s'énerver" **Fine,**

fine. **No need to get worked up.**

11. "Putain de merde! Je ne peux rien voir avec cette mau-dite tempête!" **Fucking hell! I can't see anything in this damn storm!**

12. "Entre-nous" **Between us**

13. "La douleur ne se fera pas sentir longtemps, je te le promets. Reste avec moi, Tate." **It won't hurt for long, I promise. Stay with me, Tate.**

14. "Regarde-nous, Tate," **Look at us, Tate.**

15. "Regarde comme nous allons bien ensemble." **Look how good we are together.**

16. "Que diable se passe-t-il?" **What the hell is this?**

17. "La ferme." **Shut up.**

1

TATE

Mom will show up. I haven't flown all the way to Nice, France, for nothing.

I stand with my suitcase at the front of the airport, staring at the text messages on my phone. Mom said Jerome—my new stepdad—drives an old, dark-blue Ford pickup truck, so I concentrate on the kiss 'n' go zone for any sign of the truck.

But then it occurs to me that Jerome doesn't know me, and might not even be expecting me. Mom dragged me out of my final school term to go on this impromptu holiday. She's been full of surprises lately. I don't know if it's a midlife crisis or what, but first she became obsessed with technology detoxing along with health and wellness. Then she met Jerome on a business trip, and shortly afterward had a surprise wedding.

She was busting at the seams to get back to France, saying it will be good to get away from technology. To bond as a new, blended family.

That didn't sit right with me. For one, I'd never met the guy. And two, this wasn't like Mom at all. Couldn't she wait till I graduated?

But right now, my mom's not here and I don't know what Jerome looks like. She's talked to me about him. But I don't know if she's talked to him about me.

My gut twists and I draw in a long breath, closing my eyes. There's no use in getting anxious. My mom always shows up after she's wandered off, and I end up fretting over nothing. It's who she is. I school my features into calmness.

French words are thrown around me as people greet their loved ones while moving to their cars, exchanging tight hugs and goodbyes. I may not speak their language, but I can tell that's what they're saying.

I feel empty, but I can't look away.

"Tate?"

A man stares down at me, and for a moment, I can't respond. Something about tall, older men intimidates me—and this one is pushing six feet and has the muscle mass of a bull. He looks like he stepped out of the woods after working in the sun all day with his tanned skin, short, cropped, dark-blond hair, and beard. His brow is furrowed, and his green eyes are frozen on me like he doesn't believe what he's seeing. I'd guess he's in his early forties—more than twenty years older than me.

This must be Jerome. "Hi."

The line between his brow deepens. "Where's your mom?"

My throat constricts. "I thought you would know." I force the words out, finding it hard to speak against the rising panic. If she'd made other plans, Jerome would have known. I'm always the one left in the dark. "She texted me to go ahead, that she'll meet you at the country house."

Jerome looks around as if to spot my mom, but when he can't, a muscle in his jaw jumps. "Okay. If that's what she told you, we'll head to the house."

His body briefly brushes against mine and I stumble back as he takes my suitcase. My mind is spinning so much that I'm not even paying attention to my surroundings.

Jerome cocks his head toward the truck. "Go hop in. I'll put your stuff in the back."

I nod, biting my lip. I head to the passenger side and buckle in. That was embarrassing—and now I have to spend a whole car ride with someone I don't know.

I wish my mom were here.

When Jerome jumps in and starts the truck, the radio blares to life, making my nerves lessen. At least there's something to drown out the silence. He drives out into the departing traffic, slowly making our way out of the airport onto the main road.

"Does your mom always do this sort of thing?"

I almost smirk at that. Jerome doesn't know my mom if he's asking me this question. But I suppose it's hard to tell when they've only been married for three months and their relationship has been mostly FaceTime calls and the occasional weekend trip. Mom didn't even bring Jerome back to California to meet me before the wedding—just flew to Paris for a week, came home with wedding photos and a new last name.

Despite the anxiety still simmering in my system, I nod. "It's not surprising. My mom's missed my student teacher meetings a few times because she forgot to tell me she had other things on. She used to lose me in the shopping mall or supermarket as a kid, too." I twist my fingers in my lap. "The flight staff said she landed, so maybe she's taking a detour."

Jerome frowns at that, but doesn't push it further. "Has she been weird lately?"

The only thing that comes to my head is Mom wanting to bring me here.

I turn the question back on Jerome. "Has she been weird to *you?*"

He chuckles, and I notice his cheeks dimple. "Yeah, she finally took me up on my offer for you two to come." He continues in a clarifying tone, "I can barely convince Bianca to do anything. But as soon as she found out my house is in the middle of nowhere—no signal or Internet—she jumped at the offer. That's strange for you city girls."

He's right. But then I turn over what Jerome said and realize he was the one who suggested coming here to France—that he was the one who suggested bringing me along. Something in my chest swells at that, and I look at him.

Maybe Jerome's not so bad. He just looks big and intimidating. From the way my mom spoke about him, he was a gentle and passionate man. I didn't picture him to be so…gruff.

"Just because we're city girls doesn't mean we can't survive in the country," I murmur, crossing my arms and sinking down into the seat. I hate the preconceived notion that just because we live somewhere in the valley, we can't survive without our Jimmy Choo handbags or pumpkin spice lattes. "I can like, totally do that. Y'know?" I say, laying it on thick.

Jerome laughs. "We'll see. Either way, I think you'll enjoy it. I believe slowing down from our fast-paced lives is important. It gives you time to reflect and learn more about yourself."

My tenth-grade retreat in the Adirondack Mountains feels like the closest thing I can compare. We were supposed to look inward and think about what we wanted to do better in the future, but my experience was awful. None of my friends were at the retreat, and I felt so alienated from everyone else. There was no privacy in a shared bunk room as I cried in my bed, pretending to sleep.

Not something I want to feel right now.

"Do you live out there?" I ask. "Like permanently?"

"Technically it's a charterhouse, but I've been living in it for the last six months. It needed some restoration. But it's done now, so I've been building a separate cabin with my son."

I give Jerome a look. "I didn't know you had a son."

He gives me a half smile. "You'll meet him soon enough."

Jerome focuses on the road, letting our conversation dissolve. I gaze out the window, and about thirty minutes into the drive, the scenery starts to change. Gone are the skyscrapers and metropolitan streets of the city. Grass fields stretch out in a vast landscape of gentle valleys and hills. The June sun burns bright, pouring into the window, and I close my eyes. I know once I step out of the pickup truck, the chill from the AC will be dearly missed. This is the perfect weather for a swim.

The truck jolts as we begin ascending to higher ground. Among all the greenery, I spot signs of a provincial village nestled below two cliffs. A canyon crosses its center; stone buildings scatter up the cliff face a hundred meters high.

"Moustiers is the closest village," Jerome begins. "I come down for the market, but there are cafés and shops if you want to visit."

"It's beautiful," I breathe. I could think of nothing better than spending the rest of your life in a sleepy, mountainside village. It's picture perfect, like the movies.

I'd like to visit.

"I know." He smiles softly, eyes back on the road.

Once the village ends, we drive around the mountain shrouded by juniper and oak trees. The forest goes on forever, and then I wonder, how does someone live out in the middle of nowhere? Jerome can only get so many things from a food market. What about bigger things, like in an emergency or something?

I quirk a brow at him. "How rural is your place, exactly? Tell me you have hot water, please."

Jerome snickers, a knowing glint in his eyes. "Yes, princess. We have hot water. And there are no neighbors in sight—unless you count the trees."

I release a breath. Thank God. I can survive without Internet, but not without decent indoor plumbing.

Did he just call me princess? Or was he teasing me? Either way, I turn to look out my window so Jerome can't see the small smirk stretching my face.

We finally pull up a long, gravel driveway and he cuts the engine. I look out the windshield, mouth hanging open in awe.

I turn to Jerome as if he should explain why such a beautiful home is here, hidden out of sight.

Jerome only chuckles at me. "Come on."

I exit the truck, following him as he drags my suitcase to the front doorstep. It's a lot cooler out here than I expected, with the front of the house mostly shaded by oak trees. It's a long, two-story stone house, topped with red tiles. Green vines creep up beside the wooden front door, reaching to the second-story windows, which all have blue barn-door-style shutters.

The aged theme continues inside as we enter the foyer. Black and white tiles line the floor, and a wooden staircase leads up to the second level. But the walls are a pale green, almost white, with antique French molding. But I can see the paint is worn and chipping in places. I arch my chin up toward the ceiling, seeing a bronze chandelier.

Jerome eyes me from the staircase. "Not seen anything like this in America, have you?"

I blink, not realizing he was already up there. "No." I follow him to the second level. "Just in movies. How did you get this house?"

"It was my uncle's. He died some time ago, and it was passed down to me."

He continues down a hallway, sunlight pouring through the open windows. "Many old houses are isolated like this one because of Carthusian religious life in the Middle Ages. So, my ancestor might have been a monk or a priest."

We reach a door near the end of the hall and I half smile. "Do you have any ghosts?"

Jerome gestures for me to go in first, and laughs. "Not that I've seen. But I'm sure there are."

This bedroom faces the back of the house, overlooking green fields and forests in the distance. A simple wire-framed bed lines the wall opposite a brick fireplace, with exposed beams on the ceiling.

It's mismatched and antique, but in a charming way.

"Don't use that fireplace." Jerome leans against the column of it, his finger digging into parts of the brick that chip off. "It's a hazard. Just for show."

I nod and take my suitcase, leaving it by my bed. "Thank you."

Jerome gives me a sad smile. "You want to see the rest? Or would you like some time alone?"

Before I'd gotten in the car, I'd say I wanted to be alone. But now, I don't think that's true. I haven't thought about my mom since our drive here, and I fear if I have more time to think, my anxiety will get worse.

I feel a pinch in my stomach and take a breath. "Please, show me more."

Jerome leads me back into the hallway, gesturing to each room as we pass by. "Leon's bedroom, spare room, bathroom, study. My bedroom is down the far end."

He winds down the steps and turns left, entering a dining room. I'm noticing more and more that this house is refurbished only in certain places. The floorboards are old, wooden planks. There's another stone fireplace. But the walls have been freshly painted cream.

Jerome doesn't stop walking, and we reach the end of the house.

"You'll notice there's excess space. We don't really use the dining room since there's space to eat in the kitchen." He stops at a rustic island with cabinets in the center, and points out certain features. "French range cooker. You'll need help with that if you want to cook anything, but I'm usually the one who does the cooking." He opens the fridge and looks to me. "Do you want a drink?"

I haven't had anything since I was on the plane. "What do you have?"

"Water, beer, or lemonade."

"I'll take a lemonade, please."

Jerome hands me a can and shuts the fridge, circling around to the other side of the room toward a set of double doors. I follow, cracking open the can and taking a sip.

"This house has good airflow," I say, feeling the summer breeze from outside.

"Yes. I like letting the outside in by keeping all the windows open."

He briefly shows me the spare living room that occupies the other end of the house before taking me back upstairs again. He looks at me over his shoulder. "Forgot to show you the movie room."

My heart skips a beat at that. *A movie room?*

Jerome stops at the top of the landing, pulling down a string attached to the ceiling and opening the attic. I leave my can on the floor before I climb up the stairs behind him.

It's all wood and exposed rafters up here. Four small windows let some light in, but this attic is darker than the rest of the house. I can see why Jerome chose this space as the movie room. A big screen is mounted on the wall at the opposite end, and a long, plush gray couch covered in throw blankets and pillows sits before it. There's even a pool table in the middle of the room.

"You can watch satellite TV up here, but for movies, there's only DVDs," Jerome says. He points to a laptop set up on the floor near the screen with a thick case of DVDs beside it. It reminds me of growing up in the 2000s.

I nod. "Cool."

"You don't seem too impressed by that," Jerome teases, his lips tilting into an amused grin.

"What? I am impressed. I've wanted a movie room since I was a kid," I huff, and he chuckles.

"So did Leon. But he hasn't used it all that much. I like knowing it'll be put to good use by you, though," he says. His phone ringing cuts in.

As I turn to go back down the stairs, I notice how the lines of Jerome's body are taut. He stops at the stairs.

I feel my ankles shake on the steps. It's got to be my mom. "What's wrong?"

His eyes are glazed over in horror, but he blinks out of it and stuffs his phone back in his pocket. "It's nothing. Just work."

I pick up my can and take a cooling sip. Everything is fine, I don't need to worry about Mom yet. I follow Jerome downstairs into the kitchen and he makes a surprised noise. I look up and see another man come into view, sitting on one of the bar stools at the island.

"Tate, this is my son, Leon."

I can see the resemblance. Leon is a smaller version of Jerome, with dark-brown hair slick with sweat, some strands still sticking to his forehead. He must've been out working on the cabin while Jerome picked me up, because his jeans and white undershirt have patches of dirt.

Another difference between father and son is that Leon's eyes are dark blue, where Jerome's are green. Leon's hooded gaze sears my skin, his expression empty as he takes a swill of the glass of beer clutched in his hand.

What's his problem?

I give him a small smile. "Nice to meet you."

He swallows, wiping his lips. "Hey, stepsister."

His tone is mocking, but Leon directs his gaze to his dad as he finishes, seeking to get a reaction out of him. I look to Jerome, sensing him clench his jaw as he bears the response.

He breathes through his nose. "Did you work while I was—"

A girl jogs into the room from another set of doors, but her elation is cut short once she recognizes who's in the room. She stops, her smile still evident as she comes closer before sitting down beside Leon. Her damp, blue hair dangles to her collarbone, wrapped only in a white bath towel.

Jerome scowls.

Leon grins at the girl before passing her his beer to sip. His gaze flicks back to Jerome. "A little."

Jeez, I don't want to be here. I can sense there's tension and I don't want to step on anyone's toes while I'm staying here. There's nothing more awkward than witnessing family drama that isn't my own.

Jerome only grunts, turning to the front door. I don't have anything else to do, so I follow him.

When he hears me trudge up alongside him, he gives a frustrated sigh. "I would show you the grounds, but my son didn't pick up the work I asked him to do. Are you okay to explore yourself?"

"Yeah, of course. I've got to unpack, anyway, but I'll make sure to explore later," I say, stopping on the gravel driveway, watching as he continues toward a log cabin not too far from the main house. "Thanks again."

Jerome grins at me over his shoulder and turns away. I make my way back inside, and close myself in my room.

2

JEROME

I knew Bianca was a free spirit, but leaving her own daughter alone in a foreign country is fucking unacceptable. I invited both of them here so we could finally spend time as a family.

Instead, I'm left staring at a cryptic message from Bianca. The paragraph is long, explaining the reason for her disappearance at the airport, and the whole culmination of events leading Bianca to believe she needs to drop everything and seek a new life. But one particular line stands out.

She's yours now.

My face sinks into my hands. Christ, this is beyond awful. Just when I thought I'd finally found the wife I always wanted, she bails and abandons her daughter with me. My track record in choosing women is shit.

But I'm more angry on Tate's behalf. Bianca made her daughter sound like a lazy nuisance, but all I've seen is a reserved, well-mannered girl. She looked so tense when I picked her up, mouth shut in a firm line and eyes guarded as she saw me.

I know Tate wasn't exactly comfortable—aside from the issue with her mom—she'd never met me before. And I wasn't ecstatic at having to pick her up either, it's been a while since I've interacted with an eighteen-year-old girl.

It was a lot easier than I'd expected, though.

But then on the drive here, when Tate smiled at the sight of the village, a warmth spread through my body. I don't even think I've ever seen her mom smile like that. That's all Tate.

Once I saw that smile, I knew she'd like it out here. But now...

I can't tell her Bianca's just up and left; it'll crush her.

I lean against the unfinished log wall of the cabin, looking up to assess the current state of the logs. Leon and I have built the cabin using the butt and pass method, whereby the logs are stacked on top of each other and pinned tightly in the corners with no notching needed. It's a fast way to build, and I thought it'd be easier for Leon.

But Leon doesn't care. He'd rather hang out with girls than build with his dad.

I take my axe and check the current pile of logs we have, as well as the cabin logs. The last one Leon placed on top has a hump in it, so I decide to shave it off, otherwise the gap between the logs will be too big. The logs have been pretty crooked from these trees we're using, but I think it's good. It gives us time to make sure the logs are perfect.

Sweat glides down my back as I chip away at the hump.

I probably need three more logs, then I'll start the purlins and ridge beam placement.

Making sure the cabin logs are smooth, I slowly haul another one up. I use long galvanized nails to spike the logs together, and repeat the same process three times. The sun begins dipping below the trees, but I ignore it. Lost in the grind.

"That girl is such a fucking doormat." Leon's snide voice makes me turn with a flair of anger. He still has a goddamn beer in his hand, not intending to work.

"Watch your mouth, Leon," I warn. "You need to be more sympathetic."

He scoffs. "I can't be sympathetic to someone who won't fight back. That cunt you married has Tate under her thumb."

Christ, I can't even take control of my own damn kid. He's been like this ever since he graduated high school four years ago, and his mom and I stopped sharing contact. He's always preferred me over her; Amelie was too strict on him. But now, I'm starting to see why.

Leon's not supported me and Bianca from the start, and I didn't expect him to. But he can't speak about women like that. Even if he hates them.

I have to be more firm with him. It's the only way.

"I can't be sympathetic to someone who ignores the tasks they promised to do." The log I finish peeling crashes to the pile, making Leon jump. I look at him pointedly. "I didn't bring you out here so you could fuck country girls, smoke weed, and be an ass."

"You wanna build the cabin, I don't," he shouts, scowling. "You like isolation, but I don't. It's always what you want,

Dad. Why don't you get interested in what I want to do for a change?"

I want to groan. That's the whole point, spending time together so I can learn what he's into.

I can't talk to Leon like this. I wave him off, my tone aggravated. "Do what you want then."

He walks back to the house and I feel like punching a damn wall. My grandpa built cabins to bond with me. Of course, I didn't like it in the beginning, but I was never that bad.

Nothing I've planned has come to fruition. Getting married, bonding out here in the country as a family, and a girl who's now my responsibility.

Fuck. I shouldn't have organized this trip in the first place.

A shrill scream steals my attention, coming from the forest, and the hair on my neck stands on end.

3

TATE

My phone plays Lana Del Rey's "Say Yes to Heaven" as I unpack my suitcase. I figured that listening to music would distract me from my thoughts, something to make me feel sweet and warm.

It's sort of working, but I mainly feel the absence of sweetness and warmth in myself. The music is only giving me an imitation of it.

I sigh, separating my clothes into piles on the floor by tops, bottoms and dresses. If I throw myself into the task at hand, it's better than stewing in my own worries and doing nothing.

I deal with the dresses first, hanging them up in a small wardrobe. I have a hard time believing a man chose this kind of antique furniture, but what do I know about men? I don't even know who my biological dad is.

Maybe Jerome has an eye for antiques? Again, he so doesn't look like the kind of guy who would be into that.

I pack my tops and bottoms into the drawers below. Part of me does think it's no use unpacking my stuff. Realistically, I'll be out of here in a month to graduate.

Hell, I could fly out in a week and my mom wouldn't care. She's not here.

I zip up my suitcase and place it beside the wardrobe, turning to the open window as a strong breeze kicks in.

The view out my window makes my heart skip a beat. Dusk settles over the house like a painting, too perfect to be real. A flock of birds fly across the pink sky, the lilac clouds drifting, making way for the crescent moon. The hot breeze from earlier has now cooled down enough that I don't feel so overheated.

I spot a few stars twinkling to life and one shoots across the sky. When I was a kid, my grandma told me that if you spot a shooting star, you make a wish. But she also said if I ate the crust off my bread, my hair would go curly, and that never happened.

But I like to think that if you say something to the universe, it answers back. My mom might have lost me a few times, but she'd always make up for it somehow.

I close my eyes and make a wish.

Wandering downstairs, I head to the kitchen to see if anyone's preparing dinner. But when I find no one, I check the fridge and pantry. The French stove intimidates me too much, so I'll be happy with a sandwich or two for now.

"Making yourself at home already?"

I turn, finding Leon hovering at the kitchen island. He's light-footed; I didn't even hear anyone walk in.

I close the pantry, noting the tone in his voice—friendly, but veiling something else. "I wouldn't say so. I've only been here a few hours."

"That's my point. You are raiding our food."

"I'm hungry. I wanted to see what you have." I point to the stove. "I'm not going near that thing."

Leon snickers. He walks over to the fridge and pulls out another beer bottle. His Adam's apple bobs as he takes a long swallow, his eyes never leaving me.

There's something about the way he stares at me that I don't like. It's like he's judging me at a glance. If he doesn't like me, that's no skin off my nose. But put some space between us? Or don't interact with me.

I don't need his dislike on top of everything else.

"I don't understand how our parents got together." Leon shakes his head. "My dad has dated different women, and then he choses a walking red flag."

"My mom's not a bad person," I say, my voice firm. "She's just troubled. She's always been that way." Like the way she'd have two glasses of red wine before bed when she thought I was asleep. She was dealing with demons of her own.

"Keep lying to yourself. Your mom is a narcissistic bitch." He says it so cooly, like he doesn't even care.

Anger flairs within me. "You don't know her."

"I don't need to. All I need is two eyes to see the way she treats you—to hear the way she talks about you. You know what I heard her say to my dad? Tate will never make it past the fries at Burger King, it's all that girl is good for."

My mouth thins into a straight line, and pain stabs through my chest. I brush past Leon and race outside. I need to get out of the house. I need air; I need to be alone.

19

Because I'm going to fall apart.

I glance to my right, seeing Jerome peeling logs by the cabin, and I turn away before he can see my face. I gulp in the wild breeze, thinking if I just breathe, I'll be able to calm down, but it doesn't stop. My throat is locked tight, and I don't know what to do.

My feet carry me into a copse of trees a short distance from the house, the wind dying down. I wander and arch my chin up to watch as green leaves dance in the air, twirling down to the forest floor.

It's much quieter here, and I let out a shuddering breath, the tears hot and aching. Why does my mom say that to people? It's so embarrassing and demeaning. She told her friends in front of me once, and I thought it was her brand of dark humor. A one-off.

But now it's at my expense. Now it's cruel. The anxiety I felt at the airport has now molded into something fierce—years of anxiety, anger and self-loathing on top of it. I'm boiling over. I have the urge to punch something, but all I can do is clench my fist and scream.

A startled cluster of birds bursts from the trees, their shrieks echoing off the trunks.

Who am I kidding? My mom's not coming back. I've been nothing but an inconvenience to her.

I turn around a large tree, and something cracks under my foot.

My heart stops when I see a white shell. I kneel, seeing the eggshell is empty.

At least I didn't kill a bird.

"Tate." Jerome's hoarse voice is distant, but the crunch of leaves under his boots gets closer and closer.

And I slowly look up.

He's panting, his eyes round as he takes me in. "Are you hurt?"

I stand, meeting Jerome's eyes and my mouth trembles. I open my mouth to say something, but nothing comes out.

I'm hurting so much.

My mom's never asked. But Jerome seems to care, and I try to force my guard up—to give him a smile—but then his eyes soften on me with such pity that the dam inside me breaks.

"My mom's not coming back, is she?"

Jerome closes his eyes, buckling under the weight of my statement. But I don't need him to answer, his silence is confirmation enough.

Jerome opens his eyes and takes me in his arms as I cry.

4

LEON

ONE WEEK LATER

In the silver light of dawn, I twist the old doorknob to one of the side entrances to the house and meet resistance. I try again, making the door rattle on its hinges.

I'm not so drunk I can't open a damn door. My dad's locked the fucking door. The prick.

I try another door which enters into the kitchen and it's the same. My dad never locks the doors; he's never felt the need to out in the middle of nowhere.

Now he must know I've been sneaking out. Or he's fucking tired of it—of me.

But there's another way in. I'm sure the windows aren't locked.

I unlatch one of the windows at the front of the house. The blue shutters give me no trouble, but then the glass window doesn't budge.

"Goddammit," I murmur. I could crash at Leia's house to skip all this bullshit, but I've already had my fill of her tonight.

I don't think I can tolerate more of her attention. I just want to crash in my own bed.

My eyes catch sight of the trailing wisteria above the front door, the trellis beneath it leading to a second-story window.

This could work.

Testing that the trellis won't fall, I find a hold for my foot and jump up, latching onto it.

Much of the house is old, and I don't want to find out the hard way if this trellis is too. With my heart in my throat, I try to make quick work of the climb, reminding myself to not look down. Because if I do, it's over for me.

I'm panting by the time my palms reach the window ledge, praying it will open.

The tiny latch unhooks and the window opens.

"Fuck yes," I breathe, my muscles burning as I pull myself up and through the window, my feet meeting the hardwood floor.

I swallow. Thank God.

It takes a few minutes before my mind stops reeling, and I get up off the floor, treading lightly as I pad to my room.

I catch Tate's bedroom door left open ajar, and stop at the doorframe. She hasn't come out of her room since the day she arrived, and I've never seen her leave the door open.

I take a step toward my bedroom, but something compels me to close her door. I don't feel sorry for her, and I don't like that she has to sleep next to my room.

If I close it, it's like she's not here.

As I shut her door, I hear something and narrow my eyes. It's three in the morning; I doubt that Tate's awake. But then I hear it again.

Heavy rhythmic breathing.

My pulse speeds up, and suddenly my mouth feels dry. I gently let go of the knob, my feet firmly planted to the spot.

The bedsheets rustle and an unmistakable breathy whimper escapes Tate's mouth. I swallow, a bolt of heat coursing through my body, and I know it's not from the alcohol.

I shut my eyes, trying to clear my head. What the fuck am I doing? I don't even like this girl. I hate that she's here.

But my curiosity keeps me behind Tate's bedroom door. My nostrils flair as the sound of her wet pussy reaches me, and I want nothing more than to push this door open and see what she's doing. But I can't, she'll see me if I do, and I hold in a groan.

Tate's got me so worked up, and for what? She's an American valley girl and a doormat. Not my type.

But my cock swells in my jeans, and I'm suddenly unzipping them and fisting my half-hard cock as I press my eye to the gap between the hinges.

In the dark I can barely make out anything, but the subtle moonlight through her window falls onto the bed, and I see Tate lying on her stomach, an arm reaching over her bare ass as she fingers her pussy hard and fast.

I stroke my cock slowly, making sure I'm not as loud as she is. I try to match her pace, picturing that I'm fucking her from behind.

My pathetic little stepsister.

Hate-fucking Tate isn't the same as wanting to fuck her. All she does is make me angry, so this is just a way to let off steam. When I realize that difference, I don't hold back as pre-cum streams down my fist, my hips rolling into my hand and I hiss through my teeth softly.

Tate's back bows, and she shudders as she comes, her breath hitching.

As I'm on the brink, I race into my bedroom and shut the door as quietly as I can. I grab a tissue from the box on my bedside table, and spill into it, eyes rolling to the back of my head.

Fuck.

I should feel bad about coming to my stepsister, but I don't. I chuck the tissue into the trash can under my desk, and dive into my bed.

5

TATE

My sleep schedule has been so shit. I spent the first two days crying in bed until exhaustion hit me, then I'd wake up and a full day had passed. There were no tears left to cry then, so all I felt… was empty. An unwillingness to get out of bed.

I want to hide from Jerome and Leon. I feel like such an alien. These men are so outdoorsy and active, they probably find it pathetic I stay inside.

I wish I didn't care so much. I don't like how different I feel. I want to belong. I want to be accepted.

But my mom can't even do that.

Heavy footsteps into my bedroom make me stir awake, but then the curtains are pulled back and the midday sun stings my eyes. I pull the sheet up over my face.

"I know it feels like hell," Jerome says, sounding disgruntled. "But you can't rot in bed, that does no good. C'mon."

He doesn't know what this is like, my mom fucking abandoned me. And now I want to punch something again.

I do nothing, pretending I'm still asleep. Then I feel Jerome tugging the entire sheet off my body, and I lurch up.

"Hey!" I glare up at him, grabbing the sheet. But Jerome's grip is much stronger than mine, and he tears it from me.

I bite out. "I could've been fucking naked, y'know."

My cheeks burn. Using a handsy and in-your-face approach might work with boys if that's how he raised Leon. But I don't think it's appropriate between us.

Now that I've stated the obvious, Jerome takes a few steps back to the door, avoiding my gaze. But his voice is firm. "I won't take that tone from you, Tate. I waited for you to get up these past few days, but somebody had to get you out of your rut." He turns back to me, his eyes sweeping up from my pink camisole. "I've got a job for you today. Meet me downstairs."

Geez, Jerome is already making good use of me now. This is a stark difference from the man who treated me as if I were made of glass the other day. On our way back from the forest, all Jerome could do was hold me and bring me to my room. He even brought my dinner to me later that night, and the next.

I look out the window, seeing the overcast sky and the slightly muddied grass below. If we're working outside, I guess I better be prepared to get dirty.

I dress in some overalls and a sports bra, since it's still muggy despite the rain overnight. But I don't know what's in store for me, so I guess this will do.

I head downstairs, finding Jerome in the entrance hall at the front door. He's finished pulling some boots on and has another pair beside him for me.

"This is for breakfast, too," he says, handing me a warm croissant.

I take a bite as I toe my boots on, and love the warm buttery taste flaking on my tongue. I've forgotten how hungry I am. "Thank you."

I teeter on one foot while yanking on the second boot. The croissant hovers halfway to my mouth when my ankle twists, and I lurch backward. My heart leaps into my throat.

Before I can hit the ground, Jerome's hand shoots out and grabs my elbow, steadying me. On instinct, my fingers wrap around his corded forearm. His skin is warm, tanned, and scattered with light golden hair.

"Careful there," he murmurs, his French accent thicker than usual. His green eyes catch mine, and for the first time, I notice the tiny gold flecks in them.

My face burns hot. We're so close, I smell his cologne—something woodsy and masculine that makes my head spin. His broad chest is right there, and I realize my other hand has landed on it to brace myself.

"I-I'm good," I stammer, quickly dropping my hands and taking a step back. "Just clumsy."

Jerome's hand lingers on my elbow for a moment before he lets go. "Perhaps trying to put on boots while eating wasn't the best strategy?"

I laugh nervously, tuck my hair behind my ear, and devour some of the croissant. "Yeah, maybe not my smartest move."

I perch on the stairs to tug on the other boot this time, before he leads me out of the house and we walk toward the cabin. Our boots squish into the mud.

"I know it's not my business to try and tell you what to do," Jerome says. "But I don't want you worrying about your future for now, okay? Because you can stay with us as long as you like. Your mom isn't in the picture, but you're still my stepdaughter and my responsibility."

My heart warms at that, and I nod. Now that I've got something in my belly, and I'm not stuck in my dark room, my head feels more clear. "I've got my finals in August and graduation in September. I don't know what I'm going to do after that, but I definitely want to complete high school."

I cared about graduating before I came here, but the drive I had has disappeared. It's still important though, just not like before.

"Okay, I'll sort out some flights for you when we're in town," Jerome says. "Also, don't go to the village alone—or any place outside the property. No matter if it's day or night, bring me or Leon along. I know you're used to being alone, but you're in my house and those are my rules."

"I wasn't planning to get lost on my own," I say, not even knowing where to go around here, apart from the village.

Jerome smiles. "Good."

As the cabin comes into view, I stop. "You already finished?"

Unlike when I first saw the cabin, it's now got a roof and four walls, as well as spaces cut for the door and windows.

"No, she needs a paint job. That's what we're doing today." Jerome pats down the exterior wall, assessing the logs. "Just the outside. We'll put the undercoat on first."

There's a big paint can sitting on some plywood at the side of the cabin, along with two brushes. Jerome hands one to me as I finish off my croissant, his eyes lingering on my bottom lip.

"You got some here." He points to his own lips, and I quickly wipe the flakes off my mouth. Heat rises to my cheeks, and I quickly dip the brush into the paint and start working, my brows pinched together. Jerome's looking out for me. Why am I getting so flustered by him looking at me?

I'm not some lonely girl who blossoms the moment they get any attention. Jerome's my stepdad, but he doesn't feel like one. People can have kids young, I know that. But it's still disorientating how young he looks. Jerome's at least forty.

If I saw him out on the street as a stranger, I'd say he's hot.

Maybe I'm just channeling my emotions into something else. Maybe I'm just horny. But I've masturbated every time I struggle to sleep, and even then, these weird feelings don't go away.

I sigh. Attraction isn't a bad thing if I don't act on it, I guess.

The pungent chemical smell of the undercoat hits me, and I grimace, bearing the stench. But as I paint each log, I find myself getting lost in the work. In school, I'm so used to staying in my own head, trying to think math problems through, or analyze a book.

Doing something with my hands feels nice. But it'll be even more exciting to paint some color on the cabin.

Then I think back to the antiques around the house, and call to Jerome. "Do you choose the furniture in the house? Or do you hire a designer?"

When he rounds the corner of the cabin, I get an eyeful of his shirtless torso. He's also covering the lower part of his face with a bandanna, eyes squinting from the smell. "Some are passed down from family, but otherwise I choose them. Why do you ask?"

"You have a good eye." I smile. "I mean, most of the houses I've seen keep getting turned into modern show homes. You haven't refurbished much of the place either."

"That eye comes after decades of practice. I'm a contractor, and this house is a piece of history. Old furniture and antiques give it character. And as you said, things are more modern now, and people miss the past. So, a holiday rental like this will be exactly what travelers want." Jerome glances my way. "Do you have any pointers?"

"No." I contemplate. "But I think the movie room is too dark. Maybe fairy lights?"

He chuckles like he can't take my answer seriously, and I can't help but feel defensive about it. Before I can talk back, he says, "That's not a bad idea. I'll hold you to that."

We spend the whole morning painting. By lunchtime, Jerome drops his brush on the plywood and takes me to the kitchen where he dishes out leftovers of beef bourguignon, the tender meat falling apart in its rich red wine sauce.

I dig in. The savory depth of flavor is incredible, pairing well with the crispy ham and cheese croquettes.

31

"Is there any more work to do?" I ask, wiping crumbs off my mouth.

Jerome quirks a brow at that. "You want more work?"

I nod.

He leans back against the stool's headrest, his eyes wandering in thought. "I won't have any more work for you until tomorrow. Maybe you could think of things you want to get from the village? Write them down; we'll go this week."

Well, I know I'll need more toiletries, but apart from the basics, I don't need much else. Then Jerome's words from the car ride come back to me. I believe slowing down from our fast-paced lives is important.

Maybe it's a matter of finding more things to enjoy. This is a holiday, after all. But what do I enjoy? I like watching movies, but everyone likes that and I can't buy movies from a provincial village.

I nod at Jerome anyway. I'll have to brainstorm more later.

Once we finish eating, Jerome announces he's going out to meet a friend of his, and asks if I'll be fine on my own. I still need to explore this place, so I smile and nod.

When I watch his truck leave, I feel the anguish from this morning creep in, but I quickly brush it away. I can't depend on Jerome to make me feel good.

Instead, I head upstairs to the bathroom. My overalls are muddy, and I'm pretty sure some of the undercoat is on me.

The bathroom door is ajar, and I push through without stopping.

Leon stands at the vanity. His lean torso sparkling from a fresh shower, a towel hanging low on his hips as he brushes his teeth. He gives me a look from the corner of his eye like I'm not supposed to be here.

I forgot there's only one bathroom.

Why the fuck does it have to be so awkward every time I see him? It's making me hate him more.

"Uh, you left the door open," I explain in a quiet breath.

Leon only stares at me before turning back to the mirror as if I'm not there. He doesn't hurry as he spits into the sink and cleans his mouth. God, this asshole... If I could shower somewhere else, I would. I can see Leon doesn't like sharing space. I don't either.

But stop making it so unpleasant. I hate feeling like I'm in someone's way.

By the time he's done, I've taken on a defensive stance. Arms crossed, I stare daggers at him as he passes me without a word. He looks like he barely had enough sleep, and as he steps into the sunlit hallway, I make a point of slamming the door shut.

★★★

I march out of the house in a white dress, clutching my hat to my head so it doesn't fly away with the wind. The sun hasn't burned away the cold mud from the rain yet, so I still sport the boots Jerome gave me.

I decide to circle the house first, since I haven't explored the back of the property. The gravel pathway runs to the back,

33

where a table and iron chairs are setup. In an open field of grass, there's a pool, a long distance away from the house. But when I get closer, I realize it's a really old pool, the inside made of stone, with a little fountain spewing water on the edge.

The land slopes from here, perched above the valleys intersecting below. Apart from the house itself, this view has to be the selling point. It didn't look so… expansive from my room. But standing here out in the open, I feel so small.

I remember exploring the forest at the family lake house with my cousins when I was little. The simple pleasure of discovering everything around me is something I've not experienced again till now. Because there was never another opportunity to.

I spread my fingers as I brush the long field grass, turning into the forest.

Birdsong echoes and I look up, watching out for birds and other animals in the trees. Our house in the valley isn't surrounded by nature like this; it's surrounded by other houses and empty plots of land, not much else.

But this place is buzzing with life.

I sit down against an oak tree trunk, watching the sunlight twinkle through the canopy, the wind rushing in my ears.

This would be the perfect spot to read—there are no distractions out here. And with a pillow at my back, it would be even better.

I've only been reading books for school the past few years. But it'd be nice to fall into one for pleasure. I'll try to find a book in the village, if there are any. But I doubt there'll be any in English.

A loud clicking sound brings my attention back to the house. I frown and sit up, wondering what it is, but then I spy Leon pushing a bike onto the driveway. He's dressed in a cream linen shirt and shorts, his dark-brown locks curling out from under a black cap.

Where's he going?

Part of me wants to go up to him and ask if I can join him—despite the awkwardness of it. I don't like Leon, but I don't have anyone else to show me around right now. Once I get my bearings, I can travel from place to place without asking for help.

Gaining my feet, I make my way to the forest opening, but then something hits my collarbone, skittering against my skin.

I scream.

My hands fly around, knocking the spider off me. I run out, losing my hat, and feel the bile rise in my throat.

Leon's seated on the bike, looking at me like I'm crazy. "What the hell?"

My heart races and I feel all around my body, paranoid it's still on me. "A spider fell on me."

Just when I thought the country was so beautiful and tranquil.

A slow smirk spreads across Leon's face. "Thats what you get for lying against a tree."

The adrenaline coursing through me makes the question rush out. "Can I come with you?"

I don't want to be alone after that.

Leon pushes off onto the road. "No."

The rejection hits me flush in the face. There's not a lick of politeness in this guy, and it almost makes me want to cry.

But the hurt makes me bold and I call out, "Why?"

I watch him ride past the trees, not acknowledging my question. Anger flares within me. I'm not going to be ignored like this. I quickly scan the garage for a spare bike, and find one leaning against the wall inside.

I haven't ridden a bike in… forever. But I'll take my chances to get that asshole to acknowledge me.

My heart races as I ride up the slight incline, my steering wobbly. Leon's figure is a smaller speck in the distance, but I follow him, gaining speed.

The hot summer breeze billows my hair, and I flick the bell, trying to get his attention.

Leon looks briefly over his shoulder, mutters something, and instead of slowing down, he speeds up.

"Leon, stop being a dick," I whine.

The road begins circling around the mountain, getting steeper. I don't know if it's the tires or the rocky gravel on the road, but my bike gets wobblier and my stomach twists. What if a car comes by and I can't control the bike?

I'm fighting a losing battle here. Leon's already disappeared from my line of sight, and I have no idea where I'm going.

"Leon," I shout, my voice swallowed by the wind.

The bike jolts and suddenly I'm veering off to the left. I try to brake, but I tip over and land at the lake's edge.

ARCADIA

My bike wheels click in the air, and I'm half submerged in murky, muddy water. "Shit."

Water sloshes in my boots as I trudge out of the lake, and I sit on the bank to empty them. The air stings my knees and I see fresh red grazes.

At least I didn't break a bone.

The embarrassment of the accident comes rushing to me, and I look both ways down the road to see if anyone noticed—if Leon noticed. I must've looked so stupid veering off into a lake.

But there's no one, not even Leon.

I sigh, a different kind of hurt making my throat tighten. I've got no choice but to head back to the house.

With my wet feet squeaking in my boots, I pull the bike out of the lake and walk back the way I came, the wind chilly against my skin.

6

JEROME

"You don't seem too concerned about your wife, Jerome," Carson bites out, holding nails between his teeth as he prepares to nail a horse's shoe.

I've driven out to Carson's farm, my longtime friend, thinking I'll get someone to confide in. But instead, Carson seems unsympathetic.

My tone comes out defensive. "Of course I care about Bianca. I've been in shock this past week."

"Yeah, but that's not what the police will think," he says, aligning the nails with the holes and hammering them into the shoe. "I've watched enough true crime shows to know that the victim is always murdered by someone they know, and you're the number-one suspect."

I murmur a curse under my breath. Carson's right, and now I look like a fucking idiot. The police did cross my mind when I received Bianca's text, but then what if she realized it was a big mistake and came back? I didn't know how to judge it, and on top of that there was Tate to deal with.

When I don't respond, Carson sighs, finishing his work before looking me in the eyes. "Look… Even if Bianca isn't in danger and has decided to go somewhere, you need to file a missing person report."

***

His words echo in my head as I pull into my driveway and jerk the handbrake. I'll need to take Tate to the station tomorrow and file the report.

When I get out of the truck, I notice a girl on the road.

I stop and watch her walk from the road, trailing a bike. It's Tate, her long blond hair damp and sticking to the naked skin of her shoulders. Her dress molds to her body as water drips down her muddied legs.

This wasn't what I'd expected, but it makes me grin. I'm glad to see she's stretching her legs and not cooped up in her room. My voice comes out amused. "I see you found the bikes."

But as she stops before me, I realize a little too late that her dress isn't just molded to her body.

It's see-through. She has an arm folded around her chest.

"Don't laugh." Tate sulks.

I hold up my hands, avoiding her gaze as she moves to the garage. "I'm not laughing."

I'm doing something much worse. The vision of Tate's skin showing through the fabric flashes across my eyes.

When she leans the bike against the wall inside the garage, she bends down to check something and I quickly turn away, but not before getting an eyeful of her ass visible under the white fabric.

Jesus fucking Christ. She walked home like this?

I clear my throat. "So, you're not going to tell me what happened?"

Tate straightens and faces me, her arms crossed. "I went for a bike ride, and fell in the lake that way." She nods in the general direction to the side of the mountain.

The lake is a fair distance away from the house. I don't want Tate traveling that far by herself. "What did I say about traveling alone, Tate?"

And she walked back home practically naked. What if someone kidnapped her? Or worse?

My blood is boiling.

"I'm sorry I was trying..." She sighs. "Never mind. Do you have Band-Aids?"

With the way Tate trailed off, she sounds... disappointed. And I know it's not because she fell in a lake.

There's something she's not telling me.

Did she mess around with someone out here? Like Leon does? Tate doesn't seem like that kind of girl, but when it comes to grief or pain, anyone can self-medicate with drugs, alcohol or sex.

I close my eyes, pushing down the anger rising within me. Tate's not done anything to provoke me except ride out alone, and I've got to be gentle and patient with her.

"Yes, we do," I bite out, entering the house. "But get yourself cleaned up first."

I race upstairs and into to my bedroom, closing the door. My eyes suddenly feel heavy as I sit on the bed and toe off my boots. My morning started off great, but come this afternoon, I just can't shake this shitty mood and I don't know why.

Bianca is definitely a reason. But Tate... I'm trying to keep her safe. Seeing her break down in the forest a week ago tore my heart in half.

Then my mind conjures an image of her washing the mud off herself in the shower. The water cascading over her delicate shoulders, the steam rising around her—

Fuck. It's stirring something deep inside that I haven't felt in years. I wipe a hand over my face, a heaviness in my chest overcoming me. Tate's my stepdaughter; I can't be fantasizing about her. But being with Tate, it's like I'm reliving those old days, feeling that spark of wild youth.

Or perhaps I'm jealous of it.

I grab my phone, dial Bianca's number and hold it to my ear. *Please, pick up.*

I married Bianca because I felt we were a good match. Maybe not romantically, but practically. I'm old enough to know relationships aren't just a fun, crazy rush of hormones all the time. You have to enjoy each other at your most mundane, and Bianca was that. She seemed like a safe option, and the sex wasn't bad.

But in all my relationships, it always felt like something was missing, and I still don't understand what that is.

I've given up on trying.

Bianca's voice mail reaches my ears. *Dammit.*

I strip out of my paint clothes and change into something more comfortable—a loose pair of jeans and a black t-shirt. I pad downstairs into the kitchen, switching the lights on as night rolls in.

I get the dough out of the fridge and set it down on the chopping board. Since we can't order pizza out here, I've learned how to make it myself.

Flattening the dough with a rolling pin, I spread the pizza sauce on top before drizzling olive oil, sprinkling some salt, grating the parmesan cheese, and adding the mozzarella.

Is Tate even a fan of pizza? I should've asked her what topping she likes. Leon and I usually have pepperoni or meat, but I think cheese is the safest option tonight.

I sprinkle the basil on top when footsteps enter the kitchen.

"I tried searching the bathroom cabinets but I couldn't find them." Tate comes up beside me, dressed in her pink pajamas.

My mind is blank. "What?"

"The Band-Aids," she says.

"Oh." I turn to one of the upper cabinets next to the stove and pull out a first aid kit. "That's because they're here. Are you happy to eat cheese pizza?"

She takes the box and begins sifting through its contents. "Yeah, I like pizza."

"Okay, good. If you were lactose intolerant this would've gone real bad." I chuckle, placing the pizza into the oven. "Have you seen Leon?"

I turn and see Tate's now sitting on the bar stool, her scraped knee up to her chest as she peels a fresh Band-Aid and places it on the wound. "He was bike riding."

Bike riding means he's gone to the village to see his friends. He could've at least told me if he'd be back by dinner.

"Were you bike riding with him?" I ask.

Tate shakes her head, and I narrow my eyes in thought. If Leon saw Tate and didn't offer to show her the village, I'm going to be pissed.

I know he doesn't like things getting in the way of his freedom.

"You can be honest with me—was my son being a dick?" I look Tate in the eyes.

She still shakes her head. "No."

Okay, well I tried.

Tate puts her knee down and passes me the box. "Thanks."

I put it away, and begin cleaning up the mess I made, Tate watching me.

It makes the skin on my neck prickle. Isn't she going to go off into her room or something? I'll admit I'm not used to my son always being around, and now that Tate's here lingering around me, I'm realizing just how distant we've become as father and son.

"Why don't you get the TV ready upstairs?" I suggest. "We can watch something and have dinner up there."

"Sure." Tate hops off the stool before grabbing a lemonade from the fridge and racing upstairs.

She just does what I ask, so different from Leon. I huff and grab a beer out of the fridge.

Twenty minutes later, the timer on the oven goes off and I spin to get our dinner out. I cut the slices, leaving two for Leon in case he makes it home before wrapping them up and putting them in the fridge.

I'm careful not to drop the pizza on my way up the ladder to the attic. The only light in the room comes from the projector screen and a tall lamp beside the couch.

"That smells good," Tate coos from the couch. "I've found a movie you might know."

I set down the plate onto the coffee table, grabbing a piece before settling down on the other end of the couch. "I'm listening."

Tate tears off a piece. "I'm not telling you; you'll see it for yourself."

Suddenly, an iconic piece of suspenseful music plays in an underwater scene, drawing closer to a boy's legs when he's dragged under water.

I haven't seen this movie since it came out. "*Jaws*."

Still chewing a mouthful of pizza, Tate smiles and nods.

"I didn't think anyone your age was watching these movies?" I say, curious. I think I tried showing *Gremlins* to Leon when he was little, but it just made him cry, and all my favorite movies from the eighties have a weird brand of horror.

"I've seen some," she says. "I like any movie with Robin Williams or Patrick Swayze."

"Ah, yes. Two very good movie stars," I say. "That's the main difference between movies now and back then. Actors became movie stars, whereas nowadays anyone can be an actor."

Tate nods. "I understand. It was harder back then to get into the industry."

We eat in silence for the next hour, watching *Jaws*. I sip my beer, engrossed in the movie, when Tate folds her legs up onto the couch.

"This is why I hate the beach." She cringes, watching the massive great white shark sinking the boat.

I laugh under my breath. "Sharks that big don't exist."

"Sure, but I still don't want to go where normal sharks swim. Any large body of water where I can't see the bottom freaks me out thanks to this movie."

So, she has seen it before. "Would you like me to change the movie, princess?" I ask, grabbing the remote. "If this is too scary, I can change it."

Tate's eyes narrow on me, her lip pouting. "I can handle it."

I can't help but grin. Giddiness isn't something I've felt in a while, it's refreshing.

Tate speaks up again. "You can't lie that some of these movies unlocked new fears in you. Don't you have any?"

I think for a moment. "Snakes and the wicked witch of the west."

Tate cocks her head at me. "The wicked witch of the west?"

I shiver. "She terrified me as a kid." I hate *The Wizard of Oz* because of her.

Tate laughs and I find myself chuckling along with her. I normally wouldn't admit that to anyone, even Bianca, because I thought she'd say I was stupid. But Tate's not like that. I've forgotten how nice it is to be around someone like this... just being in easy company.

Shit, I'm lonely.

"Don't tell anyone I'm scared of the wicked witch of the west," I warn.

She mimes zipping her lips shut. "Your secret is safe with me."

★★★

The next morning, we enter the reception area of the police station and a woman at the front desk greets us.

"What's the reason for your visit today?" she inquires in a pleasant voice.

I clear my throat. "My wife's gone missing."

"I'll get one of our officers to take your statement. Please follow me."

I trail behind the receptionist with Tate. The station is fairly small as she takes us down a short corridor and knocks on an office door. She quickly informs the officer of our arrival and he calls us inside.

"Hello sir, what's your name?" The officer's face is stuck in a stern expression as he gestures for us to sit.

"Jerome, and this is Tate." I look to Tate as she sits in the leather chair beside me.

She smiles meekly at the officer and speaks in French. "Hello."

The officer nods and turns briefly to his computer, clicking a few things on the screen. "I'm going to interview you and put all the details into our database. What is your relationship to the missing person?"

"Bianca is my wife. And Bianca is Tate's mother," I say.

The officer nods, typing. "What's Bianca's full name and date of birth?"

"Bianca Louise Beaumont. The 5th of August, 1975."

"Can you give me a physical description?"

"She's Caucasian with long black dyed hair. American, brown eyes, fit... I don't know her exact height but she'd be around five-foot-seven."

"Do you remember what Bianca was wearing the last time you saw her?"

"I don't know." I turn to Tate, switching to English. "Do you remember what Bianca was wearing the last time you saw her?

Tate takes a moment to recall. "She was wearing a white satin blouse and blue jeans...black sunglasses. She also had a brown Luis Vuitton suitcase."

I translate her words to the officer and he types some more before turning to a scanner. "Do you have a photograph?"

"I don't have a physical one, but I could email you one?"

"Yes, we can do that." He gives me his email and I quickly send a selfie Bianca took while we were out in Paris one night.

"Do you know her last known whereabouts?" the officer asks, scanning from me to Tate.

I repeat the question to Tate, and she brings her attention to the officer.

"My flight landed before my mom's. When her plane landed, I looked everywhere but couldn't find her. Then when I asked the flight staff, they said my mom had boarded the plane. But then she texted me to meet her at Jerome's house."

I repeat her information to the officer and add, "We took Bianca's word for it, but it's been a week now since she left the airport.

"Okay, but when did you physically last see Bianca, Tate?"

I translate the officer's words again.

"The morning we left for Nice. We hung out at the airport until I boarded my flight first," Tate clarifies.

The officer stops typing and arches a brow at me. "Why did you not report this sooner?"

"Bianca's always been… flighty. Tate wasn't surprised that Bianca had wandered off," I answer. "But then I received this text message from Bianca." I know the officer can't read English but I hold out my phone for proof. "She said that she was sick of her life, and wanted to leave everything behind. Even her daughter."

"Take a screenshot and send that in an email," he commands.

I shoot off the screenshot in an email, and watch the officer silently as he focuses on his computer screen, clicking and tapping away.

After a short wait, he turns the screen to face me. "This will be the official missing person's report for your wife." He points to a series of numbers listed at the bottom of the document. "For any follow-up inquiries, you need to remember this reference number."

I nod, typing it into my notes app.

A printer behind the officer whirs to life and he turns to gather the documents. "I'll need you to review and sign that all this information is correct."

He passes me Bianca's report and I scan all the information Tate and I provided, and nod, grabbing a spare pen sitting on the officer's desk.

"What should we expect from here on?" I ask, handing the officer the signed report.

"Thank you. As for what to expect, we'll look at surveillance footage from the airport and expand from there. But we'll need your contact information as well, for updates on the investigation."

I give the officer my phone number, email and address. When he stands from his desk, Tate and I follow.

"We'll do our best to find your wife and mother," the officer says with a small smile, looking from me to Tate.

"Thank you," she answers quietly.

He holds the office door open for us, but before I can step through the threshold he says in a lower voice, "If your daughter is struggling, I'd recommend checking out Red Counseling and Therapy in Manosque."

The word daughter makes me cringe, but I bear his response with a quick nod. "Will do. Thank you, officer."

Tate is the first one to make it back to the car, and I can sense the damper on her mood.

I fire up the ignition and look at her slumped in the passenger seat. "I'm sorry for putting you through that."

She shakes her head. "It needs to be done. And I couldn't understand a word that was said, so it wasn't bad."

But it still makes Tate think of her mom. The radio fills the silence in the car as I drive out of the police station. Tate leans her head against the window, her eyes vacantly staring out at the fields.

I hate this. It's like she's retreated back into her shell.

Instead of taking the left road that leads back to the house, I veer right. I need to get Tate's mind off Bianca.

"Did you make your list?" I ask.

"What list?"

I laugh. "So that's a no."

I can feel Tate's eyes on me, confused and annoyed.

"You said you wanted to see the village," I clarify, giving her a grin.

7
TATE

The air smells of freshly baked bread and lavender as we exit the truck. At first, it's a steep walk up to the village. The cobblestone path winds between clusters of rustic buildings with pale shutters, some even have beautiful flowers crawling up to their roofs.

When the ground levels, we're inside the town square. Vendors hawk their wares and children laugh as they run through the crowds lining the market stalls.

"I need to restock on some food." Jerome holds up the two net bags he brought. "Then we can see the shops if you like?"

I nod. It's better than staying home after this morning. The cop had a discriminating look about him, and I didn't like it at all during the interview. Jerome and I are automatic suspects to him, and it just makes me so angry.

If they knew what my mom was like, they could understand why I'm so cold about her.

I follow Jerome as he slowly makes his way past the stalls. We spend time looking at the fresh produce. Plump sun-ripened tomatoes, soft peaches, and glossy cherries. Something about them being homegrown makes them look so much better than the ones from the supermarket.

"Is there anything you want?" Jerome asks as he bags the tomatoes he bought.

I smile. "I'm good for now. You don't need to worry, I've got French money."

"You're under my roof." He says it like it justifies his reasoning. "You'll run out of money fast if you're buying this stuff. Save it for your souvenirs. I'm happy to get you anything you need."

"Thank you, but I'm fine." I walk past Jerome to see what the other vendors are selling. I spy dried herbs and lavender, as well as pastries and sweets. When I turn to look at the shops in the buildings, I'm drawn to what looks to be an artisanal shop. Ceramic plates line the front with beautiful blue and white designs. My grandma used to have fine china like this; no one could ever use it, only look at it locked away in a cabinet.

I head inside the shop to find that there's not only earthenware, but all kinds of nicknacks. Crystals, art books, yarn, and small home decor.

Browsing down an aisle of notebooks, I find one that catches my eye and pick it up. It's not leather bound like the others around it, instead it's made of white crochet and embroidered with flowers.

It's pretty, but I don't know what I'd put in it.

"Hey," Jerome calls to me, heading down the aisle. "Did you buy anything?"

"No." I place the book back on its shelf. "Just looking. How did you do with the food?"

I follow him out of the shop. "Good. There was no goat cheese, but I found a replacement. I'm making a platter tonight."

Jerome is very creative with his choice of food. "That sounds very French."

"Cheese, wine, and baguette." He grins. "No, not just those. But I thought you might want to try something French that wasn't a croissant or frog legs."

As we turn back into the market, something catches Jerome's eye and we stop at a stall. Zoning out, I scan the town square. I meet eyes with Leon.

Shirtless and with a gold chain around his neck, Leon's resting at the fountain in the square, biting into a juicy peach. When he realizes it's me, he pulls away from it, mouth glistening, and smirks, licking his lips.

My heart skips a beat and I frown, turning away. I don't want to give Leon the time of day, but I do want to get him in trouble. He didn't come home last night.

I tug on Jerome. "Leon's here."

A splash makes both of us snap our heads in one direction. Children laugh as they're drawn to the fountain, and Leon peeks up behind the lip before stumbling up to his feet, saturated.

Did he just try and hide in the fountain?

"What the fuck is he doing?" Jerome protests, and I can't help but snort. I watch as he heads for Leon with a determined stride. "Quit avoiding me, Leon. It's about time you come home."

When Jerome tries to help Leon out of the fountain, Leon pushes his hand away, murmuring angrily at Jerome. They exchange a few tense words I can't hear, but I assume Jerome is ordering Leon back home.

Leon stays in one spot as Jerome turns away. Leon's gaze hooks on me with razor-sharp eyes, and I know then that I've successfully ruined his day.

I smile at him and he flips me off.

"We'll have to see the shops another time," Jerome announces, anger still lingering in his voice. "I'm sorry."

"That's okay," I chirp, taking one of his bags. "I'm ready to go home."

Instead of driving with us, Leon took his bike, not caring for the thunder rumbling in the distance. He doesn't say a word to me at dinner, in fact he ignores me, eyes never straying my way. Not even when I'm talking to Jerome.

"You look so tired." I break the ice, and Leon pauses, looking up from his plate full of leftover pizza. "What did you get up to in the village?"

The question is innocent, but I know Leon isn't the type to open up easily. Especially with his dad around.

I want to push him more.

Leon's eyes flick between Jerome and me before taking another bite of his pizza slice. "Partying."

"The usual group?" Jerome asks.

Leon casts his gaze to his plate. "Yeah."

The silence is thick as we eat. Seeing this family have dinner, I realize Jerome and Leon have some distance between them. Not in a neglectful way, like with my mom, but it's like they don't know how to be around one another.

Once I'm getting ready for bed, the unspoken grievances between me and Leon make me restless, and I know I won't be able to sleep unless I address him now.

I can also smell weed, and it's coming from outside my window.

When I peer over the window frame, I see Leon smoking a blunt. He recoils when he notices me from the corner of his eye. "Merde."

"Don't walk away." My command makes him stop in his tracks. "I want to talk."

"What every guy wants to hear," he remarks.

"You hate my mom and that means you must hate me. But I'm not her. The other day, I rode after you and fell in the lake and you didn't even think to check if I was ok."

"I didn't know, and I told you not to come."

Regardless, I think someone would at least look back to check if the person riding behind them disappeared.

"You didn't want me to come," I counter.

He laughs through his teeth and shakes his head. "You can read my mind, can you? Fine, I didn't feel like bringing you along. Are you happy? Is that what you wanted to hear?"

A rush of anger surges to my brain. "Why?"

Leon takes a long drag of the blunt, considering me. "Why are you so agitated about this? You need one of these." He flicks the blunt in his fingers.

I can't find the words to speak. Leon's telling me to calm the fuck down, and that what he did was nothing.

I stare at the blunt and for a split second, I consider it. Leon's driving me so crazy, I'm actually considering it.

The chemicals in my brain burn and bubble. All I can respond with is a laugh before slamming the window shut.

I slump in my bed and scream into the pillow.

***

A deafening crack jolts me awake. Thunder crashes, shaking the walls around me, and my heart pounds. The room flickers between black and white as lightning flashes outside.

I pull my knees to my chest, counting the seconds between thunder and lightning like I used to as a kid.

One, two, thre—

Another boom shakes the house before I reach three.

The storm's right on top of us.

Rain pelts against the glass like someone's throwing handfuls of pebbles. Through the flashes, I catch glimpses of tree branches whipping violently in the wind outside.

My phone says it's 3:27 AM. The battery's at 12 percent—I forgot to plug it in before bed.

ARCADIA

A particularly bright flash makes me flinch. The thunder follows instantly, so loud it feels as if it's splitting my skull. The power flickers on once, twice, then dies completely.

Great.

Each new sound makes me jump, my nerves fraying further with each passing minute. Sleep feels impossible with nature's fury raging outside my window.

Voices drift through the walls—low and urgent. I recognize Jerome's deep timbre and Leon's sharper tone, though I can't make out their words.

I slip out of bed, bare feet silent on the wooden floor. The hallway's pitch black, but another flash of lightning shows me Leon and Jerome standing together in conversation.

"Awful way to wake up, huh?" Jerome says as I approach, his hair bed tousled.

I nod, still too sleepy to speak. I glance at Leon, and he too looks barely awake.

"Check the fuse box," Jerome says to Leon, his tone low but urgent.

"Dude, it's not the fuses." Leon's voice comes out gravelly. "I'll go check the generator."

"Tate." Jerome gestures toward Leon as he heads down the stairs. "You follow him and check if he's right. Because I'm certain he's not, and he'll need help. I'll check the fuse box."

I close my eyes and sigh, but I don't have the energy to complain.

On my way down, I spot a raincoat and a spare pair of boots near the back entrance and put them on before following Leon out through the downpour. Even then, the rain soaks through my thin pajamas in seconds. Lightning illuminates the path ahead as we sprint toward the generator shed behind the house.

Leon yanks open the metal door and we stumble inside the cramped space. The generator sits in the darkness, silent and useless. Water drips from Leon's hair as he crouches beside it, his raincoat clinging to his shoulders.

"Hold this." He hands me his phone to use as a flashlight.

I aim the beam where his hands work, watching as he pops open a panel with practiced ease.

I break the silence. "Why are you checking the generator first? Isn't it normally the fuses?"

Leon glances at me with a slight smirk, keeping his focus on the generator. "The fuse box? Please. It's usually the easy fix. But I know generators. I've dealt with them before. Trust me; it's probably just a fried starter. Just part of the routine."

I arch an eyebrow, curiosity piqued. "You sound like you've done this a few times."

"More than a few," he replies, his voice confident. His fingers trace along wires and connections, checking each component methodically. "You don't want the house to go dark in a storm like this, and I'd rather fix it myself than wait around for someone else to do it."

"Why not let Jerome handle it?" I ask, genuinely questioning.

His eyes flicker up to meet mine, and I catch that gleam of pride. "Because I can. Didn't you want to see me do something besides just party all the time?"

I pause, considering that. "Yeah, I guess I did."

He looks back at the generator, and a small smile tugs at his lips. "Well, let me do my thing."

Leon pulls tools from a nearby shelf—wire strippers, electrical tape, a multimeter. His movements are quick and precise as he strips back insulation and bridges connections. The confidence in his hands is mesmerizing.

The generator sputters, then roars to life. Leon's smile widens as he closes the panel, clearly pleased with himself. The lights flicker on in the main house, casting long shadows through the shed's doorway.

"Not the fuses after all," he says, cocky grin playing on his lips as he looks back at me.

***

When I wake up, the sun is well above my window and I realize it must be lunchtime. I couldn't sleep last night, not after going to bed angry, one of the worst feelings in the world.

Second to being abandoned by your mom.

I head downstairs, still in my pj's and bed hair, fishing some cereal out of the cupboard when someone clears their throat.

"Morning Tate," comes the deep baritone of Jerome's voice, and I turn, seeing him and Leon seated at the dining table by the windows. Leon's finishing off an apple core.

"Morning sis," he says through a mouthful.

"Uh, morning. Sorry I didn't see you two there," I say quietly, still waking up.

"Leon wants to tell you something," Jerome announces, sitting back firmly in his chair. He looks to Leon and Leon doesn't miss a beat.

"My friends and I are going to the gorge. You can come if you want?"

There's no doubt in my mind that Jerome is forcing him to say this, so instead of feeling excited about the gorge, I just nod my head. "Sure."

Forty minutes later, I'm standing awkwardly by the front door, watching a beat-up van pull up to the house. The squeal of brakes cuts through the quiet afternoon, and I can feel my heart racing. I'm not sure if it's excitement or anxiety.

Leon strolls past me, his shoulder brushing mine as he heads toward the van. I follow, trying to ignore the weight of unfamiliar gazes on me. As we approach, the side door slides open with a rusty groan.

"Allez, monte," Leon says, gesturing for me to get in.

I climb into the van, the smell of stale cigarettes and pine air freshener hitting me as I settle into one of the single seats. Leon hops in after me, taking the seat directly across. His friends chatter in rapid French, their words flowing over me like water.

Leon reaches into his pocket and pulls out a blunt, twirling it between his fingers. He leans forward, exchanging a few words with the guy in the passenger seat. Their voices are low, conspiratorial, and I can't help but feel like an outsider.

Suddenly, the blond guy in the front twists around in his seat, flashing me a bright smile. "Hey there! I'm Gilles," he professes in accented English. "Welcome to our little adventure crew."

I open my mouth to respond, but before I can get a word out, Leon cuts in.

"This is Tate," he says, his tone flat. "She's staying with us for a while."

Gilles' eyebrows shoot up. "Oh? Interesting. Well, Tate, you're in for a treat. The gorge is beautiful this time of year."

I nod, trying to muster up some enthusiasm. "Thanks, I'm looking forward to it."

As the van lurches into motion, I catch Leon's eye. He's watching me with an unreadable expression, the blunt smoking between his lips. I have a feeling this is going to be an interesting day.

***

The craggy white cliffs tower over the Verdon River hundreds of meters high. Tufts of greenery cling to the rocks. The vibrant turquoise river is dotted with little boats of tourists and some swimming in the water.

It's like a holiday postcard come to life. So picturesque it's unreal.

I make sure to take a photo as our group starts crossing a bridge over the canyon.

"Aren't we going down there?" I point at the boats, and Gilles slows down to my pace till he's at my side.

"We will. I hope you're not afraid of heights." He smirks.

Oh no. My eyes skim the cliff faces, all of them at different heights with numerous overhangs and perches.

The ocean scares me, but rivers or lakes like this are fine. I'm not scared of heights, but I'm not keen to jump off a ledge.

"Right, Leon?" Gilles says it like a challenge as he reaches over my shoulder to roughhouse Leon.

"Right," he says tightly. Leon's face is blank in front of all the beauty of the gorge, and he's not walking with his friends, but trailing behind with me.

Is he scared?

When Gilles runs up to the others, I address Leon quietly. "We don't have to do this, you know?"

He scoffs at me. "You think I'm scared?"

Smoking so much weed in the car makes sense now. He's calmed down since this morning.

"There's nothing wrong with being scared. I don't really want to jump off a cliff either." I look pointedly at Gilles, who's currently hooking his arms around the girl I first saw with Leon at the house. "And he doesn't feel like your friend."

"It's always a competition with him," Leon admits. "And I'm competitive, even if there's no competition."

I nod slowly. "So, he just wants to look cool in front of everyone?"

"Probably. Or for the girls."

We sink into silence as we approach the rock face. Leon's friends lead us into the brush on top of the cliff side first, finding a jagged trail that takes us lower and lower until we emerge in a clearing.

Immediately my stomach flips. The solid rock beneath my feet doesn't feel so safe anymore as I see the steep drop to the glistening river. One of Leon's friends throws a measuring tape over the edge, and leans down to the rock to see the number.

"21 mètres de haut," he says.

"Fuck." 21 meters high? I can't do that.

Leon's friends are pumped up, full of adrenaline as they marvel at the height and begin stripping their shirts off. The other girl besides me isn't budging an inch closer to the edge, but she's already stripped to her one-piece. Way more game than me.

Then I look to Leon. Behind his friends, he's crouching against a tree, face drained of color.

Jesus. Leon looks like he's about to faint at any second.

Gilles takes the first spot at the ledge, determined to impress. He gives a loud speech in French before taking a few steps back. He runs to the edge, pouncing off the cliff. Collectively, we all rush to the edge, watching his fall. His body curls in forward somersaults until he hits the water, and there's an uproar of cheering as he resurfaces.

That was insane.

I watch as more people jump off the cliff. Some make it look effortless with their flips and graceful drives, while others fumble but laugh once they resurface. The exhilaration in the air is so infectious, and now it doesn't feel so impossible to do.

"It's your turn, American girl." One of Leon's friend's comes up to my side, trailing water from his previous dive. "Or are you too chickenshit?"

My bravado from moments ago shrivels. I shake my head and give out a nervous laugh. "My bikini will rip off when I hit the water."

Before the guy can respond, Leon's at my side. He pulls his shirt over his head and hands it to me, leaning into my ear. "If you jump, I jump."

I stare at him as he passes me and stops at the edge. His sudden bravery is betrayed by his trembling hands.

"Are you sure?" I ask.

He nods.

I pull his brown shirt over my head and get a waft of his scent. Musky body spray and fabric softener and a little sweat. The shirt reaches down to my thighs, which is enough.

The drenched guy cheers, giving me an encouraging clap. "That's right. Jump!"

"Leon's going first," I say before moving behind him.

Leon takes a few steps forward, assessing the drop. He shakes his arms and jogs on the spot, trying to psych himself up.

But I hear Leon's breath trembling, and he suddenly blurts out, "This is insane. I'll probably just panic."

No one that's jumped so far has shown such open terror. Even though I'm scared, I somehow feel worse for Leon.

It compels me to step forward and grip his hand. "If they can do it, we can too."

Leon's eyes round on me, mortified. But he doesn't push me away, in fact, his hand turns into a vise grip.

Leon's fucking terrified.

One part of me is scolding myself. Leon doesn't deserve my kindness. After all, he's treated me like shit. I still hate him for it.

But if he can't extend that kindness, I will. I can't stand to see someone else suffer like this. I will be better than Leon.

I will be better than my mom.

And if I can jump, I suppose it means I can get over anything. Even if it feels impossible. Like the way we're holding hands right now.

"On three," I command, wanting to suddenly get this over and done with before I change my mind. "One. Two. Three!"

We leap off the cliff, my hand still clasped tightly in Leon's. For a split second, my stomach lurches, but then—

Weightlessness.

The wind rushes past my ears, drowning out the cheers from above. My hair whips around my face as we plummet toward the turquoise water below. It's terrifying and thrilling all at once.

Time seems to slow down. I steal a glance at Leon, his eyes wide with a mix of fear and exhilaration. A laugh bubbles up from my chest, turning into a scream, pure and unrestrained. I feel alive, more alive than I've felt in weeks.

The fall stretches on, a moment of perfect freedom. No worries about my mom, no anxiety about my new life here. Just me and the open air.

I close my eyes, bracing for impact.

We hit the water with a thunderous splash. The shock of the cold water jolts me back to reality. I try to kick up to the surface, but the impact knocked the wind out of me. My lungs burn, desperate for air that I can't find.

I struggle, my limbs feeling heavy and uncooperative. The peaceful weightlessness from moments ago is replaced by panic. The water presses in around me, and no matter how hard I try, I can't break the surface.

My vision starts to blur. I can't breathe. I can't—

Suddenly, strong arms wrap around me, pulling me upward. My head breaks the surface, and I gasp, gulping in air. My lungs burn as I cough and sputter, trying to clear the water from my airways.

"Tate! Tate!" Leon's voice is frantic. He's holding me tight, treading water for both of us. "Tout va bien ? Dis-moi."

I can't understand what he's saying, but the panic in his voice is clear. My vision is still blurry, and I can't seem to catch my breath. Leon's face swims in and out of focus as he continues to speak rapidly in French.

"Ne t'inquiète pas, je te tiens." His words are a jumble to me, but his tone is soothing despite the edge of fear.

Leon starts swimming, pulling me along with him. I try to help, but my limbs feel like lead. He's practically dragging me through the water, his arm secure around my waist.

"Tiens bon, on y est presque," he mutters, his eyes scanning the cliff face.

Finally, we reach a small outcropping of rock jutting out from the cliff. Leon hoists me up onto it, his hands gentle but firm as he helps me sit. I slump against the cool stone, still coughing and gasping.

Leon pulls himself up next to me, his chest heaving. His eyes scan over me. "Tu t'es fait mal?"

I shake my head, not understanding but wanting to reassure him. "I'm okay," I manage to croak out between coughs.

Leon's eyes widen, and he realizes he's been speaking French this whole time. He switches to English, his voice rough with emotion. "Are you hurt? Can you breathe?"

I nod, finally catching my breath. "I'm fine," I rasp. "Just... winded."

Leon's shoulders sag with relief. He doesn't move away, though. His hand remains on my arm, as if he's afraid I'll slip back into the water if he lets go.

As I catch my breath, I notice Gilles and the others swimming toward us. Their faces are a blend of concern and curiosity.

"What happened?" Gilles calls out, treading water near our perch.

I wave a hand dismissively, not wanting to make a big deal out of it. "Just got the wind knocked out of me. I'm fine now."

Leon nods, backing me up. "She's okay. Just needs a minute."

Gilles looks skeptical for a moment, but then breaks into a grin. "Well, that was quite the dramatic first jump! You two certainly know how to make an entrance."

The others laugh, and I feel the tension dissipate. They start splashing each other and joking around in the water.

"You sure you're alright?" Leon asks quietly, his hand still on my arm.

I nod, offering a small smile. "Yeah, thanks for pulling me out."

The tension in his body loosens as he lets go of me. Brushing his hands over his face, he leans back onto his hands. We sit in silence for a while, watching the others play in the water. The sun is warm on my skin, and I start to feel better as my breathing returns to normal.

"You want to go back in?" Leon asks after a bit.

The initial shock of the jump has worn off, and now I'm itching to get back in the water. "Yeah, I think I'm ready to swim now."

Leon nods, his eyes still watchful. "Okay, but stay close."

We slide off the rock and into the cool water. It feels refreshing against my skin, washing away the last of my anxiety. I start to swim, moving my arms in slow, steady strokes. Leon keeps pace beside me, his movements fluid and graceful.

We spend the next hour exploring the gorge with his friends, swimming from one spot to another. Every now and then, Leon glances at me, as if checking that I'm still okay. But instead of feeling smothered, I find his presence comforting.

***

The van rumbles along the winding mountain roads, the setting sun painting the sky in streaks of orange and pink. I'm exhausted, but it's the good kind—the type that comes from a day well spent. My hair is damp, dripping onto Leon's t-shirt that I'm still wearing.

Leon sits beside me in the back, his head resting against the window. His eyes are half closed, but I can tell he's not sleeping. The radio plays softly in French, and the gentle sway of the van is almost hypnotic.

My muscles ache from swimming, and my skin feels tight from the sun. But I can't stop thinking about that moment when we jumped together, his hand gripping mine tight enough to bruise.

Leon shifts in his seat, and I feel his knee brush against mine. Neither of us moves away.

"Hey," he says quietly, his voice rough with fatigue. "There's this waterfall not far from here. Cascade de Sillans."

I turn to look at him, surprised he's breaking the silence. "Yeah?"

"Want to check it out tomorrow morning? Before it gets too hot." His eyes meet mine briefly before looking away. "It's a half an hour hike."

The invitation catches me off guard. After today, I expected us to go back to our usual dance of avoidance and sharp words. But there's something different in his voice now—less guarded, maybe.

"Sure," I find myself saying. "What time?"

"Seven?"

I nod, and we fall back into comfortable silence. The van continues its journey home, and I close my eyes, letting the gentle motion lull me into a half sleep.

***

I trudge through the front door, my legs feeling like lead. The house is quiet, save for the soft clinking of dishes coming from the kitchen. A warm, savory aroma wafts through the air, making my stomach growl.

"Nous sommes de retour," Leon calls out, his voice hoarse from the long day.

Jerome appears in the hallway, wiping his hands on a dish towel. "How was your day?"

"We went cliff diving," I say. I leave out the part about nearly drowning. No need to worry Jerome.

"Cliff diving?" Jerome's eyes widen and he looks between Leon and I. "That's… quite adventurous. You both okay?"

I nod, forcing a smile. "Yeah, we're fine. Just tired."

"And hungry," Leon adds, sniffing the air. "What's for dinner?"

Jerome gestures toward the dining room. "I made coq au vin. Why don't you two go get cleaned up, and we'll eat when you're ready?"

Leon and I exchange a glance, both of us eager to wash off the day's grime and change into comfortable clothes.

"Sounds great," I say, already heading for the stairs.

I take a quick shower, letting the hot water soothe my aching muscles. As I dress in soft pajamas, I can hear the shower running down the hall. By the time we both make it back downstairs, Jerome has set the table and is pouring wine into glasses.

"Wine?" Jerome quirks a brow at me as he extends the wine bottle over a spare glass.

I shake my head. "I can't drink alcohol yet."

"Oh right." He laughs, putting the bottle down. "America is different. Here you have to be 18."

I nod and quickly grab a lemonade out of the fridge.

We settle into our seats, the aroma of the coq au vin making my mouth water. Then we dig into our food, Leon and I too hungry and tired for much conversation.

***

I lie in bed, staring at the ceiling, my mind replaying the events of the day. The cliff, the jump, the rush of adrenaline—it all seemed so surreal now. I'd been terrified, sure, but I'd done it anyway. I'd come out the other side.

My thoughts drift to my mom, to the day she left me here. The pain of it still stung, a raw wound that throbbed with each passing day. But today, for the first time since it happened, I feel a glimmer of hope.

A gentle gust wafts into my room through the window, bringing along the smell of weed.

I slip out from under the covers and peek outside. Bathed in moonlight, the rear lawn reveals Leon stretched out on the turf, a wispy tendril of smoke ascending from his vicinity.

For a moment, I hesitate, unsure if I should disturb him. But something pulls me toward him—and before I can talk myself out of it, I slip on my shoes and head downstairs.

The night air is cool against my skin as I step outside, making my way toward Leon.

I approach Leon quietly, not wanting to startle him. "Hey," I say softly.

Leon turns his head, his eyes meeting mine in the dim light. For a moment, I think he might tell me to go away, but he just nods and returns his gaze to the sky.

Taking that as an invitation, I lower myself onto the grass beside him. The coolness of the blades seeps through my thin pajamas, sending a slight shiver down my spine.

"What are you doing out here?" I ask, my voice barely above a whisper.

Leon takes a long drag before answering. "Stargazing," he remarks, exhaling a plume of smoke. "Decompressing."

I wait for him to elaborate, but he doesn't. His eyes remain fixed on the vast expanse above us, as if searching for something in the twinkling lights.

"You did good today," I say, and Leon's eyes flick to me. "I didn't think you'd jump."

He clicks his tongue. "You almost drowned."

I don't think till I say it. "I feel great."

Leon gives me a confused look. "That's fucked up."

There's a brief silence before I start cracking up, and Leon follows suit.

"Yeah, I don't recommend adding one trauma to another. But I feel like nothing can scare me anymore, it's strange."

"You have perspective," Leon explains.

I lean back on my elbows, following Leon's gaze upwards. The sky is a canvas of stars, more than I've ever seen before.

Away from the city lights, the Milky Way stretches across the sky in a breathtaking display.

"I wish I felt content," Leon says suddenly. "I felt it during the fall. But once the rush of it was over, I felt awful."

"Why?" I ask.

"My brain just does it sometimes." He gives out a bitter laugh. "I can't reason with it."

I look at him with dawning realization. Fighting your own brain, fighting for control over your emotions. I know what that's like. Leon opening up like this makes me feel less alone.

"I feel like my brain works against me too," I say, watching the stars twinkle above. "I bottle up my anxiety because I feel it all the time. I've tried mindfulness, practicing meditation, even therapists. I hate it, but I don't know what else to do."

Leon stares at me for a moment, something dawning in his eyes. He extends his blunt to me.

I watch the end burn in the night air, smoking and red. Leon makes me hurt, but in a good way. My mom was supposed to love me, when all she did was hurt me. I've been in denial about it for so long, I don't know how to take my armor off.

But Leon ripped it off for me.

I take the blunt and press it to my lips, inhaling.

"I thought you were so calm and mellow when I first saw you," he says. "But you're like me; my brain won't shut the fuck up."

I blow smoke into the air and turn, finding his eyes already on me. And for the first time since I met Leon, he looks so earnest and vulnerable.

"I can't promise it will ever go away. But it gets easier, especially with this."

I feel his fingers brush my lips as he takes the blunt from my mouth. Leaning over, he looks down at me as he takes another deep drag.

Warmth spreads through my belly. He has such a pretty mouth.

Smoke trails from his lips. "Acknowledging your shit mom is a start." He snickers, grinning so hard, I can see the sharp points of his canines.

And I laugh.

***

The morning mist clings to the trees as we follow the narrow trail to Cascade de Sillans. Leon walks ahead, occasionally glancing back to make sure I'm keeping up. The sound of rushing water grows louder with each step, until finally, we emerge into a clearing.

The waterfall thunders down a limestone cliff, the water a pristine white curtain against the dark rock. Spray fills the air, creating tiny rainbows in the early morning light.

"It's beautiful," I breathe, taking it all in.

We find a spot on some rocks near the pool at the base of the falls. The roar of the water creates a private bubble around us, making it feel as if we're the only two people in the world.

"I used to come here a lot when I was younger," Leon says, his eyes fixed on the falling water. "Whenever things got too intense at home."

"With your dad?" I ask carefully, remembering our conversation from last night.

Leon shakes his head. "After my mom left." He picks up a small stone, turning it over in his hands. "I was seven. She just... couldn't handle it anymore. The quiet life, being a mom, any of it. She lives in Marseille now, runs a little art gallery."

I can't help but snort.

Leon's eyes widen, and he looks at me, really looks at me for the first time. "Shit, Tate. I'm sorry. Here I am whining about ancient history when you're dealing with fresh wounds."

"It's fine," I say, but my voice cracks a little. "I guess we're both members of the Shitty Moms Club."

Leon laughs. "Yeah, I guess we are. Honorary president and vice president."

We sit in silence for a moment, the waterfall roaring in the background.

"You know what the worst part is?" I say finally. "I keep thinking, what did I do wrong? Was I not good enough? Smart enough?"

Leon nods, his eyes distant. "I get that. For years, I thought if I was just... better somehow, she'd come back." He pauses, then adds, "Dad tried to fill both roles after that. He'd make these elaborate breakfasts, help me with school projects, try to talk about feelings." Leon's laugh is hollow. "But he was trying so hard to be her that he stopped being himself. And I... I just wanted my dad back."

"Is that why you two clash so much?" I ask, remembering their tense interactions.

Leon's fingers trace patterns in the dirt. "Yeah, I think so." He looks at me, a hint of vulnerability in his eyes. "But with you here, it's different. He seems... I don't know, less tense or something."

The weight of his words settles between us. I think about Jerome's gentle guidance, his quiet strength. About how Leon's sharp edges seem to blur around me now.

"I understand," I say finally. "About parents trying to be something they're not. At least your dad tried. Mine just... vanished."

Leon looks at me, his expression softening. "It's not you, Tate. It's her. Trust me on this."

I feel tears pricking at my eyes. "How do you know?"

"Because I've met you," Leon says simply. "And you're nothing like what she says. You're pretty alright."

I laugh through my tears. "You're not so bad yourself, when you're not being an ass."

Leon's expression flickers between surprise and something else I can't quite read. He looks away, back toward the waterfall. We fall silent again. The waterfall fills the space between us, loud enough to drown out thoughts but not the weight of what we've shared. I watch the water crash against the rocks below, feeling strangely hollow and full at the same time.

"We should head back," Leon says finally, standing and brushing dirt from his jeans. He extends a hand to help me up, then pulls it back, as if second-guessing the gesture.

I stand on my own, suddenly unsure what to do with my hands, with this fragile thing we've created. "Thanks," I say. "For showing me this place. And... you know."

Leon nods, his eyes meeting mine for just a moment before sliding away. "Yeah. Same." He turns toward the path, then pauses. "Your mom's an idiot, by the way."

The words hang in the air, simple and unexpected. I feel something tighten in my chest.

"So is yours," I reply.

A ghost of a smile crosses his face. He doesn't look back as he starts down the trail, but his pace is slower now, making space for me to walk beside him.

We don't speak on the way back, each lost in our own thoughts.

8

TATE

TWO WEEKS LATER

I take the paint swatches from Jerome, my fingers tingling where they brush against his. I try to focus on the array of soft blues and greens, but it's hard to concentrate with him standing so close.

"What do you think?" I ask, holding up two similar shades of pale blue. "Sea Spray or Jade Mist?"

Jerome leans in, his shoulder pressing lightly against mine as he examines the swatches. The scent of sawdust and something uniquely him fills my senses.

"Hmm, Jade Mist," he murmurs near my ear. "It'll brighten up the space nicely."

I nod, not quite trusting my voice. We've been spending a lot of time together lately, painting and cooking side by side. And with each passing day, I find myself more and more drawn to Jerome's calm strength and quiet humor.

"Brings the outside in," I manage to say, handing the swatch back to him.

Jerome smiles, his eyes warm as they meet mine, making my stomach flutter. I stole his phrase. "I'll go mix up the paint while you finish taping off the trim."

As he walks away, I take a steadying breath and grab the ring of tape, stepping up the small ladder. I begin taping off the corner edges of the ceiling. I hum along to the French music playing on the Bluetooth speaker. A few minutes later, the door shuts, and I turn to see Jerome has returned with the paint mixed in the tray, and his shirt discarded.

I swear to God. This is a lot more challenging when he doesn't wear a shirt.

I make a conscious effort to look Jerome in the eyes as he hands me a small paint roller, then I quickly look away.

We start painting the walls, working in companionable silence. The soft strokes of our rollers blend with the gentle French music playing in the background. But every now and then, I steal glances at Jerome as we work.

My eyes are drawn to the way his muscles flex and ripple under his tanned skin. Each movement is a testament to his years of physical labor, sculpting his body. The definition in his arms and back speaks of countless hours spent building, lifting, and creating.

I watch as he reaches up to paint a high corner, his biceps bulging with the effort. A bead of sweat trickles down his spine, and I find myself mesmerized by its path. The image of him, shirtless and focused on his work, stirs something deep within me.

Realizing I've been staring, I quickly return my attention to my own section of the wall. But I can't shake the image of Jerome's strong hands gripping the roller, the same hands that have been so gentle with me since I arrived.

What would those hands do to me? Heat pools in my core before I shake off the thought.

The sun begins to dip below the horizon, casting the cabin in a warm, golden glow. As we continue painting, I'm acutely aware of Jerome nearing my side of the wall, closing the last section of white paint.

I feel a sudden coolness on my cheek and reach up to touch it. My fingers come away with a smear of green paint. I look at Jerome, who's trying to suppress a grin, his eyes twinkling with mischief.

"Did you just…?" I ask, incredulous.

He shrugs, a playful smirk on his lips. "Maybe you needed a little more color."

I narrow my eyes, a slow smile spreading across my face. "Oh, it's on," I say, dipping my paint roller into the tray and flicking it in his direction. A splatter of Jade Mist hits his chest, dripping down his bare skin.

He looks down at the paint, then back at me, his eyebrows raised. "You're going to regret that," he asserts, his voice low and promising.

I squeal and try to dart away, but he's quicker. He grabs a paintbrush, loads it with paint, and advances on me. I'm laughing so hard I can barely breathe, trying to dodge his attempts to paint my face.

In my haste to escape, I stumble over the small ladder, my feet tangling in the rungs. I gasp, my heart leaping into my throat as I start to fall. But Jerome is there in an instant, his strong arms wrapping around me, pulling me against his chest.

The laughter dies in my throat as I look up into his eyes. They're dark, the green of his irises almost swallowed by his pupils. His breath is coming as fast as mine, his chest rising and falling rapidly beneath me.

"Be careful, Tate," he murmurs, his voice barely more than a growl.

I'm acutely aware of every point of contact between us. His hands on my back, his chest pressed against mine, his thigh wedged between my legs. The heat of his body seeps into mine, igniting a fire in my core.

His gaze drops to my lips, and I feel a shiver run through him. The air between us is like electricity. I can feel his heart pounding, or maybe it's mine, I can't tell anymore.

I part my lips, not sure what I'm going to say, but no words come out. Instead, I find myself leaning closer. His breath hitches, and he leans in, his lips a whisper away from mine.

Every nerve ending in my body is alive and tingling.

The cabin door swings open. I jump back from Jerome, my heart racing into my throat. Jerome clears his throat, running a hand through his hair as he turns to face Leon.

"Hey," Leon greets, his brow furrowing as he looks at us. "What's going on?"

SAINT BRYDE

"Nothing," I say quickly, my voice coming out breathier than I intended. I feel the heat rising to my cheeks, and I hope Leon can't see the blush spreading across my face.

Jerome nods, his voice gruff as he says, "Just finishing up the painting."

Leon's eyes narrow, and I can see the confusion written all over his face.

I try to act casual, grabbing the paint roller and dipping it into the tray, but my hands are shaking slightly, and I can feel Jerome's gaze on me.

"You both look...weird."

Jerome chuckles, but it sounds forced. "We had a paint fight, and Tate almost fell."

Satisfied with that answer, Leon drops the subject. "Alright, well, Dad there's someone here. I think it's the detective?"

Jerome quickly grabs a rag and wipes the paint off his torso. I feel his eyes on me, but I can't bring myself to look at him.

"Finish it off for me," he orders breathlessly.

I nod and dip the roller back into the paint as he exits.

I press a hand to my chest, feeling the wild thrum beneath my fingers. What just happened? And why do I feel like we were caught doing something wrong when it felt so... *good*?

The rhythm of the roller against the wall is soothing, the soft *shush-shush* filling the silence. I focus on the sensation, the push and pull, the give-and-take. Anything to distract myself from the memory of Jerome's touch, his breath on my skin, his lips a whisper away from mine.

The door creaks open behind me, and I turn to see Leon, his dark-blue eyes piercing as they meet mine. He steps into the room, his gaze flicking from me to the wall and back again.

"You missed a spot," he insists, nodding toward the corner.

I look, and sure enough, there's a small patch of white peeking through the green.

I clear my throat, turning back to the wall. "Thanks," I murmur, my voice barely more than a whisper. I can feel Leon's gaze on me, the weight of it heavy on my back.

"You okay?" he asks.

I duck my head, hoping to hide the blush. "I'm fine," I say, my voice steadier this time. "Just hot in here."

Leon grunts, and I can hear him moving closer. I tense, my body suddenly hyperaware of his presence. He stops beside me, his arm brushing against mine as he reaches out for the roller.

"Here," he says, his voice quiet. "Let me help."

I look at him, his dark-blue eyes locked onto mine. There's something in his gaze, something intense and unreadable.

"Okay." I hand him the roller, our fingers brushing briefly.

Leon starts to paint, his strokes sure and confident. I watch him, the way his muscles flex and ripple under his white shirt. The way his dark hair falls into his eyes, the way he pushes it back with a casual flick of his hand.

I can't help but compare him to Jerome. Where Jerome is all rugged strength and mountain man, Leon is lithe and graceful, his movements fluid and effortless. But there's a tension in him, a coiled energy that's just as powerful, just as intense.

I shake my head, trying to clear my thoughts. This is dangerous territory, this comparing, this noticing. I'm treading on thin ice, and I can't afford to fall in.

"That should do it," he states, stepping back to admire his work.

We begin cleaning up without a word. I gather the brushes and rollers, while Leon picks up the paint tray.

As we pack everything away, I notice his jaw is set, a slight furrow between his brows. I wonder what he's thinking, if he sensed the tension between Jerome and me earlier.

We make our way back to the house, the gravel crunching beneath our feet. The evening air is cool against my skin, a welcome relief after the stuffy cabin.

Leon holds the door open for me as we enter the house. I mumble a quiet "thanks" as I pass him, my arm brushing against his chest. The doors to the living room are closed, and I can hear Jerome talking, along with another male voice. Leon and I make sure to avoid that side of the house, and turn into the kitchen.

We begin cleaning the brushes and rollers in silence. The sound of running water fills the room, punctuated by the soft clink of brushes against the sink.

"What do you think they're talking about?" I ask to fill the silence. Have the police found leads? Places my mom might've gone?

Leon shrugs his shoulders.

"I hope they've found something," I say, but there's a weird pang in my heart when I say it.

Leon's quiet for a moment, his eyes fixed on the brush he's cleaning. "Don't get your hopes up too high," he murmurs softly. "These things can take time."

I feel a lump form in my throat. It's been weeks since I last mom, and the uncertainty is eating away at me. I focus on scrubbing a particularly stubborn spot of paint, channeling my frustration.

"I know," I reply, my voice barely above a whisper. "It's just… hard, you know? Not knowing."

Leon reaches for the wet cloth. "I can't imagine what you're going through," he admits, his voice subdued and gentle. It's a side of Leon I haven't seen much of—this softer, more empathetic version. "As much as your mom is a bitch, you're not alone in this, Tate. We're here for you."

I look up at him, surprised by the sincerity in his eyes.

"Thanks, Leon," I murmur, offering him a small smile. "That means a lot."

We fall into a comfortable silence as we finish cleaning up. As I dry my hands on a nearby towel, I hear the muffled voices again coming from the living room. My curiosity gets the better of me this time, and I find myself inching closer to the door, straining to hear what's being said.

Leon notices and raises an eyebrow. "Eavesdropping?"

I feel a blush creep up my cheeks. "I just… I need to know if they've found anything."

He sighs, running a hand through his hair. "Look, if it's important, Dad will tell you. You shouldn't—"

Before he can finish, the living room door opens, and Jerome steps out, his face unreadable.

Jerome's eyes meet mine, and I can see a mix of emotions swirling in their depths. My heart races, partly from the anticipation of news about my mom, and partly from the vivid image of our almost-kiss in the cabin.

"Tate," he states, his voice low and gravelly. "Can we talk?"

I nod, my throat suddenly dry. I follow him into the living room, acutely aware of Leon's gaze on my back as I pass.

The detective is gone, leaving behind only the faint scent of cologne. Jerome gestures for me to sit on the couch, and he takes a seat across from me in an armchair.

"They've found a lead," he begins, his eyes never leaving mine. "Your mother's credit card was used at a gas station in Marseille three days ago."

My heart leaps into my throat. "Marseille? That's... that's not far from here, right?"

Jerome nods, his expression guarded. "About two hours away. The detective is following up on it, checking security footage from the gas station and surrounding areas."

I lean forward, hope blooming in my chest for the first time in weeks. "So, she's okay? She's alive?"

Jerome's face softens, and he reaches out to take my hand.

I resist the urge to pull away. I don't want Jerome to touch me right now, not like this.

"It seems that way, yes. But Tate, we need to be prepared for the possibility that someone else might be using her card."

The hope in my chest flickers. "Oh," I say, my voice small.

Jerome squeezes my hand gently. "I know this is hard, but we're making progress. We'll find her, Tate. I promise."

I nod, forcing a tight smile.

"You also still have..." Jerome gestures to my cheek, and then I remember the paint.

"Oh," I scrub at the dried paint on my cheek. "I'll go... wash it off." Before I head upstairs, I round back on Jerome. "Um, tomorrow can you drop me off at the library? I need a place with Internet and computers to look at my grades."

Jerome nods. "Of course."

I thank him and race upstairs. My overalls are hot and sticky from sweat. I want nothing more than to rip them off, but as I pass the bathroom Leon comes out of his room, startling me.

"Hey," he interjects. "Some of my friends are heading to a bonfire tonight. Wanna come?"

I hesitate, my hand still on the doorknob. The thought of staying in the house, facing Jerome's loaded glances after our almost-kiss, makes my stomach churn. Plus, I could use a distraction from the news about my mom.

"Yeah, sure," I say, surprising myself with how eager I sound. "That sounds fun."

Leon's eyebrows rise slightly, as if he wasn't expecting me to agree so readily. "Cool. We're leaving in an hour. Nothing fancy, just throw on something warm, it'll be cold tonight."

I nod, a small smile tugging at my lips. "Thanks for inviting me."

He shrugs, but I catch a hint of a smile on his face. "No problem. See you downstairs."

As he heads back to his room, I slip into the bathroom, my mind already racing with thoughts of what to wear. I quickly wash the paint off my face and hands, then hurry to my room to change.

I stand in front of the mirror, smoothing down my oversized sweater. It's soft and warm, perfect for a bonfire night. I've paired it with some high-waisted jeans and my trusty sneakers. My hair falls in loose waves around my shoulders, and I've even put on a touch of mascara.

As I head downstairs, I hear voices coming from the kitchen. I pause at the bottom of the stairs, listening. But of course, I can't understand what they're saying in French.

"Ce n'est qu'un feu de camp, Papa," Leon's voice carries, tinged with frustration. "Tu l'as dit toi-même. Elle a besoin de sortir, de rencontrer des gens de son âge."

A beat of silence follows, and I can almost see Jerome's furrowed brow in my mind's eye.

"Juste... garde un œil sur elle, d'accord?" Jerome's deep voice rumbles, concern evident in his tone.

"Je le ferai," Leon responds, his voice softening. "Ne t'inquiète pas."

What if they're speaking about the incident in the cabin? *Oh God.*

I inhale deeply and step into the kitchen. Both men turn to look at me, and I feel a flush creep up my neck under their scrutiny.

"Ready?" Leon asks, grabbing the keys from the counter.

He doesn't appear angry, and the tension releases from my body. They must have been talking about something else.

I nod, offering a small smile. "Yeah, let's go."

Jerome clears his throat. "Have fun," he replies, his eyes meeting mine for a brief moment before flicking away. "Don't stay out too late."

"We won't," Leon assures him, ushering me toward the door.

As we step outside, the cool night air hits my face, and I take a deep breath. The sky is cloudy, but stars twinkle overhead. Jerome's truck is parked in the driveway.

"You don't own a car?" I ask as I hop into the passenger seat.

The engine rumbles to life. "Mine's in the city. We need a truck tonight though."

I raise a brow. "Is it a long way?"

Leon swerves onto the road and drives. "It's off-road."

We drive in silence for a while, the darkness of the countryside enveloping us. The headlights cut through the night, illuminating the winding road ahead. I watch the shadows of trees flicker past, lost in thought.

"So." Leon's voice breaks the silence, startling me slightly. "You've never been to a bonfire before?"

I shake my head. "Not really. I mean, I've seen them in movies, but…"

He chuckles, a low, warm sound that sends an unexpected electricity through my body. "Well, it's not quite as dramatic as the movies make it out to be. Just some friends, music, drinks, and a fire."

"Sounds nice," I murmur, fiddling with the hem of my sweater. "Back home, it's mainly just house parties."

As we continue driving, the paved road gives way to a dirt track. The truck bounces and jolts, and I grip the door handle to steady myself. Wide plains of grass stretch out before us as we descend a hill. Leon navigates the rough terrain with ease, his hands sure on the steering wheel.

"Almost there," he says, glancing at me. In the dim light of the dashboard, his eyes look almost black. "You okay?"

I nod. "Are these the same people from the Verdon Gorge?"

Leon scratches his neck. "Yeah, same crowd. You'll see some familiar faces."

The truck jolts over a particularly rough patch, and I grab the dashboard to steady myself. Leon swears under his breath, his hand brushing against mine as he reaches for the gear shift. I pull my hand back quickly, my skin tingling where we touched.

As we round a bend, I see a warm glow in the distance, flickering against the dark sky. The bonfire is in the middle of a field.

Leon pulls the truck to a stop a little ways away from the fire. I can see figures moving around, hear the faint sound of music and laughter carried on the night breeze.

"Ready?" Leon asks, turning to face me.

I breath in, steadying myself, and nod. "As I'll ever be."

He locks the truck and we make our way to the bonfire.

As we approach the fire, I recognize some faces from the Verdon Gorge. A few people wave at Leon, calling out greetings in rapid French. He introduces me, but their names blur together in a haze of unfamiliar sounds.

I settle onto a log near the fire, the warmth seeping into my bones. The crackling flames cast dancing shadows across the faces around me. Snippets of French conversation float through the air, incomprehensible but melodic.

Leon plops down beside me, his knee brushing against mine. "You good?" he asks, his voice hushed.

I nod, offering a small smile. "Yeah, just… taking it all in."

He studies me for a moment, then stands. "Want a drink?"

I hesitate. "I… I don't know what to have."

A mischievous grin spreads across his face. "I'll surprise you. Wait here."

He disappears into the darkness beyond the fire's glow. I fidget with the hem of my sweater, hyperaware of the curious glances thrown my way.

Leon returns, a bottle of clear liquid in his hand. He sits back down, closer this time, and leans in. His breath tickles my ear as he whispers, "Don't tell Dad."

I look at the bottle, recognizing the Cyrillic script. "Vodka?" I whisper back, eyes wide.

He places a finger against his lips, that impish grin still playing on his face. "Shhh," he says, uncapping the bottle and offering it to me.

I hesitate for a moment, eyeing the bottle. The responsible part of me wants to refuse, but the rebellious side—the part that's been suffocated by anxiety and uncertainty for weeks—wins out. I take the bottle.

The vodka burns as it goes down, and I can't help but cough. Leon laughs, a deep, rich sound that makes my cheeks flush—though that could just be the alcohol.

"Easy there," he remarks, taking the bottle back. "Small sips."

I watch as he takes a drink, his Adam's apple bobbing as he swallows. The firelight dances across his features, highlighting the sharp angle of his jaw and the curve of his lips.

"What do you guys usually do at these things?" I ask.

Leon shrugs, passing the bottle back to me. "Talk, mostly. Sometimes we play games. Truth or dare is popular."

I take another sip, smaller this time. The burn is less intense, and a pleasant warmth begins to spread through my body. "Truth or dare? Isn't that a bit… high school?"

I might be finishing high school, but Leon's not. He's older, and I'm sure his friends are too.

He grins. "What, are you scared?"

I roll my eyes, but I can't help smiling. "As if. I'm just not sure I want to bare my soul to a bunch of strangers."

"They're not strangers," Leon asserts, gesturing to the group around us. "They're friends. And besides, you don't have to play if you don't want to."

I consider this for a moment, taking another sip of vodka. The alcohol is making me feel loose, relaxed in a way I haven't felt in a long time. "Okay," I say finally. "I'm in."

Leon's eyes light up, and he calls out to the group. Soon, we're all sitting in a circle, the bottle of vodka being passed around. I catch snippets of English here and there, enough to understand the basic rules.

As the game begins, I feel a combination of excitement and nervousness bubbling up inside me. I'm not sure what to expect.

The game starts off innocently enough. Someone has to lick their elbow. Another person reveals their most embarrassing childhood memory. I relax a little, the vodka warming my insides and loosening my inhibitions.

Then it's my turn.

"Truth or dare?" a girl asks me in accented English. It takes me a moment to recognize her, she's the girl I first saw with Leon at the house. And I still don't know her name.

I hesitate for a moment. "Truth," I say, figuring it's the safer option.

She grins, leaning forward. "Have you ever kissed someone?"

The question catches me off guard. I feel heat rising to my cheeks, and not just from the fire. "I... uh..." I stammer, suddenly very aware of Leon's presence beside me.

"Come on," the girl urges, her eyes sparkling with mischief. "It's just a kiss."

I take breath, steeling myself. "No," I admit finally. "I haven't."

There's a chorus of surprised exclamations and giggles. I duck my head, embarrassed, but when I glance at Leon, I'm surprised to see him looking at me with an expression I can't quite read.

The game continues, and I start to relax again. The questions and dares become more bold as the night wears on and more vodka is consumed. I find myself laughing at the antics of Leon's friends, feeling a sense of belonging despite the language barrier.

Eager and uneasy feelings roil within me. The vodka has made everything fuzzy around the edges, and I'm feeling bolder than usual.

"Tate!" someone calls out. "Truth or dare?"

I hesitate for a moment, then decide to throw caution to the wind. "Dare," I say, my voice stronger than I feel.

The group erupts in cheers and excited chatter. I catch Leon's eye, and he raises an eyebrow at me, a hint of a smile playing on his lips.

The girl from earlier leans in, her eyes glinting mischievously in the firelight. "I dare you… to kiss Gilles."

My heart skips a beat as I follow her gaze to Gilles sitting across the circle. Under normal circumstances, I'd probably be too shy to even consider it. But the vodka has loosened me up, and a part of me wants to prove that I'm not as inexperienced as they all think.

I take a steadying breath. "Okay," I say, surprising myself with how steady my voice sounds.

There's a collective gasp, followed by more cheers. Gilles looks surprised but not displeased. He stands up and makes his way over to me, the firelight casting flickering shadows across his face.

As he kneels in front of me, I'm suddenly very aware of everyone watching us.

Gilles leans in, his hand gently cupping my cheek. "Ready?" he whispers, his breath warm against my skin.

I nod, unable to form words. My heart is pounding so hard I'm sure everyone can hear it.

He closes the distance between us, and then his lips are on mine. They're soft and warm, and he tastes faintly of beer and smoke.

The group erupts in cheers and wolf whistles, but I barely hear them. My mind is spinning, a mix of alcohol and adrenaline making everything feel surreal.

I glance at Leon, expecting to see him laughing along with the others. Instead, his jaw is clenched tight, his eyes dark and stormy. He's staring at Gilles with a look that could freeze hell over.

"Well done, Tate!" someone calls out, but Leon stands abruptly, silencing the group.

"I need another drink," he mutters, his voice low and tight. He stalks off toward the coolers, his shoulders tense.

The atmosphere around the fire shifts, becoming uncomfortable. I feel a twinge of guilt in my gut, though I'm not sure why. It was just a dare, after all. Why does Leon look so... angry?

As the group's attention shifts away from us, Gilles takes Leon's seat beside me.

"So, Tate," he slurs, "how are you liking France so far?"

I force a smile. "It's beautiful. Everyone's been very welcoming."

Gilles grins, leaning in closer. "I can show you more of the beauty, if you like. There's a great spot just over there…" He gestures vaguely toward the darkness beyond the fire's glow.

My stomach tightens. "Oh, um, that's okay. I'm good here."

But Gilles doesn't appear to get the hint. His hand reaches for my knee.

"Come on, bébé. Let me give you the real French experience."

Before I can react, a shadow falls over us. Leon stands there, his jaw clenched tight.

Leon's voice cuts through the air like a whip. "Elle a dit non, Gilles. Reculez."

Gilles looks up, his eyes narrowing. "Cela ne te regarde pas, Léon."

Leon's jaw clenches, his eyes flashing dangerously. "Je t'ai demandé de reculer," he growls, his voice low and threatening.

For a moment, tension crackles in the air. Then Gilles stands, raising his hands in mock surrender. "D'accord, d'accord. Pas besoin de s'énerver."

Gilles stumbles to his feet, muttering under his breath as he wanders off toward the coolers.

I watch Gilles stumble away, my heart still racing from the uncomfortable encounter. Leon drops down next to me.

"You okay?" he asks, his voice gruff.

I nod, wrapping my arms around myself. "Yeah, I'm fine. Thanks for… you know.

Suddenly, a cold drop hits my cheek. I look up, just as the sky opens and a torrent of rain pours down. Chaos erupts. People scramble, grabbing blankets and half-empty cups. Someone kicks dirt onto the fire, extinguishing it with a hiss.

Leon grabs my hand, pulling me toward the truck. "Come on!" he shouts over the downpour.

We race through the rain, my heart hammering against my ribs. He opens the passenger door for me, and I clamber in, soaked to the bone.

Leon jumps into the driver's seat, his dark hair plastered to his forehead. He starts the engine, the windshield wipers working overtime.

"Putain de merde!" he shouts, squinting through the windshield. "Je ne peux rien voir avec cette maudite tempête!"

I can't understand the words, but his tone makes the meaning clear. The rain is coming down so hard it's like a solid wall of water. The truck lurches forward, following the line of cars snaking away from the field.

I clutch the door handle as Leon navigates the muddy field, the truck sliding slightly in the slick grass.

"Are you okay to drive?" I ask, my voice shaky.

Leon nods, his eyes fixed on the road ahead. "Yeah, I'm fine. We just need to get to the main road."

The truck jolts as we hit a particularly deep rut, and I yelp, my hand instinctively reaching out to steady myself. It lands on Leon's thigh, and I quickly snatch it back, my cheeks burning.

"Sorry," I shout.

He doesn't respond. We finally reach the paved road, and Leon lets out a sigh of relief. The rain is still coming down in sheets, but at least we're on solid ground now.

As we drive, the silence in the truck grows heavy. I can't help but replay the events of the night in my mind—the dare, the kiss with Gilles, Leon's anger. I sneak a glance at him, his profile illuminated by the occasional flash of lightning. His jaw is clenched tight, his eyes focused on the road ahead.

"Leon," I start, not sure what I'm going to say but feeling like I need to say something. "About earlier—"

"Don't," he cuts me off, his voice tight. "It's fine."

I fall silent, hurt and confusion swirling inside me.

Lightning flashes across the sky, illuminating the road ahead for brief, blinding moments. I grip the edge of my seat, my knuckles turning white as Leon struggles to keep the truck on the road.

Suddenly, a deafening crack of thunder shakes the air. Leon groans under his breath, his hands tightening on the steering wheel.

"I can't see a damn thing," he mutters, leaning forward and squinting through the windshield.

The wipers are working overtime, but they're no match for the deluge. Water streams down the glass in thick rivulets, distorting our view of the road.

Another flash of lightning reveals a turnoff ahead. Leon signals and carefully guides the truck onto the shoulder, pulling as far off the road as he can.

"We're going to have to wait it out," he concedes, turning off the engine but leaving the hazard lights blinking. "It's not safe to drive in this."

I nod, relief and anxiety warring within me. I'm glad we're not driving anymore, but being stuck here with Leon, after everything that happened at the bonfire, makes me nervous.

9

LEON

Like hell I'm driving in this storm, not when Tate's with me. It's too risky.

I can't focus on anything but the rain pounding against the windshield and Tate's presence beside me. The storm came out of nowhere, forcing us to pull over. Now we're stuck here, alone in the truck.

Part of me is happy we're finally alone. I couldn't stand that shit at the bonfire. Gilles thought he could make a move on Tate, then so many of the other guys kept checking her out. The hot new American girl.

And Tate kissed him.

Fuck. Why did I bring her? And why am I so agitated? It's not my business what she does or who she gets involved with. I've slept around.

But I don't like the idea of Tate doing that.

I grip the steering wheel and sigh at the rain pelting the windshield. "Looks like we're not going anywhere for a while," I mutter, stealing a glance at her. "It's too dangerous driving in this weather."

Tate shifts in her seat, wringing out her wet blond hair. "Good choice."

The silence stretches between us, broken only by the rhythmic tapping of raindrops. I reach around the back of the cab, feeling a blanket under the seat. I pull it over to Tate and she lights up.

"Thanks." As she pulls it over herself, I realize it's actually a picnic blanket. But it'll do. "Aren't you cold?"

I nod, peeling my wet sweater over my head. "I'll dry."

There's only one blanket in this truck as far as I know. One of us was going to strip, and I imagined Tate wasn't going to do it.

I wouldn't be against it though. Suddenly, an image of Tate's glistening skin and taut stomach reach my mind. Like the night I was watching her…

My cock stiffens against my jeans.

I try to refocus on wiping down the rain from my arms with my sweater.

"Do you think rain makes you sick?" Tate asks.

I give her a quizzical look and shake my head.

"I wondered why anyone thought rain caused colds. A Portuguese guy I dated once worried about storms for that very reason."

"Maybe it's a cultural thing." I hear myself say. She dated a Portuguese guy?

Tate nods, pulling the blanket tighter around her shoulders. Her wet clothes cling to her body, and I force myself to look away. The rain continues to pound against the truck, creating a cocoon around us. It's so loud, I can barely hear my own thoughts.

Tate *kissed* Gilles. All that replays in my head is them leaning in close by the bonfire, and anger rises within me. I can't help myself. The question burns on my tongue, demanding to be asked. "Why did you kiss Gilles?"

Tate's eyes widen, caught off guard. She shifts uncomfortably under the blanket. "It was just a dare. I wanted to prove myself."

I scoff, my jaw clenching. "That's a stupid reason to kiss someone."

Her cheeks flush, a blend of embarrassment and anger. "Excuse me? Who are you to judge who I kiss?"

"I'm not judging. I'm stating a fact. It was stupid to kiss him." The words come out harsher than I intend, but I can't stop myself. "You know I don't like him."

"You're not my keeper," Tate snaps, her eyes flashing. "You don't get to decide who I kiss or why."

Her words hit me like a punch to the gut. I lean closer, my voice low and dangerous. "You're right. I'm not your keeper. But I am the one who has to deal with Gilles' smug face every time I see him now."

"Oh, poor you," Tate mocks, rolling her eyes. "How terrible it must be for you to see someone happy."

"Happy?" I bark out a laugh. "You think that asshole cares about you?"

Tate's face flushes red with anger. "And you do?"

The question hangs in the air between us. Lightning flashes across Tate's face, and I can see the challenge in her eyes.

Something snaps inside me. Before I can think, I've grabbed her face in my hands and crushed my lips against hers. It's rough, desperate, nothing like the gentle kiss she shared with Gilles. I want to erase every trace of him from her memory.

Tate gasps against my mouth, her body stiffening in surprise. But then she melts into me, her hands circle my neck, pulling me closer. I growl, deepening the kiss, my tongue demanding entrance. She opens for me, and I taste her, sweet and intoxicating.

My hands slide down her damp neck, over her shoulders, gripping her waist. I want to touch every inch of her, to claim her as mine. The blanket falls away as I pull her onto my lap, pressing her against me. A loud bolt of thunder shakes the earth, and my heart jolts.

Tate's moan sets my nerves on fire, electrifying every inch of me. She fists her hands in my hair, and I let out a rough sound. I tear my mouth from hers, peppering kisses down her jaw and throat.

"Leon," she gasps, her voice breathy and desperate.

I pull back, looking into her eyes. They're dark with desire, her lips swollen from my kisses. I've never seen anything more beautiful.

"We shouldn't do this," Tate whispers.

"You don't sound convincing." I grin, grazing my tongue along her lower lip before tugging it between my teeth.

Tate's eyes flutter closed, relishing my touch. She laughs weakly, shaking her head. "No, I'm not."

I can smell the scent of Tate's fruity shampoo as locks of her damp hair hang in my face. Her heavy-lidded gaze is stuck on me as I graze my fingers along the naked skin of her midriff, toying with the hem of her sweater.

"You're so soft," I mutter, my fingers digging into her flesh. I peck her chin. "So warm. I bet you're even warmer between your legs for me."

Tate's breath is warm on my lips as she leans in, pressing her mouth to mine in a slow, deep kiss.

I pull her closer, my hands roaming her body as our kiss deepens. Droplets streak down the windows, blurring the world outside. The rhythmic drumming on the metal roof drowns out everything else, leaving only Tate and me. Warmth radiates from her body, a stark contrast to the chill seeping in from the storm. All I can focus on is the feel of her soft skin under my fingers, the taste of her lips, the way she moves against me.

My heart races as Tate grinds her hips down, creating delicious friction. I groan into her mouth, my hands sliding up her sides, taking her damp sweater with them. She raises her arms, allowing me to pull it off completely.

"Fuck," I breathe, taking in the view of her in just her bra. My hands cup her breasts, thumbs brushing over her hardened nipples through the fabric. Tate arches into my touch, her breath hitching.

I trail kisses down her neck, nipping and sucking at her pulse point. Her fingers tangle in my hair, tugging slightly as I make my way lower. I reach behind her, fumbling with the clasp of her bra.

"Leon," Tate gasps as I finally unhook it, letting it fall away. But her hands instinctively come up, covering her tits. I silence her with another kiss, before sliding my hands over her wrists.

"Do you want me to stop?" I ask, holding Tate's eyes.

Her chest rises and falls, and she swallows, conflict clear on her face. But then she shakes her head. "No," she whispers. "Don't stop."

That's all the encouragement I need. I gently pull her hands away from her chest, and begin kneading her tits, kissing along her jaw. There's a rigidness to her body, like she's not used to this.

Since she'd never kissed anyone before taking the stupid dare, she must be a virgin. I don't know why, but the realization makes me incredibly... pleased?

The hard ridge of my cock rubs against Tate's inner thigh through my jeans, and it's driving me crazy. I capture a nipple between my lips, swirling my tongue around the sensitive bud. Tate throws her head back, a low moan echoing through the truck.

As I work my mouth and knead her flesh, Tate's trembling, her breath coming in quick, shallow gasps. I want to touch her, to feel her heat, her wetness. I want to make her scream my name.

"You're soaking wet for me, aren't you?" I whisper, my lips brushing against her ear. "Just begging for me."

My free hand slides down her stomach, fingers toying with the button of her jeans.

I can feel the heat radiating from her core as I pop the button open, slowly lowering the zipper. Tate's breathing quickens, her hips rocking against me. I slip my fingers beneath, groaning when I cup her panties.

"Fuck, Tate," I growl, palming her heat.

Tate's hips buck against my hand, seeking more friction. I tease her, applying pressure then easing off, driving her wild.

"Please," she gasps, her nails digging into my shoulders. I smirk, enjoying the spectacle of her coming undone. I slip my fingers beneath her panties, finally touching her bare flesh. She's smooth, wet, and incredibly hot.

I explore her folds, spreading her wetness up to her clit. Tate jolts at the contact, a soft moan escaping her lips. I circle the sensitive bud, applying gentle pressure. Her breath comes in quick pants, her body tensing.

"You're so hot, Tate," I murmur, my voice hoarse with desire. She gasps as I slide my finger inside her, body tensing. I can feel her discomfort, so I don't move, giving her time to adjust, my thumb stroking her clit softly. I've seen Tate finger herself, but I guess it's different when someone else is doing it to you for the first time.

"Leon," she whispers, her voice trembling.

I can see the mix of fear and desire in her eyes. "Shh, it's okay," I murmur, leaning in to kiss her gently. "I've got you."

I start to move my finger slowly, gently exploring her. She's tight, so fucking tight, and I can feel every ripple of her muscles as she starts to relax. I curl my finger slightly, searching for that spot that will make her see stars.

Tate's breath hitches, her hips jerking slightly. I can feel her growing wetter, her body responding to my touch. I keep my movements slow and steady, letting her get used to the sensation.

I take in Tate's face. Her eyes are closed, lips slightly parted, and her cheeks are flushed. She's breathtaking, a vision of pure, unadulterated need. Then, when we hit a good pace, her eyes flutter open, meeting mine, and I see a flicker of surprise mixed with something deeper, something more primal.

Tate holds my gaze, biting her lip.

"That's it," I whisper, my lips brushing against her ear. "Just feel, Tate. Feel how good it is."

She moans softly, her head falling back against the wheel. I see the pleasure starting to take over, her hips moving in time with my hand. I increase the pressure on her clit, circling it faster as I slide a second finger inside her.

Tate gasps, her nails digging into my shoulders once more. "Fuck," she pants, her eyes fluttering closed.

"You're doing so good," I growl, my dick bulging painfully. I'd fuck her given the chance, but it doesn't feel right to do it in my dad's truck. But I promise myself I will later.

Her hips buck against my hand, her breath coming in quick gasps. I can feel her getting closer, her muscles tightening around my fingers.

"Leon, please," she begs, her voice breathy and desperate.

"Please what?" I ask, my voice low and husky. "Tell me what you want."

Her eyes meet mine, her cheeks flushed and her lips parted. "Make me come, Leon," she whispers. "Please make me come."

I growl at her words. Hearing Tate beg for release is intoxicating. I capture her lips in a searing kiss, swallowing her moans as I increase the pace of my fingers.

"Come for me, Tate," I whisper against her mouth.

My thumb circles her clit faster, applying more pressure. I curl my fingers inside her again, and her body tenses.

"Leon, I'm... I'm..." Her hand flies to the grab handle above.

"That's it, baby," I encourage, feeling her walls start to flutter around my fingers. "Come for me."

Her body convulses, inner muscles clamping down on my fingers. Tate cries out, her orgasm crashing over her. Her hand falls to the window, streaking across the condensation before bracing against me. I continue to stroke her, prolonging her pleasure until she collapses against me, spent.

I withdraw my hand, bringing my fingers to my mouth. I suck her taste off them, savoring the sweetness, my eyes locked onto Tate's. She watches me intently, cheeks flushed a deep pink, chest still heaving as her breath slowly returns to normal. I can see the mixture of satisfaction and uncertainty in her gaze.

"That was..." Tate stammers, her voice barely above a whisper. She pauses, swallowing hard before composing herself. "Don't tell your dad."

I grin, feeling a rush of power and excitement course through me. "You don't need to worry, stepsis," I assure her. Leaning in closer, my lips brush against her ear. "This is our little secret."

10

TATE

By 1:00 AM, it's safe enough to drive through the last dregs of the storm. Leon starts the engine, and the rain patters softly against the windshield as he navigates the wet roads.

I feel... rejuvenated in a way I've never felt before. There's a sting between my legs, but also an ache—the good kind of ache. I came into the truck soaked to the bone and freezing, but after my little tryst with Leon, I'm radiating warmth.

And I'm so ready for bed. My eyes keep fluttering shut, my head lolling back against the headrest. The motion of the truck rocking me to sleep like a baby.

But my mind still races. The impression of Leon's mouth comes back to me, hot and demanding. The pressure of his lips against mine, the way his tongue explored every inch of skin. My body tingles with the recollection of his passionate kisses, leaving me aching for more—despite exhaustion tugging at my consciousness.

I've never been intimate with someone before. And it's Leon of all people who made me feel so good.

But I know he does this with girls; I'm not expecting anything from it. He was jealous of Gilles and wanted to let off steam, and I don't know what came over me in that moment. As soon as his mouth latched onto mine, I was under a spell and wanted him so bad.

Even though Leon's my stepbrother. Even though Jerome's my stepfather, and would absolutely lose it if he found out. Guilt twists in my gut at the thought of him, but I push it away. I can't deal with that right now. And my mom…

I don't want to think about her.

Leon pulls up to the house, the engine quieting as he turns the key. For a moment, we sit in silence, the only sound the soft patter of rain on the roof.

"We're here," he murmurs, his voice husky and low.

I nod, suddenly feeling awkward.

Leon opens his door, and the spell breaks. I fumble with my seatbelt, my fingers clumsy with fatigue and lingering desire. The cool night air hits me as I step out, making me shiver.

We walk to the house, our footsteps hushed on the wet gravel. Leon opens the door, holding it for me. I slip past him, careful not to brush against him. I'm not sure I could handle more contact right now.

The house is dark and quiet. Jerome must be asleep.

We climb the stairs, our feet whispering against the wood. At the top, we pause, facing each other in the dim hallway. Leon's eyes gleam in the darkness, intense and unreadable.

"Goodnight, Tate," he murmurs softly.

"Goodnight," I whisper back.

For a heartbeat, I think he might kiss me again. My breath catches, my body leaning toward him almost involuntarily. But he just gives me a small nod and turns away, disappearing into his room.

I stand there for a moment, my heart pounding. Then I shake myself and head to my own room, closing the door behind me with a soft click.

***

I sit at an old desk retrofitted for the library's computers. It's a cozy little nook, surrounded by shelves of thick books.

Jerome dropped me off this morning. Unlike his house, the village has Internet and a small but functional library. I need to focus on schoolwork today since I've caught up on the previous class schedule.

I log into my school account and pull up the assignment list. A science report on climate change and some algebra problems stare back at me. Sighing, I open a new document and start typing.

The hours slip by as I dive into research on rising global temperatures and melting ice caps. It's depressing stuff, but I force myself to focus. I've always been good at science, and I don't want to fall behind just because I'm in a different country.

Around noon, I take a break to stretch my legs and grab a sandwich from the small café next door. The old woman behind the counter smiles at me, her wrinkled face kind. I stumble through ordering in French, and she chuckles, switching to heavily accented English.

Back at the computer, I tackle some math homework. Numbers have never been my strong suit, but I work through the problems methodically. By midafternoon, my brain feels like mush, but I've finished both assignments.

Now, I need to check my grades.

My fingers hover over the mouse, hesitating for a moment before I click the link. As the page loads, I can't help but glance around. The library's quiet, save for the soft rustling of pages and the occasional whisper.

I brace myself with a purposeful breath for what I'm about to see.

The page loads, and my heart sinks as I scan the rows of numbers and letters. C's and D's stare back at me, mocking my efforts. I blink hard, willing the grades to change, but they remain stubbornly disappointing.

A lump forms in my throat as I scroll through the report. Each low score feels like a punch to the gut, reminding me of all the times I'd struggled to focus on the schoolwork my teachers emailed me, too preoccupied with my mom's disappearance to pay attention.

What does this mean for my future? College is around the corner, but it feels like a distant dream now with these shit grades.

My mom's voice echoes in my head, harsh and cutting. *You'll never make it past the fries, Tate.* The memory of her words stings, and I feel tears prickling at the corners of my eyes.

I close the browser window, unable to look at my failure any longer. If I don't get good credits in my finals this August, I won't make it to college. The library suddenly feels suffocating, the silence oppressive.

What if my mom was right? What if all I'm destined for is a life of flipping burgers and living paycheck to paycheck?

I stand abruptly, the chair scraping loudly against the floor. A few heads turn in my direction, but I barely notice.

Outside the library, Jerome's truck pulls up, and I hurry over, eager to escape my own thoughts. As I climb in, I feel his eyes on me, studying my face.

"Everything alright, Tate?" he asks, his brow furrowing with concern.

I force a smile, not wanting to burden him with my academic failures. "Yeah, just tired from all the schoolwork."

Jerome nods, but I can tell he's not entirely convinced. He shifts the truck into gear and pulls away from the curb. As we drive through the village, I stare out the window, trying to push away the anxiety gnawing at my insides.

"We're going to make a quick stop at the car wash," Jerome announces, breaking the silence. "The truck could use a good cleaning after that storm you drove through."

I nod absently, barely registering his words. Heat rises to my cheeks as I'm reminded of last night with Leon, but my mind flicks back to those stupid grades. The gentle rumble of the truck's engine fills the cab as we leave the village behind, heading toward the outskirts.

Jerome pulls into a small, rundown car wash. The place looks deserted, with faded signs and rusty equipment. He parks the truck in one of the bays and turns to me.

"Alright, Tate. Time to get your hands dirty," he states, a mischievous glint in his eye.

I roll my eyes. I'm not in the mood for his method of helping me today. He's going to make me work again? "What do you mean?"

He nods toward the self-serve washing equipment. "You're going to wash the truck. It'll do you good to focus on something physical for a while."

I want to protest, but the determined look on his face tells me it's pointless. With a sigh, I climb out of the truck and approach the washing station, smelling old soap.

Jerome leans out the window, calling instructions. "Put some coins in the machine, grab the pressure washer, and start with the wheels. Work your way up."

I follow his directions, inserting a handful of euros into the slot. The machine whirs to life, and I pick up the pressure washer. It's heavier than I expected, and I struggle to aim it at first.

As I start spraying the wheels, the powerful jet of water kicks up dirt and grime. I can't help but feel satisfied seeing the truck's rims begin to shine. The repetitive motion and the sound of rushing water are oddly soothing.

I move on to the body of the truck, watching as sheets of water cascade down the sides, carrying away dust and mud.

Jerome winds down the window a little. "Don't forget the roof!"

I stretch up on my tiptoes, trying to reach the top. I struggle to reach the roof, the water splashing back onto my face and shirt. Frustrated, I glance at Jerome through the windshield. He's watching me with an amused expression, clearly enjoying my predicament.

"I can't reach," I call out, gesturing at the roof.

Jerome gestures to the hood and mouths *be careful.*

For real? He could just get out of the fucking truck and do it himself. This is too complicated for no reason.

I hesitate for a moment, then set the pressure washer down. Carefully, I hoist myself onto the hood. The metal is cool and slick under my hands and knees. I grab the pressure washer again and start spraying the roof.

As I stretch to reach the center of the roof, I feel my shirt clinging to my skin, soaked through from the splashing water. I glance down and realize with a jolt that the wet fabric is practically see-through.

For a fleeting second, I catch Jerome staring at me. His gaze intense and dark, honed on my thighs, then my chest. It's enough to send a bolt of heat through my body, the pressure washer forgotten in my hand. But then, I meet his eyes through the glass.

And he knows then and there, I saw what he was doing. His Adam's apple bobs as he swallows, lips thinning into a strained line.

My heart thunders in my chest. I should feel embarrassed, should scramble off the hood and cover myself, but I don't. It's subtle, but I can see Jerome's chest rising and falling rapidly, like I'm making him nervous.

Slowly, deliberately, I slide my hand down the windshield, leaving a trail of water droplets in its wake. Jerome's eyes follow my movement, his gaze burning into my skin. I feel powerful, desirable, in a way I never have before.

I like feeling Jerome's eyes on me.

Suddenly, the spell is broken by the beeping of the car wash machine, signaling the end of our time. I startle, nearly slipping off the hood. Jerome blinks, shaking his head as if coming out of a trance.

Again, he cracks the window down an inch, and his voice comes out rough. "We should... we should go."

I nod, unable to form words. As I slide off the hood, my legs feel shaky. I grab a towel from the back of the truck and hastily try to dry myself off, avoiding Jerome's gaze.

I climb into the passenger seat, my heart still racing. Jerome starts the engine, his movements stiff and controlled. As we pull out of the car wash, I sneak glances at him from the corner of my eye.

His jaw is clenched, a muscle ticking in his cheek. I can see his knuckles are white where he grips the steering wheel. The silence between us is deafening, filled with all the things we can't say.

I want to say something, anything, to break this awkward silence, but words fail me.

As we drive along the winding roads back to the house, I can't help but replay the moment on the hood of the truck in my mind. The way Jerome looked at me, like he wanted to devour me… Part of me is thrilled by the intensity of his gaze, but another part is terrified of what it might mean.

Does he regret what happened? Is he angry with me? The uncertainty gnaws at my insides.

We're about halfway home when Jerome finally speaks. "Tate," he says, his voice low and gravelly. "What happened at the car wash, and the cabin that day…"

I hold my breath, waiting for him to continue. My stomach twists.

Jerome takes a deep breath. "It can't happen again. Do you understand?"

I nod quickly, relief and disappointment warring inside me. "I understand," I whisper.

He glances at me then, his green eyes softening slightly. "You're young, Tate. And I'm… I'm supposed to be taking care of you. We can't blur those lines."

I swallow hard, fighting the urge to argue. Nothing happened, he just looked at me. Instead, I nod again. "Okay."

Jerome clears his throat, shifting gears in both the truck and our conversation. "So, what was really bothering you at the library? You seemed upset when I picked you up."

I bite my lip, debating whether to tell him the truth. His concerned gaze breaks down my resolve, and I sigh. "I checked my grades. They're… not great."

"How bad?"

"Mostly C's and D's," I admit, my voice barely above a whisper.

Jerome's brow furrows as he processes this information. "I see," he remarks, his voice thoughtful. "And how do you feel about that?"

I shrug, trying to appear nonchalant even as anxiety churns in my stomach. "It sucks, but what can I do? I've missed a lot of school, and it's been hard to focus with... everything."

He nods, understanding in his eyes. "Of course. It's been a difficult time for you. But Tate, these grades don't define you. You're intelligent and capable. We just need to figure out a plan to get you back on track."

Jerome's words of encouragement catch me off guard. I've been so used to hearing the opposite, especially from my mom, that I don't know how to respond at first. I fidget with the hem of my damp shirt, trying to find the right words.

"I... I don't know," I finally mumble, staring down at my hands. "It's just... everyone always acts like I'm stupid because I don't get straight A's. Like, if you're not acing every class, you might as well give up, you know?"

I take a shaky breath, feeling the weight of years of criticism pressing down on me. "My mom... she always said I'd never amount to anything. That I was too dumb to make it past flipping burgers." My voice cracks a little as I continue, "And now, seeing these grades, I can't help but think maybe she was right. Maybe I'm just... not smart enough."

The words tumble out before I can stop them, all the insecurities and self-doubt I've been carrying spilling into the open. "It's like, no matter how hard I try, I'll never be good enough. And everyone can see it."

I risk a glance at Jerome, half expecting to see pity or disappointment in his eyes. Instead, I'm met with a look of understanding and something that almost seems like anger—not at me, but at the situation.

Jerome's voice is firm but gentle. "I need you to listen to me very carefully… I'm telling you right now, Tate, most people are stupid, but you're not one of them."

His words hit me like a punch to the gut, and I feel tears welling up in my eyes. I try to blink them away, but they spill over, hot trails down my cheeks.

"What are we even defining as smart here? Someone who goes to college? Just because someone has a degree doesn't make them smart. What did your mom do with her college degree?"

"Nothing," I mumble, wiping at my face.

"See? She's not holding herself to her own standard then. But you know what you are, Tate? A reliable worker. You're always helping me out, and you don't complain even when things get tough. And that's something your mom never had."

I sniff, considering his words. "I feel like I'll be missing something crucial if I miss college."

Jerome sighs. "I used to think that too when I was your age. I hated high school so much, I dropped out, but even then, I'd envy my friends. Then they told me college isn't all it's cut out to be." He pauses, then adds, "The point is, if you don't get into college, you'll wonder about all the stuff you could've done with a degree. And if you were in college, you'll wonder about all the stuff you could've done without it. This isn't the be-all and end-all of your life, Tate. Trust me."

Jerome's words settle over me like a warm blanket, offering comfort I didn't know I needed. I take a shaky breath, trying to process everything he's said.

"I... I never thought about it like that," I admit, my voice barely above a whisper. "It's just, everyone always made it out like college was the only way to be successful."

Jerome nods, his eyes still on the road. "That's what society tells us, but it's not the whole truth. There are many paths to success, Tate. And success itself can mean different things to different people."

I wipe the last of my tears away, feeling a strange mix of relief and uncertainty. "So... what should I do then? About school, I mean."

He glances at me, a small smile tugging at his lips. "Well, first things first, we need to get your grades up. Not because they define you, but because they open doors. Options are always good to have."

I nod, feeling a spark of determination ignite within me. "Okay. Yeah, I can do that."

"I know you can," Jerome replies, his voice filled with a confidence I wish I felt. "We'll work on it together. Set up a study schedule, maybe get you some extra help if you need it."

As we drive, the tension from earlier appears to dissipate, replaced by a comfortable silence. I marvel at how Jerome can make me feel so... seen. It's a stark contrast to how my mom always made me feel. It's like he knows me better than I know myself.

11

JEROME

The truck smells of damp earth and sex. It's been like that since this morning, and even after Tate washed the truck, I can still smell it. It's driving me crazy.

I wasn't pleased at seeing the outside sprayed with mud from the storm last night, but I can't blame Leon for the weather. I can, however, blame him for not cleaning up after his sex trysts. I made sure to wind the windows down so Tate couldn't recognize it when she got in. Although, I don't know if she knows what—

My mind can't go there. No matter how much it wants to.

As we drive home, the memory of her toned thighs in those little high waisted shorts against the windshield flashes before my eyes, and I swallow. Then the memory of back at the cabin, her paint-streaked face inches from mine. If Leon hadn't interrupted us, I would've kissed Tate. Possibly done more than that.

I don't know what came over me at the car wash. She's such a reliable, good girl, and doesn't cringe at the prospect of spending time with me—not that she has to. But I've worked on the cabin with Tate more than I have with Leon.

Bianca wouldn't even spend time with me like that. The more I think back, the more I realize she and I have very different interests.

But with Tate, I've never felt this way about anyone, and it's scary how much I want to just give in.

Thankfully, she hasn't brought up the almost-kiss. And I'm hoping she doesn't.

I pull into the driveway, cutting the engine as darkness settles around us. Tate's been quiet the whole ride home, her mind clearly elsewhere. I will help her set up a study schedule, but that's something we can do tomorrow. As we both step out of the truck, I remember she wanted me to show her how to use the French range cooker.

"Are you up for a cooking lesson?" I ask.

Tate's eyes light up and she nods. "Yeah, I want to cook on the stove."

It's cute that she calls it a stove. I hold the front door open for her. "It's a French range cooker. Have you ever made French onion soup?"

She purses her lips, curiosity peeking in her voice. "No, never."

"Well, you'll love it."

"Great, let me get changed first," Tate says, racing upstairs in her damp clothes.

I head into the kitchen to get everything ready, and Tate comes back dressed in her pajamas.

I roll up my sleeves. "First things first, let's fire up the cooker."

I walk Tate through the process of lighting the cooker, explaining each step. Her hands tremble slightly as she turns the knob, but soon enough, a steady flame dances beneath the burner.

"Look at that, you're a natural." I wink at her.

A small smile tugs at her lips. "Now what?"

"Now, we chop onions." I grab a few from the pantry, tossing one her way. She catches it, fumbling slightly. "Think you can handle that?"

Tate nods, determination setting her jaw. I show her how to slice the onions thinly, our hands working in tandem. The kitchen fills with the sharp scent, and I catch her wiping her eyes.

"Gets to everyone." I chuckle, sliding the onions into a pot with a generous pat of butter. "Here's where the magic happens."

I guide her through the process, explaining each step as we go. She listens intently, asking questions and following my lead. The onions caramelize, filling the kitchen with a rich, sweet aroma.

"Now for the secret ingredient," I say, reaching for a bottle of cognac. Her eyes widen as I pour a splash into the pot, the alcohol igniting in a brief, dramatic flame.

"Whoa!" Tate jumps back, then laughs—a genuine, carefree sound that warms me more than the French range cooker ever could.

As we finish up the soup, ladling it into bowls and topping it with crusty bread and melted cheese, I can't help but feel a sense of pride.

"Ready to taste your creation?" I ask, sliding a bowl her way.

"You helped me," Tate clarifies, toasting her spoon of soup toward me. As she takes her first bite, her eyes close in appreciation. "Oh my God, this is amazing."

I grin, settling in across from her. "See? You've got more talent than you give yourself credit for."

"We'll see." She smiles, stirring her soup. "The real test is when I cook alone."

The kitchen door swings open and Leon strolls in, his hair still damp from a shower. His eyes narrow at the scene of Tate and me at the table.

"Something smells good." He grabs a bowl from the cabinet.

"Your timing's perfect." I gesture to the pot. "Tate made French onion soup."

Leon pauses, spoon hovering over the pot, and I catch a hint of possessiveness in his tone. "You taught her to use the range?"

"She did great." I nod. "Grab some bread and cheese."

He joins us at the table, his chair scraping against the floor. The silence stretches as he takes his first bite.

"It's good." Leon's voice carries surprise. He glances at Tate, who keeps her eyes fixed on her bowl.

I watch them both, noting the careful way they avoid looking at each other. They've fought again? I take a spoonful of soup.

"Thanks." Tate's voice is barely above a whisper.

"You should learn to make coq au vin next." Leon breaks off a piece of bread. "Dad makes the best in the region."

"That's because your great-grandmother's recipe is unbeatable." I smile at the recollection of learning it myself. "Though I had to practice for months to get it right."

A few minutes later, Leon clears his bowl and heads upstairs with a mumbled, "Bonne nuit."

Tate stacks our empty dishes in the sink. "Mind if I watch something in the attic?" she asks.

"Not at all." I dry my hands on a dish towel. "Want company?"

She nods, already heading upstairs. I follow her up to the attic where she settles by the laptop on the floor. The projector flickers to life, casting a blue glow across her face as she leafs through the DVD options in the case.

"Oh, Bridget Bardot!" Her eyes light up at *And God Created Woman.*

"Ah, a classic." I sink into the couch cushions, watching her insert the DVD and hit play.

Tate settles down on the couch beside me and the film starts. I find myself more aware of her than the screen. She draws her knees up, wrapping her arms around them. The soft light plays across her delicate features, highlighting the curve of her cheek, the slight part of her lips.

Bardot's character dances on screen, sensual and free-spirited. Tate shifts beside me, and her shoulder brushes against my arm. Neither of us move away. My heart picks up speed, beating an irregular rhythm against my ribs.

"She's beautiful," Tate whispers, her voice carrying a note of something I can't quite place.

"She is," I murmur, but my eyes aren't on the screen. They're fixed on Tate's profile, the way the projector's light dances across her features. Her blond hair catches the glow like spun gold, and her hazel eyes reflect the flickering images. "Beautiful in a natural way. The kind of beauty that doesn't need artifice."

Tate turns to me, perhaps sensing my gaze. But my eyes dart back to the screen. "She caused quite the scandal back then."

"Because she owned her sexuality?"

The question hangs in the air between us, heavy with implication. Heat creeps up my neck. Onscreen, Bardot's character kisses her lover passionately.

Tate looks away, but not before I catch the flush spreading across her cheeks. My fingers itch to brush against her skin, to trace the path of that blush.

I grip the armrest instead, forcing my attention back to the movie.

An hour passes, and Tate's fallen asleep against my shoulder, her breathing soft and even. I should wake her, send her to bed, but I can't bring myself to move.

The second my eyes are back on the screen, a splash of cold hits my face. I jolt, water dripping down my chin.

Suddenly, Tate stands before me, a half glass of water in hand, fighting back laughter. She must have been fake sleeping. "Payback for the paint."

I wipe my face with my shirt. "You little—"

She bolts, giggling. I chase her down the attic stairs, our footsteps echoing through the quiet house. She darts into the kitchen, using the island as a barrier between us.

"Think you're clever?" I circle left.

She moves right. "Very." Her eyes sparkle with mischief.

I fake going one way, then cut back. She squeals, trying to escape, but I catch her around the waist. Water from my shirt seeps into hers as I pull her close.

"Got you." My voice comes out husky.

Tate's laughter dies. She tilts her head back, meeting my gaze. Her lips part slightly, and I feel her pulse racing under my fingers where they rest against her hip.

A drop of water trails down my neck. Her eyes follow its path, then flick back to my mouth. The air grows thick between us. I should step back, let her go, but my body won't obey.

She rises on her tiptoes, her breath warm against my chin. My head dips lower, drawn by some magnetic force I can't resist.

"Tate," I say in a warning tone. "Don't do this to me."

"What?" She breathes, playing coy.

It takes everything in me to back away. I stalk out of the kitchen, down through the foyer and into the end living room that's shrouded in darkness. My mind is spinning, and I can hear Tate's footsteps behind me.

I make sure to keep my voice low, only loud enough for her to hear. "We can't do that, Tate. You're a nice girl. But you know exactly what it looks like."

She frowns like she's been reprimanded. "Nothing happened, Jerome. Calm down."

"I *can't*," I say savagely, coming in so close, my heart spikes. "What did you feel?"

"I feel…" Her lips part, and she looks up at me with doe eyes. They're like hooks pulling me in, inescapable. "Like I wanted it."

I make an effort to breathe, but my voice still comes out harsh. "If anyone saw us, I'd be in jail. The police will think I removed Bianca just to get to you." I don't want this thing we feel to be a slimy, dirty secret. The implication of me being a predator to Tate—I'm not some sick fuck who would take advantage of her, but that's exactly what everyone will see. "It's disgusting."

Tate considers my words for a moment, the whirlwind it could be if we act on these urges. Instead of being shaken by it, there's a stout reasoning and calmness in her voice as she looks me in the eye. "Jerome, none of that is true. It's not happened, and we didn't kiss." Seeing how freaked out I am, Tate gives me distance, leaning against a set of drawers by the window. "But I'm capable of making my own choices, and I'd be lying if I said I didn't want it to happen. No one has to know."

I blink, not believing this is real. Tate's in over her head.

My hand grips the edge of the drawer next to me, knuckles turning white. The room feels too small, the air too thick.

"Listen to yourself," I say, running a hand through my hair. "You're eighteen, Tate. I'm old enough to be your father."

"But you're not my father." Her voice carries a stubborn edge.

"No, I'm your stepfather. Your mom trusted me—"

"My mom abandoned me!" The words burst from her like a dam breaking. "She left me here, with you. And maybe..." She takes a shaky breath. "Maybe that's the only good thing she's ever done for me."

The raw honesty in her voice hits me like a physical blow. I turn away, pressing my forehead against the cool glass of the window. Outside, the night is pitch black, reflecting our silhouettes.

"This isn't right," I whisper, more to myself than her. "You're confused, vulnerable—"

"Don't." Her voice hardens. "Don't treat me like I'm some stupid kid who doesn't know what she wants."

I hear her footsteps approaching, but I don't turn around. Can't turn around. If I look at her now...

"Jerome." Her hand touches my shoulder, and I flinch. "I know what I'm feeling. And I think you do too."

God help me, I do. That's the problem. That's been the problem since she first stepped off that plane, looking lost and beautiful and so goddamn young.

"Go to bed, Tate." My voice comes out rough. "Please."

I feel her arms wrap around my waist from behind, her cheek pressing against my back. My resolve crumbles like sand.

"Please don't push me away," she whispers.

I turn in her arms, my hands finding her shoulders to create distance, but the moment I look into her eyes, I'm lost. She rises on her toes, and this time, I don't stop her.

Her lips meet mine, soft and tentative. A groan escapes me as I pull her closer. She melts into me, her fingers sliding up my chest to tangle in my shirt.

I turn us around and back her against the window, deepening the kiss. She sighs into my mouth, the sound undoing the last threads of my control. My hand cups her face, thumb brushing across her cheek as our lips move together in a desperate dance.

Reality crashes back when she whispers my name against my lips. I break away, breathing hard, my forehead resting against hers. Her eyes flutter open, dark with desire.

"We shouldn't have done that," I murmur, but fuck I can't stop now. Goddammit. I capture her lips again, harder this time.

"Then stop," Tate challenges against my mouth, her breath hot on my skin.

I pull back just enough to look at her. "You first."

She shakes her head, a wicked smile playing on her lips. "Make me."

"Christ, Tate." I groan, pressing her harder against the window. My hand slides into her hair, tilting her head back and kissing her neck. "You're playing with fire."

"Maybe I like getting burned." Her fingers hook into my belt loops, pulling my hips against hers.

132

She gasps, feeling the hard ridge of my cock in my jeans, and the contact makes me hiss.

"You're too young to know what you want."

"Really?" She nips at my bottom lip. "Because I feel pretty clear on it."

I catch her wandering hands, pinning them above her head. "You're trouble."

"And you're stalling." She arches against me, testing my grip.

"Brat," I murmur, claiming her mouth again.

She laughs into the kiss, the sound turning into a soft moan when I release her hands to cup her face.

"Old man," she teases back, fingers threading through my hair.

My thumb traces her jawline as I explore her mouth, each sweep of my tongue drawing another sweet sound from her. She tastes divine—like forbidden fruit, like everything I shouldn't want but desperately need.

Her hands snake around my neck, pulling me down harder against her lips. The kiss turns fierce, hungry. I move her against the set of drawers, lifting her onto it. Her legs wrap around my waist, and I groan into her mouth.

The rational part of my brain screams at me to stop, but her mouth is intoxicating, her little gasps addictive. I trail kisses down her neck, and she arches into me, exposing more of her throat.

"Jerome," she softly moans, the sound of my name on her lips nearly undoing me.

Her hands slip under my damp shirt, her touch scorching against my skin. I capture her mouth again, pouring all my pent-up desire into the kiss. She matches my passion, kiss for desperate kiss, touch for burning touch.

A floorboard creaks overhead, and reality slams back into me like a bucket of ice water. Leon. My son is upstairs, probably still awake.

I break the kiss, pressing my forehead against Tate's. "Not here," I manage between ragged breaths. "Not tonight."

"Why?" She tries to pull me back, but I grip her shoulders, keeping her at arm's length.

"Leon could come down any second." The words taste bitter in my mouth.

Her eyes widen with realization, then narrow. "So?"

"So, this isn't happening. Not like this." I step back, putting space between us. My body screams in protest.

Tate slides off the set of drawers, her cheeks flushed with anger now instead of desire. "You're just making excuses."

"I'm being realistic." I run a hand through my hair, trying to steady my breathing. "This isn't some game, Tate."

"No, it's not." She straightens her cami, jaw set in a hard line. "But you're too scared to admit what you want."

"What I want doesn't matter." The words come out harsher than intended.

She flinches like I've slapped her. "Fine."

Before I can respond, she storms past me and up the stairs. Her bedroom door slams shut moments later, the sound echoing through the quiet house.

ARCADIA

I slump against the wall, my heart still racing. The ghost of her kiss lingers on my lips, and my cock tents my pants painfully, a torturous reminder of what I just pushed away.

12

TATE

The old floorboards creak under my feet as I make my way down the hall, avoiding Jerome's quiet "good morning." I mumble a response without stopping, the memory of our argument still a raw, burning thing inside me.

My fingers clench into fists, nails digging into my palms. The slam of my bedroom door last night echoes, the sound rattling in my bones. I can still feel the ghost of his lips on mine, the memory searing under my skin.

I pace the familiar space, the air thick with tension. Everything feels tainted now—the gentle brush of his hand, the warmth in his eyes. I push away the ache, the longing, focusing instead on the anger that flares hot and bright.

Sinking onto the bed, I drag my hands through my hair, gripping the strands. It not easy sharing a house with him now. Every time Jerome tries to engage me in conversation, I give him short answers. Even helping me organize my study schedule, I made sure to make no room for genuine connection.

I'm avoiding him as much as I can so he knows how it feels. But Jerome still tries—fresh coffee is always waiting for me in the morning, my favorite snacks appearing in the pantry.

Yesterday he asked about my latest art project and I pretended not to hear him.

The guilt in his gaze only fuels my resentment.

Leon's noticed, of course. "You two fighting?" he'd asked, sprawled across my bed just yesterday. I'd shrugged, not ready to unpack the mess of emotions Jerome has left me with.

But tonight, I want to test something. I need to see if I can still get a reaction from him, if I can make him break. Because what infuriates me more than anything is Jerome being a coward.

I stand at the stove, shifting from foot to foot as steam rises from the oven. The rich aroma of wine and herbs fills the kitchen, but my stomach churns with nerves. My bare skin prickles in the cool air, and I tug the apron higher, double-checking the knot at my neck.

My phone screen glows with the screenshot of the recipe I'd found online at the library. "Coq au Vin – Traditional French Recipe." The words blur as I scan them again, my hands trembling. The chicken thighs simmer in Jerome's Burgundy—the bottle had been tucked away in his wine rack, probably saved for a special occasion. I'd recognized the label from when he'd pointed it out weeks ago, explaining how the best coq au vin needed proper Burgundy wine.

Pearl onions and mushrooms float in the dark purple liquid alongside chunks of bacon. The scent reminds me of Jerome's stories about his grandmother's cooking, how she'd taught him this dish when he was young. My heart flutters as I imagine his reaction—will he be pleased I remembered? Or furious?

The kitchen clock ticks steadily. He should be home any minute. He's spent the day at the police station helping with my mom's investigation. I stir the pot gently, watching the steam curl upward in lazy spirals. The house feels too quiet, too still. Even the birds outside have gone silent.

My skin burns everywhere the apron doesn't cover. I've never done anything this bold before. The fabric barely covers what it needs to, leaving my back completely exposed. Each brush of air against my bare skin sends chills through me.

The sound of tires on gravel makes me suck in breath, trying to calm my nerves. Headlights sweep across the kitchen window. I grip the wooden spoon tighter, my pulse racing as a car door slams outside.

The kitchen door swings open as Jerome's heavy boots thud against the floor. His sharp intake of breath cuts through the kitchen's silence, and I stand there, frozen, as Jerome's eyes burn into me. I don't turn around, keeping my eyes fixed on the bubbling pot while my heart hammers against my ribs.

"What the hell do you think you're doing?" His voice is a low growl.

I swallow hard, my heart thrumming. "I wanted to surprise you."

Jerome runs a hand through his hair, frustration radiating off him. "Surprise me?" His voice rises, and I flinch. "The detective could walk in any minute, Tate! Have you forgotten your mother's still missing?"

His words hit me like a slap. Tears well up in my eyes, and I wrap my arms around myself, suddenly feeling exposed, ridiculous. I bite my lip, trying to maintain a straight face.

The tears streaming down my face turn hot with anger. How dare he throw my mother in my face like that? After everything he's put me through—pretending nothing happened between us.

"You don't get to talk to me like that." My voice comes out stronger than I feel, even as it shakes. I grip the counter behind me. "I was trying to do something nice for you."

A muscle in his jaw jumps and his eyes narrow. "This isn't a game."

He said the same thing a week ago.

"You can't take me seriously, can you?" I swipe angrily at my tears. "I saw how you looked at me that night. I felt it when you touched me."

His jaw clenches. "Tate—"

"No!" My voice rises. "The next time you slither your way in with a gesture, flirtation or what have you—just know you'll never get another chance with me. You're dead to me," I say, my voice hitching. The tears spill over, trailing down my cheeks. I turn to flee, but he grabs my wrist, stopping me.

"Tate, wait." His voice is softer now, but I can't look at him.

I tug my wrist free and run, his calls echoing behind me.

I take the stairs two at a time, my vision blurred. I slam my bedroom door shut, leaning against it as sobs wrack my body. I feel stupid, humiliated. I thought... I don't know what

I thought. Of course, Jerome would react this way—I'm just a kid to him, playing at being grown up.

I sink to the floor, burying my face in my knees. I can still hear him downstairs, his muffled curses, a door slamming. I hug my legs tighter, wishing I could disappear.

***

I press my face deeper into the pillow, trying to drown out Jerome's voice from behind my door. Three days of this—his gentle knocks, the quiet "Tate, please" that makes my stomach twist.

The tray of food he left yesterday still sits untouched by my door. I'd only grabbed the water bottle when my throat felt like sandpaper, waiting until his footsteps faded down the hall.

The humiliation burns too hot, makes me want to crawl out of my skin every time I remember standing in that kitchen, thinking… God, I was so stupid.

"I made breakfast." Jerome's voice filters through the door. "Chocolate chip pancakes."

I curl tighter into myself, pulling the blanket over my head. I love chocolate chip pancakes. The smell drifts under my door, but instead of making my mouth water, it makes me want to scream. How dare he try to bribe me with food after what he did?

The image of his face that night—the disgust, the anger—plays on repeat behind my closed eyes. Every gentle word he ever said to me feels tainted now. Every smile, every casual touch, every moment I'd thought meant something... it was all just pity for the poor abandoned girl.

"I know you're hurting," he states softly. "Please let me explain."

"Go away!" I finally snap, my voice hoarse from disuse. "I hate you!"

The silence that follows feels heavy, suffocating. I hear him sigh, then his footsteps retreating down the hall. Good. Let him hurt like I'm hurting. Let him feel what it's like to be rejected, humiliated.

I grab my pillow and hurl it at the door, wishing I could throw away every feeling I ever had for him just as easily. The tears come again, hot and angry, and I let them fall. I'm done crying over Jerome Beaumont. Done being the stupid little girl with a crush.

A soft knock at my door makes me burrow deeper under my blankets. Not Jerome again.

"It's me." Leon's voice. "I come with food."

I peek out from my cocoon. "Just you?"

"Scout's honor. Dad's out in the cabin."

I drag myself up, shuffling to unlock the door. Leon slips in with a plate of chocolate chip pancakes and something wrapped in pink tissue paper tucked under his arm.

"Gives you something to do while you're locked away," he says, setting both items on my desk.

I pick at the edge of a pancake, my stomach growling despite myself as I stare at the box. "What is it?"

"Open it and see."

I tear at the pink tissue paper and pull out a book. The cover is made of beige fabric, embroidered with different types of colorful flowers. A button buckle seals it tight. It's the diary I was admiring in the village shop weeks ago.

"You don't need to be alone with your thoughts, Tate," Leon remarks softly, "I think it's therapeutic to write them down."

I run my fingers over the delicate stitching, then flip it open. On the first page, in Jerome's careful handwriting: "Entre-nous."

"What does that mean?" I ask.

"Something between us," Leon answers, picking at the pancake.

My heart twists. But when I turn the page, there's another note in Leon's messy scrawl: "spill your guts out - from L."

I trace both messages with my fingertip, feeling the slight indentations in the paper. It's not addressed from Jerome and Leon together, but individually. Even in a gift, their rivalry bleeds through. The thought makes me want to laugh and cry at the same time.

I stare at the two different handwritings side by side—Jerome's controlled, measured strokes next to Leon's bold, impatient scrawl. Father and son, so different, yet somehow both pulling at parts of me I didn't know existed.

My thumb brushes over Jerome's message again. "Entre-nous." Something between us. The memory of his lips against mine rises unbidden, making my chest tighten. That brief, stolen moment in the kitchen—his hand cupping my face, the scratch of his beard, the gentle pressure that somehow felt like falling and flying at the same time.

Then came the regret in his eyes. The way he'd pulled back, muttering something about it being a mistake.

"You okay?" Leon asks, his voice cutting through my thoughts. He's stretched across my bed, arms folded behind his head, watching me with those piercing blue eyes. "You went somewhere else for a second."

"Yeah, just..." I close the journal, suddenly afraid my thoughts might somehow be visible on my face. "Just thinking."

Leon shifts on the bed, propping himself up on one elbow. His proximity sends a different kind of heat through me—the memory of rain drumming against the truck windows, his hands tangled in my hair, the hungry urgency of his kiss.

I swallow hard, acutely aware of how twisted this all is. Father and son. Both under the same roof. Both making my heart race for entirely different reasons.

"Thinking about what?" Leon presses, a hint of suspicion in his voice.

"About how complicated everything is right now." It's not a lie, just not the whole truth.

Jerome is stability, protection, wisdom—everything I never had growing up with mom. When he looks at me, I feel seen for the first time in my life. Not as a burden or disappointment, but as someone with potential.

But is that why I'm drawn to him? Because he fills the void my mother left? Because he's the first adult who's ever truly cared about my well-being?

And Leon—unpredictable, challenging, exciting. He pushes me out of my comfort zone, makes me feel alive and reckless in ways I never allowed myself before. With him, I'm not the anxious, obedient girl I've always been.

But we're practically family now. All three of us.

"Yeah, well, life's complicated," Leon says with a shrug, oblivious to my internal crisis. "You just gotta decide what you want and go for it."

If only it were that simple. What do I want? Who do I want? Who am I when I'm with either of them?

The only thing I know for certain is that I can't have both. And eventually, I'll have to choose—or lose them both.

"So," Leon continues, sitting up fully now. "Are you going to write in it?"

I clutch the journal tighter, as if it might contain the answers I'm looking for. "I will. I think I need to sort through some things."

"That's the idea," he says, reaching out to tap the journal's cover. "Some things are too messy to keep locked up in your head."

He has no idea how right he is.

"He can be a real asshole sometimes." Leon picks at a loose thread on my comforter. "Trust me, I know exactly what those lectures feel like."

I curl up in my desk chair, hugging my knees to my chest. "Yeah?"

"When I was sixteen, I borrowed his truck without asking. Wanted to impress this girl." Leon's lips twist into a bitter smile. "He caught me sneaking back in. Man, I've never seen him so angry. Called me irresponsible, reckless—said I was turning out just like my mother."

I listen quietly as Leon continues, his words weighing heavily in the silence of my room.

"He apologized later, but..." Leon shrugs, but I can see the hurt in his eyes. "That's how he is. When he's scared or worried, he lashes out. Makes you feel about two inches tall."

I think about Jerome's reaction in the kitchen, how he'd thrown my mother's disappearance in my face like a weapon.

"I get it now," I say quietly.

I fiddle with the leather strap on the new journal, the weight of it comforting in my hands. My gaze drifts to the scattered school notes covering my desk. Jerome has helped me study a few times, but I still need to do more. With everything that's happened, I've barely had the mental energy to study.

Leon follows my line of sight, his brow furrowing. "Are these your study notes?"

I nod and I give a frustrated sigh. "I just... I can't focus. Every time I try to read, I end up staring at the same page for an hour."

He nods, reaching out to gather my notes into a neat pile. "Why don't we go to the library? I can quiz you on your notes, make sure you're retaining everything."

I blink at him, momentarily stunned by his unexpected offer. "You'd do that? Help me study?"

Leon shrugs, the corner of his mouth quirking up. I watch as he moves with purpose, grabbing his backpack from his room. His fingers brush against the worn fabric, and I notice the faded patches sewn onto the canvas—remnants of his own high school days.

"Here," he says, unzipping the main compartment. "Let's get your stuff organized."

I gather my scattered notes, trying to arrange them in some semblance of order. My hands shake slightly as I sort through the papers—biology notes mixed with literature essays, math formulas scrawled in the margins of my Chinese homework.

Leon takes each stack from me, carefully sliding them into different sections of his backpack. He grabs my spare notebook—the one with the blue cover that's barely been used—and adds it to the pile. A handful of sharpened pencils follow, along with an eraser.

The simple act of watching him pack my school supplies makes my chest tight. It's such a normal thing—something an older brother might do for his sister.

"Thanks," I mumble, finishing off the pancakes. For a moment I remember our kiss in his truck, his hands on my body, the rain drumming against the windows. I push the memory away, focusing instead on zipping up the backpack.

"Um, I need to get dressed so..." I gesture for him to get out the door as he shoulders the backpack on.

"Right." He grins. "Meet me in the garage when you're ready."

I nod, grateful for this chance to escape the house—and my thoughts—even if it means studying.

I pull on my favorite jeans and a cropped top, then head downstairs. The garage door creaks as I push it open, and my jaw drops. There, gleaming under the fluorescent lights, sits a sleek black motorcycle.

Leon leans against it, now dressed in a leather jacket, two helmets dangling from his hands. "Ever ridden before?"

I shake my head, mesmerized. The handlebars sweep back like wings, and the single round headlight reminds me of a watchful eye. "I didn't know you had a motorcycle."

"Dad doesn't exactly approve." He runs his hand along the fuel tank. "Keeps it under wraps, you know?"

He holds out one of the helmets—matte black with subtle pinstripes. My fingers tremble slightly as I take it, the weight unfamiliar.

"Here, let me help." Leon steps closer, his hands replacing mine on the helmet. "You want it snug, but not too tight." His fingers brush my neck as he adjusts the strap, and I hold perfectly still, caught between wanting to lean into his touch and pull away.

"How's that feel?" His voice is soft, professional. No hint of our kiss in the truck, no suggestion of anything beyond brotherly concern.

I nod, not trusting my voice. The helmet feels secure but not uncomfortable, like a firm hug around my head.

"Good." He taps the top of my helmet lightly. "Safety first, right?"

The garage suddenly feels too small, too intimate. I focus on the motorcycle instead, admiring how the morning light plays across its polished surfaces.

Leon turns to retrieve something from the cupboard before making his way behind me. "Put this on too."

I slip my arms into a leather jacket that is way too big for me. Then he hands me the backpack.

I eye the motorcycle warily as Leon swings his leg over the seat and clips on his helmet. The engine roars to life, making me jump.

"Come on," he says, patting the space behind him. "Just swing your leg over and hold on tight."

My hands tremble as I grip his shoulders for balance. The leather of his jacket is smooth under my fingers as I awkwardly mount the bike, trying not to wobble.

"Wrap your arms around my waist," Leon instructs. "And keep your feet on the pegs."

I hesitate for a moment before sliding my arms around him. The position forces me to press against his back, and I can feel the solid warmth of him through our jackets. My heart pounds so hard I wonder if he can feel it too.

"Tighter," he says, and I comply, linking my fingers over his stomach. "When we turn, lean with me. Don't fight it."

The bike rumbles beneath us as Leon kicks up the stand. I squeeze my eyes shut as we start moving, my grip around his waist becoming viselike. The wind whips at my clothes as we pick up speed, and I press my helmet against his back, seeking stability.

"You okay?" Leon calls over his shoulder.

"Yeah," I manage to squeak out, though my stomach is doing somersaults. Every bump makes me clutch him tighter, and I can feel the vibration of his chuckle through his back.

The morning air is crisp against my exposed neck, but despite my fear, there's something exhilarating about the speed, the way the world blurs past us. Leon's body is solid and reassuring against mine, and gradually, I find myself relaxing into him, my terror giving way to excitement.

The motorcycle purrs beneath us as we wind through narrow country roads. My initial terror fades with each mile, replaced by a giddy freedom I've never felt before. The wind whips at my clothes, and even through the leather jacket, I can feel the rush of cool morning air.

Leon takes a sharp turn, and I lean with him instinctively, my arms tightening around his waist. The countryside stretches out before us—rolling hills painted in shades of green and gold. We pass endless rows of lavender, their purple blooms swaying in our wake. The sweet, herbal scent fills my nose, even through the helmet.

The rumble of the engine vibrates through my entire body, matching the wild beating of my heart. Leon's back is warm against my chest, solid and steady. Each time we accelerate, I press closer, grateful for his anchoring presence.

The sun climbs higher in the sky, warming the leather of my borrowed jacket. We pass ancient stone walls covered in climbing vines, their shadows dancing across the road. A flock of birds takes flight from a nearby field, startled by our passing.

I rest my helmet against Leon's shoulder blade, watching the landscape blur past us. More lavender fields stretch into the distance, their purple haze meeting the horizon. The scent mingles with the crisp morning air and something distinctly Leon—leather and cologne and summer warmth.

The bike hugs each curve of the road, and I find myself anticipating the turns now, moving in sync with Leon's body. It feels like flying, like freedom, like everything I've been missing since coming to France.

The library appears ahead—Leon parks the motorcycle in a small courtyard, the engine's rumble echoing before falling silent.

My legs feel wobbly as I dismount, and Leon steadies me with a hand on my elbow. "First ride's always the wildest," he says, helping me with my helmet.

Inside, the library is all dark wood and filtered sunlight. The scent of old books and polished furniture fills the air. Leon navigates the space with surprising familiarity, leading me past towering shelves to the secluded study area.

"Best spot in the house," he whispers, pulling out a chair.

I raise an eyebrow. "Spend a lot of time here?"

"More than I'd like to admit." He runs his fingers along the worn edge of the table. "Dad wanted me to go to university in Paris. I practically lived here my last year of school, trying to get my grades up."

The admission surprises me. I'd pictured Leon as the type to skip class, not the kind to hole up in libraries studying.

"What happened with Paris?" I ask softly.

He shrugs, unpacking my notes. "Decided it wasn't for me. I prefer working with cars. "

The colored light from the window catches his profile, painting him in shades of blue and gold. For a moment, I glimpse a different Leon—younger, more vulnerable, bent over textbooks at this very table.

"Anyway," he says, spreading out my study materials. "Show me what you're working on."

I log on to one the computers, and find my next subject to focus on is derivatives, the equations blurring together. "I'm supposed to find the derivative of this function, but…"

"Okay." He takes my pencil, his voice dropping to match the library's hushed atmosphere. "First, what's the rule for finding the derivative of x squared?"

"Two x?"

"Right. So, for this problem…"

Hours pass as Leon guides me through problem after problem. His explanations are clear and patient, breaking down complex concepts into manageable pieces. There's no condescension when I don't understand, no frustration when he has to explain something twice.

"Holy shit," I whisper, staring at the problem I just solved. "I actually get it."

Leon's smile is genuine. "You always knew how. You just needed someone to show you the steps."

I look at him—really look at him. The bad boy facade has slipped, replaced by something softer, more real. In this moment, surrounded by books and afternoon sunlight, I see a different side of Leon Beaumont.

"Thank you," I say quietly.

He meets my eyes. "Anytime."

The ride home feels different. I'm more relaxed, my arms wrapped comfortably around his waist. The afternoon sky is shades of pink and gold, and for the first time today, I'm not thinking about Jerome at all.

When we pull up to the house, I hand Leon back his helmet. "I didn't know you were such a math nerd."

"Don't tell anyone." His eyes sparkle with amusement. "I have a reputation to maintain."

I laugh, and it feels good. Natural. "Your secret's safe with me."

I shrug off Leon's leather jacket and hand it to him, still buzzing from the motorcycle ride and our study session. The late-afternoon sun beats down, making sweat bead at my temples.

"Want to cool off?" Leon nods toward the back of the house, referring to the pool. "You can borrow one of my old t-shirts if you don't have a swimsuit."

My skin prickles with heat, and the idea of slipping into cool water is tempting. "I've got my bikini."

"Alright." He's already heading toward the house, peeling off his jacket.

I hurry upstairs to my room, digging through my dresser until I find the blue two-piece. The fabric feels flimsy in my hands as I change, and I study my reflection critically. I wore this at the gorge and yet, butterflies flutter in my stomach.

Why am I so nervous all of a sudden? Leon's seen me in this before.

But it feels different now.

Grabbing a towel from the bathroom, I pad barefoot back outside. The concrete is warm under my feet, and I wrap the towel tighter around myself, suddenly self-conscious.

Leon's already in the pool, his dark hair slicked back and water droplets running down his chest. He floats lazily on his back, eyes closed against the sun.

"Water's perfect," he calls without looking at me.

I drop my towel on one of the loungers and quickly slide into the pool before I can overthink it. The water is cool but not cold, and I let out a contented sigh as it envelops me.

"Better?" Leon asks, and I nod, dunking under to wet my hair.

When I surface, he's watching me with an unreadable expression. Water drips from his eyelashes, and I find myself tracking a droplet as it trails down his neck.

"You're staring," I say, amusement in my voice. I splash at him. "Don't you know it's rude to stare."

Leon wipes the water from his eyes, grinning. "Can you blame me? I haven't seen you all week."

The admission surprises me, and for a moment, I wonder if it's true. But the weight of his gaze confirms it—I have missed him. I just didn't realize how much.

I glide toward him, treading water in the deep end. "I've been right here."

Leon closes the distance between us, his hands finding my waist under the water. He pulls me against him, our bodies flush, and I can feel the heat of his skin despite the cool water.

"Tate," he murmurs, his breath tickling my ear. "I can't stop thinking about you."

My heart races at his confession, and I find myself pressing closer, my hands sliding up his chest to rest on his shoulders. "Leon…"

His fingers tighten on my hips, and he dips his head, his nose brushing against mine. "Tell me to stop," he whispers, his lips a hairsbreadth from mine. "Tell me you don't want this."

But I can't. Because I do want this. I want him.

I close the last bit of distance, capturing his lips with mine. The kiss is different from the one in the truck—slower, more deliberate. Leon's hands roam my back, tracing the string of my bikini top, while mine tangle in his wet hair.

He walks me backward until I'm pressed against the pool wall, the concrete rough against my skin. His tongue teases the seam of my lips, and I open for him, deepening the kiss. He tastes like chlorine and something uniquely Leon, and I can't get enough.

His hands skim my sides, his thumbs brushing the undersides of my breasts, and I gasp into his mouth. Every nerve ending feels electrified, every touch igniting a fire under my skin.

Leon breaks the kiss, trailing his lips down my neck. "God, Tate," he groans against my pulse point. "I've missed you."

I arch into him, water lapping at our bodies. "Leon, please…"

But what I'm pleading for, I don't know. More of his touch, more of his kisses, more of this feeling that consumes me whenever I'm near him.

He seems to understand, because he recaptures my lips, kissing me with a fervor that steals my breath. His hands grip my thighs, hitching my legs around his waist, and I can feel his arousal pressing against me.

Leon pulls away, resting his forehead against mine, his breathing ragged. I'm breathless too, my heart hammering in my chest, my skin tingling from his touch.

"Leon," I whisper, my hands tangled in his hair. "What are we doing?"

He nuzzles his nose against mine, his thumb brushing my bottom lip. "I want to taste you, Tate."

The confession washes over me in a wave of heat. I know what he means, what he's asking for. And a part of me wants to let him.

But…

"Leon, I…" I can't find the words to express the storm of emotions inside me.

He drops his gaze, and I reach out, cupping his cheek. He covers my hand with his, his fingers lacing with mine.

"You don't have to say anything," he murmurs, raising my hand to his lips. "Just let me show you."

His eyes are darker now, hooded with desire. His thumb strokes my knuckles, sending shivers down my spine.

"Trust me," he whispers, and it's more of a plea than a command.

Trust him.

Do I?

My heart pounds as I consider his request. This is Leon—my stepbrother, my nemesis, and maybe something more. He hasn't always been kind to me, but in this moment, all I see is the raw need in his eyes.

The silence stretches between us, heavy with unspoken words. I search his face, seeking reassurance or a sign that I'm making a mistake. But all I find is that same unguarded vulnerability, and my heart falters.

"Okay," I hear myself say, my voice barely above a whisper. "Show me."

For a moment, he just looks at me, his eyes searching mine as if to confirm my answer. Then he's moving, lifting me up onto the pool's edge.

He settles between my legs, his hands firm as he parts them wider. I bite my lip, unsure of what to expect, but all he does is lean in and press a soft kiss to the inside of my left thigh. Then another delicate kiss, this time on my right thigh. His lips are gentle, breath warm against my skin. I can feel his smile as he teases my skin with soft brushes of his lips, my legs still slick from the pool.

He moves down my thighs, then back up. Licking water droplets off my skin. My toes curl at the sensation.

"Sensitive here?" He kisses my upper inner thigh, his hot breath brushing my core, and I shiver.

I nod, unable to speak. My heart is practically in my throat.

He looks up at me, his eyes glittering with desire. "Tell me what you want, Tate."

I hesitate, my cheeks burning with embarrassment. "I want..." I close my eyes, the words sticking in my throat. "Touch me."

He hums, placing a chaste kiss on the join of my leg. "Where?"

I'm tempted to cover my face with my hands, but something about Leon's gaze keeps me transfixed. Holding his eyes, I reach down and skim my fingers along my bikini bottoms. "Here."

His gaze follows the movement, and I see his Adam's apple bob as he swallows. "Here?"

My cheeks flame even hotter, but somehow, I manage to hold his gaze. "Yes."

Then he's kissing the inside of my thighs again, his lips trailing higher with each peck, approaching the edge of my bikini.

"I want to taste you," he whispers against my skin. "Will you let me?"

Will I let him? I can feel the wetness between my legs, the need pulsing through me. And somehow, I know Leon can sense it too. The confirmation sits between us, heavy and unspoken.

I nod, my eyes never leaving his. "Yes."

I watch as Leon's eyes darken further, the last vestiges of the sun reflecting in the depths. Slowly, he dips his head, his breath ghosting over me, and I hold my breath.

His lips press against my bikini, just below where I need him most. "This okay?"

"Yes." The word comes out strangled, my entire body tense with anticipation.

Then his tongue darts out, tracing the fabric's edge, and I gasp.

Leon's eyes flick up to mine, a spark of something wicked in their depths. He smirks and pulls my bikini bottoms to the side with his teeth, baring me to his gaze. The position is obscenely intimate, and I feel a rush of wetness at the exposure.

Jerome could walk into the backyard and see us.

Leon's eyes travel over me, drinking me in. "You're beautiful," he murmurs, his thumb skimming my inner thigh. "So fucking beautiful."

He's drawn this out so long now that it's agonizing.

My cheeks flame, and I feel my core pulse. "Leon, please…"

He licks his lips, and then he's pressing a soft, open-mouthed kiss to my core.

Every muscle in my body tenses at the contact, electricity zinging through me. I have to lean back, my palms against the concrete. Leon's tongue teases my slick folds, his mouth gentle as he explores.

Pleasure shoots through me, unlike anything I've ever felt before. It's more intense than our kisses, more intense than his fingers, more intense than my wildest fantasies.

A whimper escapes my throat, and I thread my fingers into his hair, holding him to me. I can feel the heat of his breath, his tongue laving me slowly, skillfully.

I writhe under his touch, every nerve ending sparking to life. "Don't stop."

He chuckles against me, the vibrations sending shivers through me. "Not going anywhere, bébé."

He resumes his leisurely exploration, his tongue flicking and swirling, finding all my sensitive spots. Every touch elicits a new sensation, a new burst of pleasure.

"Leon," I moan, my hips arching off the pool's edge. "Oh, God, right there."

He chuckles, his hands gripping my thighs. "You like that?"

"Yes," I pant, my fingers tightening in his hair. "Harder."

"Bossy." He teases my bundle of nerves, and I cry out, my body bowing off the concrete.

Beyond words now, I clutch my hand over my mouth. Leon growls, and his mouth closes over me, his tongue delving deeper. I tug at him, my body writhing as he sucks my hyper-sensitive clit into his mouth. A coil tightens in my belly, and I know I'm close.

"That's it, bébé," he murmurs, his hands kneading my thighs.

I let go, my body bowing and twisting as pleasure rockets through me. Leon holds me up, his hands gentling on my thighs as my release crashes over me.

It consumes me, takes me apart, and leaves me limp and gasping.

When I come to, fully satiated, I sit up to meet Leon's triumphant eyes. Water drips down the sides of his face, lips red and swollen, his hair messed up from my fingers. The sight makes heat pool low in my belly again.

He wipes his mouth with the back of his hand, a satisfied smirk playing on his lips. Heat rushes to my cheeks as the reality of what just happened hits me.

"You okay?" Leon asks, yanking me into the pool. The cool water wakes up my drowsy body, and I quickly circle my arms around his neck. He plants a soft kiss on my lips and I can taste myself on him.

"Yeah," I whisper, still trembling slightly. "Are you?"

I glance down, feeling the tent in Leon's trunks. My heart pounds in my chest, a mix of curiosity and nervousness churning within me. Just the hint of him, eager and aroused, sends a shiver down my spine. It feels unfair to leave him like this.

Leon notices my gaze, and a smirk plays on his lips. "See something you like?" he teases, his voice husky with desire.

I swallow hard, my mouth suddenly dry. "I... I've never done this before," I admit, my voice barely a whisper.

His eyes soften, but the hunger in them remains. "It's okay," he says, his hand gently cupping my cheek. "I'll guide you."

Leon swims us both to the shallow steps in the pool and sits down. He takes my hand, slowly leading it to the bulge in his trunks. I can feel the heat radiating from him, the hardness beneath the fabric. My fingers tentatively trace the outline of his cock, and I hear his sharp intake of breath.

"Like this," he murmurs, his hand covering mine, guiding me to grip him firmly beneath his trunks. His cock is hot and hard in my hand, the skin surprisingly soft. He shows me the rhythm, the pressure he likes before his hand falls away. I can see the pleasure in his eyes, the way his breath hitches with each stroke.

Emboldened, I explore the length of him, my fingers tracing the veins, the tip.

Leon groans, his head falling back. "God, Tate," he breathes, his hips moving in sync with my hand.

I lean in, my heart pounding in my chest. I can do this. I want to do this. I take a deep breath, my lips parting as I take him into my mouth. The taste of him is strange, musky, but not unpleasant. I swirl my tongue around the tip, earning a hiss from deep within his chest.

Leon's hand finds its way to my hair, guiding me gently. "Just like that," he encourages, his voice ragged with desire. The pool water laps at his thighs with each movement. I can feel his body tense, his muscles coiling with anticipation.

I continue to explore, to taste, to pleasure. The sounds he makes, the way his body responds to my touch, it's intoxicating. There's a sense of power and control. It's exhilarating, addictive.

But as I delve deeper into this new experience, a small voice in the back of my mind whispers: What if I'm not good enough? What if I can't live up to his expectations? The doubts creep in, threatening to overwhelm me.

I push them aside, focusing on the moment, on Leon. His pleasure is my pleasure, his desire my desire. I want this, I want him.

I look up at him through wet lashes. Leon's breath hitches, his body tensing as he grips my hair. I feel him throb in my mouth, a low groan escaping his lips. "Tate," he whispers, his voice ragged with pleasure. He pulses against my tongue, his release hot and salty. I swallow, taking all of him, my own body aching with new unfulfilled desire.

His body relaxes, slumping back against the steps. Leon's eyes are closed, his chest rising and falling rapidly. A small smile plays on his lips, a look of pure contentment.

I sit back, my heart pounding in my chest. The taste of him lingers in my mouth. I feel a mix of pride and uncertainty, wondering if I did it right, if he enjoyed it as much as I think he did.

Leon's eyes flutter open, his gaze meeting mine. His smile widens, his hand reaching out to cup my cheek. "That was… incredible," he murmurs, his thumb brushing against my skin.

I lean into his touch, feeling a warmth spread through me at his words.

Gripping the back of my neck, he pulls me up and our lips meet in a deep kiss.

13

JEROME

I push open the door to the village café, the familiar jingle of the bell overhead breaking the soft murmur of conversation inside. The rich aroma of coffee and baked goods wafts over me, but today even the enticing scents can't soothe my nerves or guilt.

Detective Louis is already seated at a corner table, tapping at his phone, his brow furrowed in concentration. I spot him immediately and make my way through the tables.

I'm grateful for this meeting. It's a much-needed escape from the suffocating silence of the house. My argument with Tate has been weighing on me like a lead blanket. The way she looked at me when I yelled—hurt, contempt—I can't shake that image. I wish I could take it back, but she hates my guts now. The fear driving my anger felt overwhelming at the time. Now, it just hangs over me, festering in the back of my mind.

"Jerome," the detective greets as I approach, sliding his phone into his pocket and offering a curt nod. "Thanks for coming."

I slide into the iron chair across from him, my heart pounding. "What do you have?"

He hesitates for just a moment, pushing a fresh cup of coffee into my hands. "There's a remote area about twenty miles from here," he professes, lowering his voice. "Rumors are surfacing about a cult operating there."

Cult. The word hits me hard, and I lean back, struggling to process what that means. "What do you mean—Bianca's in a cult?"

"It's a possibility. People have gone missing recently," he explains, urgency lacing his tone. "They've been drawn into whatever the cult is doing. We traced Bianca's last known contacts to that region. If she's there, she could be in real danger."

My hands clench around my coffee cup. "What kind of danger are we talking about?"

"I can't share specifics right now." Detective Louis leans forward, keeping his voice low. "We're still gathering concrete evidence of their activities, but we suspect it's focused around fitness or a naturalistic approach to life. If we confirm Bianca's involvement, we'll coordinate with the tactical unit for extraction."

"Extraction?" The word tastes bitter on my tongue.

"These situations require delicate handling." He drums his fingers on the table. "First, we'll establish surveillance. Once we have visual confirmation of Bianca, we'll monitor the compound's routines, entry points, security measures. Then we'll develop an operational plan with minimal risk to all parties involved."

"And Tate? What happens with her if—"

"For now, nothing changes." He cuts me off with a raised hand. "But I need you to understand something, Jerome. If Bianca's there willingly, if she's chosen this… lifestyle, we can't force her to leave. We can only intervene if there's evidence of criminal activity or immediate danger."

I take a long drink of coffee, trying to steady myself. The thought of Bianca choosing to abandon Tate for some cult… it makes my blood boil. I'm missing the days when I only had to worry about Leon. "How long until you know for sure?"

"A few days, maybe a week. We have undercover officers in the area gathering intel." He checks his watch. "That's all I can share for now. I'll contact you as soon as we have confirmation either way."

I drain the last of my coffee, the bitter liquid matching my mood. The ceramic cup clinks against the saucer as I set it down.

"Thanks for meeting me," I tell Detective Louis, rising from my chair. My joints protest after sitting tensely through our conversation. "Keep me updated on any developments."

"Of course." He nods, his expression grave.

I step out of the café into the afternoon sun. The village square bustles with its usual activity—tourists browsing shop windows, locals going about their errands. Their normalcy feels jarring against the weight of what I just learned.

The drive home is a blur. My hands grip the steering wheel too tightly as my mind races through scenarios. A cult. Of all the possibilities, this wasn't one I'd considered. The thought of Bianca getting caught up in something so dangerous…

I pull into my driveway, cutting the engine. The house looms before me, and I know Tate's up there somewhere, probably still hurt and angry. Probably thinking the worst of me.

Taking a deep breath, I step out of the truck. One problem at a time. First, I need to fix things with Tate. Then… then we'll deal with whatever comes next.

I should call Carson. He'd know what to say to make this less overwhelming. He's always been better at talking through emotional messes than I am. But that conversation will have to wait.

I turn away from the house, my boots crunching on gravel as I head toward the cabin.

Laughter rings out from behind the house. Young, care-free—so different from the tension of the past few days. My feet carry me toward the sound before I realize what I'm doing.

I round the corner of the house and freeze. The sight before me steals the air from my lungs.

Leon has Tate pressed against the pool's edge, his hands on her waist. Water droplets glisten on her skin in the afternoon sun. She's wearing a tiny blue bikini, one that shows too much. Her fingers trace patterns on Leon's shoulders as he whispers something in her ear.

My jaw clenches. This is wrong. They're stepsiblings. I should stop this, march over there and…

Tate giggles, wrapping her legs around Leon's waist under the water. He pulls her closer, nuzzling her neck. The intimate gesture makes my stomach turn.

My hands curl into fists at my sides. The rational part of my brain screams to look away, to give them privacy, to pretend I never saw this. But I can't move. Can't tear my eyes from the way Leon's hands roam over her body, the way she arches into his touch.

My vision blurs red at the edges. Every touch between them sends fresh waves of rage through my body. The possessive way Leon's hands slide down Tate's sides makes my teeth grind together. She's too young, too vulnerable. He's taking advantage of her emotional state after our fight.

They're both adults, I have no right to these feelings of possession. But logic crumbles under the weight of my instincts screaming to tear Tate away from Leon.

I watch his lips brush against her neck, and my fingers dig into my palms so hard they'll leave marks. The worst part is how she responds to him, tilting her head back, offering more access. Each soft sigh that carries across the water feels like a physical blow.

Anger burns in my chest—at Leon for touching her, at Tate for letting him, at myself for caring this much. She was supposed to be under my protection, not writhing against my son in the pool. The image of her cooking in just an apron flashes through my mind, making this betrayal cut deeper.

My boot scuffs against the gravel as I try to turn away, the sound impossibly loud in the quiet afternoon air. Tate's head snaps up, her eyes meeting mine across the distance. The color drains from her face.

We're caught in this moment, this forbidden tableau. Each second that passes makes it more obscene, more charged.

"Merde," I mutter under my breath, forcing myself to turn away. My feet feel like lead as I stride toward the cabin, needing to put distance between myself and that scene. But the image is burned into my mind—her fingers in his hair, his hands possessing what I'd denied myself.

I slam the cabin door behind me, my chest heaving as I brace myself against the rough wooden wall. The grain digs into my palms, but the physical pain is nothing compared to the storm raging inside me.

What is wrong with me?

I push away from the wall, pacing the cabin's length. The half-finished walls mock me with their emptiness. This space where Tate and I worked together, where I felt that dangerous pull growing stronger each day. Where I pushed her away to protect her, only to drive her straight into Leon's arms.

"Putain!" The curse rips from my throat as I slam my fist into the table. Pain shoots up my arm, but it doesn't dull the ache in my ribs. I'm old enough to be her father. She's younger than my son, for Christ's sake. I have no business feeling this... this jealousy burning through my veins.

The image of her in that apron floods back—innocent and seductive all at once. I'd done the right thing sending her away. Hadn't I? But seeing her with Leon now... The thought of his hands where I'd refused to touch makes me want to tear this cabin apart board by board.

I need to stop this before it's too late.

14

TATE

The thunderstorm rages outside, rain pelting against the attic windows. I drag the brush across another toenail, coating it red. The polish bottle rests precariously on an old trunk beside the couch, threatening to tip with each boom of thunder.

Up here, I can almost pretend I'm invisible. Almost forget the way Jerome's face twisted when he caught Leon and me in the pool. When I told Leon, he didn't even flinch.

"Let him see," he said.

To make matters worse, Leon had to leave me alone in the house for tonight. One of his friends called, asking for help because they were stuck on the mountain with a broken car. I'd begged him to take me along, but Leon said there wouldn't be enough room in the truck for all his friends.

And judging by the weather, I doubt he'll be coming home.

Another crack of thunder makes me jump, smearing polish across my skin. "Shit." I grab a tissue, dabbing at the red stain. The floorboards beneath me creak as the house settles, and my heart skips—but it's just the wind.

Everything's ruined now. Jerome probably wishes he never agreed to take me in. And Leon will hate me and his dad once he realizes what's been going on.

The attic doesn't hold the comfort it once had, with shadows filling every corner. The only light comes from a singular tall lamp. But it's still better than being downstairs, where Jerome's silence fills every room. Where his footsteps make my skin prickle with anxiety.

I switch to my left foot, pulling my knee to my chest, my fingers trembling with careful precision as I paint. My stomach growls—I haven't eaten since breakfast, too afraid to venture to the kitchen. I'll stay up here as long as I need to. Until I figure out how to fix this mess. Or until Jerome decides he's had enough and sends me away.

The attic stairs creak under heavy footsteps. My hand freezes mid-stroke, polish brush hovering over my toe. Jerome's familiar cologne reaches me before he does—sawdust and spice mixing with the sharp chemical scent of nail polish.

I force myself to keep painting, even as my pulse races. The old floorboards groan under his weight as he moves closer. I can feel his presence looming behind the couch, but I don't look up.

"Tate." His voice is low, controlled.

I dip the brush back in the bottle, focusing on the way the red liquid drips off the tip. "Hmm?"

He circles around to face me. I catch his boots in my peripheral vision but keep my eyes fixed on my toes.

"Look at me." The command in his voice makes my stomach flip.

I carefully drag the brush across another nail. "I'm kind of busy right now."

The nail polish bottle topples as Jerome snatches it, red polish spilling across the old trunk. I finally look up, meeting his blazing green eyes.

"Don't do that again," Jerome bites out lowly.

Heat floods my cheeks. "Do what?"

"What you did with Leon. It's not right."

I push to my feet, hands clenched at my sides. "And how long were you watching, Daddy? Oh, but you're not my dad. You're just a grumpy old man, so it doesn't matter."

Thunder rumbles and Jerome steps closer, forcing me to tilt my head back to maintain eye contact. My pulse quickens.

"No, I'm not. But I am responsible for you."

"I never asked for that!" The words burst out of me. "I never asked for any of this! My mom dumped me here and you're just—you're just trying to control everything!"

"Control?" He catches my wrist as I try to push past him. "You think that's what this is about?"

The heat from his hand sends tingles up my arm. I try to pull away but he holds firm.

"Let go."

"Not until you understand something." His voice drops lower, and heat unfurls in my belly. "*Don't do that again.*"

"You can't tell me what to do." My words come out quiet but determined. "You missed your chance."

SAINT BRYDE

When I attempt to shove Jerome away and push past him, he pivots me sideways, shoving me against the wall. Nothing about it gentle. I look him dead in the eyes, appalled. But my anger burns so hot, I lash out. Punching and beating against his chest as he cages me into the wall.

"I hate you!" I cry out. "You jealous, stubborn old man. You're angry because you can't have me, but your son could."

He catches my wrists, effortlessly pinning them above my head with one hand. I'm shocked by his strength and my own helplessness. My heart pounds as I struggle. I keep fighting, throwing my body against his, trying to break free.

Jerome's grip on my wrists tightens, his face darkening with anger and something else—something primal. Before I can react, he flips me around, pressing me hard against the wall. His body pins me in place, breath hot on my neck.

"You little fucking brat," His voice is a low growl. "You think you can just tease me and walk away?"

I try to push back against him, but he's immovable, a wall of muscle.

"Is this what you want?" His hips grind into me, and I can feel the hard length of him against my ass.

A shiver runs down my spine, a mix of fear and desire coursing through me.

"You've driven me insane, Tate." His voice is thick with contempt, but there's something else there too—something raw and primal and undeniable. "Every day, every fucking night, you're all I can think about. I'm sure Leon made you feel good—he's my son. I expect no less of him as a man."

172

I'm about to correct Jerome, to say Leon and I haven't gone as far as he thinks we have, when his breath swirls hot on my ear. "But I'm going to make you squirt; he's too young to know how."

Liquid heat pools in my core at Jerome's promise. But I'm still angry, so damn angry. I squirm against him, pushing back as much as his grip allows. "You. Missed. Your. Chance," I spit the words out savagely

Jerome's grip on me loosens just enough for me to swirl around, and before I can utter another word, his lips crush mine in a punishing kiss. His tongue invades my mouth, demanding and insistent.

I try to resist, to push him away, to scream and fight and make him pay for every moment of pain and uncertainty he's put me through. But at the same time, I want to pull him closer, to lose myself in his touch. Jerome's grip is unyielding. His hands move to my face, holding me in place as his tongue explores every corner of my mouth with a hunger that leaves me breathless.

I twist my head away.

No. He can't have me.

His lips keep seeking mine, but I deny him, twisting my head away each time he leans in, refusing to meet his hungry kisses.

"Tate," Jerome groans against my ear, his breath hot on my skin. "Look at me."

"No—" My words die in my throat as he sucks on the sensitive spot just below my earlobe, sending shivers through me. "Don't." I keep my tone defiant, but my body betrays me, arching into him despite my best efforts.

I hear the sharp pop of buttons scattering as Jerome yanks my shirt apart, stripping the fabric from my body. A gasp tears through my lungs as thunder splits through the house.

Jerome chuckles, the vibrations tickling my skin. "Liar." His teeth nip at my earlobe, sending a bolt of pleasure straight to my core. My ruined shirt crumpling to my feet.

Anger flares within me, but it's tinged with need. How can he still affect me like this? I try to focus on the contempt I feel toward him, but it's increasingly difficult as his hands map my body, gently squeezing and caressing.

Now I'm fighting not to wrap my arms around him.

Jerome's hand moves to my thigh, dragging my skirt upward. He squeezes my ass, his fingers biting into my skin. I gasp into his mouth, my struggles forgotten. Need spirals through me, making my head spin.

"Let me show you how good it can be," he whispers tenderly, and I claim his mouth.

Please.

Jerome lifts me as if I weigh nothing, my legs automatically wrapping around his waist. My heart is pounding so hard I can barely breathe. He carries me to the couch, arms strong and sure beneath me. He lays me down gently, eyes never leaving mine.

Jerome pulls his shirt over his head in one smooth motion, revealing the tanned muscles beneath. My breath catches at the sight of him, all hard lines and raw power. I can't help but reach out, my fingers tracing the ridges of his abs, the unshaven expanse of his chest. His skin is warm, almost feverish, and I can feel his heart pounding beneath my touch.

Jerome's hands move to my waist, his fingers hooking into the fabric of my skirt. He slides it down my legs, the cool air a stark contrast to the heat of his touch. I lift my hips to help him, my breath coming in short gasps as I'm left in just my bra and panties.

His gaze roams over my body, lingering on the curves and dips, the soft swell of my breasts and the delicate lace of my underwear. I can see the desire in his eyes, the raw need that mirrors my own.

Without a second thought, Jerome unbuttons his jeans and shucks them down enough to pull out his cock.

I'm shocked by it—it's bigger than I expected, thick and long, with the foreskin still intact, sliding smoothly over the head with each slow, deliberate stroke.

His breathing is steady, but I can see the tension in his jaw, the way his muscles flex as he pleasures himself. The sight of his cock, so close and so real, sends a wave of heat through me. I feel my body responding, my core tightening with a need I've never felt before. It's both exhilarating and terrifying.

I yelp as Jerome suddenly tugs me down beneath him, his hand pinned down at the side of my waist. I feel the fabric of my panties rip away, before his bulbous head dips into my folds, rubbing up and down my wet slit.

My head falls back. "Oh God."

My words turn into a moan as he roughly pushes my thighs apart, rubbing his full length against me.

"You want this." It's not a question.

I know there's no turning back now. I want Jerome, all of him, and I'm ready to give myself completely.

My face burns, but I can't deny it. "Yes."

His mouth moves along my jaw, teeth nipping at my skin. "Say it."

"I want this," I whisper. "I want *you*."

Jerome's grip on my thighs tightens, his fingers digging into my flesh as he pushes my knees up to my chest. I'm exposed, utterly vulnerable, as he lifts my hips upwards. My feet press against the hard plane of his chest, the coarse hair there tickling my soles. He grinds against me, his cock hot and heavy against my clit. The sensation is overwhelming, pleasure and pressure that sends waves of heat coursing through my body.

He leans back, his green eyes locked onto the point where our bodies meet. The image of him, tanned and muscled, looming over me, is dominating, possessive, every inch the alpha male. His hips move in a slow, deliberate circle, grinding against me with a rhythm that's both torturous and amazing.

"Regarde–nous, Tate," he growls, his voice thick with desire. "Regarde comme nous allons bien ensemble."

I can't help but obey, my gaze drawn to his cock sliding against my wetness. The sensation is intense, almost too much to bear. I can feel every ridge, every vein, as he moves against me. My clit throbs, swollen and sensitive, each grind of his hips sending a jolt of pleasure through me.

Jerome's hips move faster, the grinding of his cock against my clit becoming more insistent, more demanding. I can feel it building, the pressure inside me growing with each thrust of his hips. My breath comes in short, sharp gasps, my heart thudding in my chest. I'm close, so close. And Jerome knows it. He can see it in my face, feel it in the tension of my body.

I want to feel him inside me, filling me.

"That's it, Tate," he murmurs, his voice soft and commanding. "Come for me. Let me see you come."

And with those words, I shatter. My orgasm rips through me, a wave of pleasure so intense it leaves me gasping for breath. My body convulses, my hips bucking against his as I ride out the wave. And through it all, Jerome watches me, his eyes dark with desire and satisfaction. He's done this to me. He's made me feel this way. And he knows it.

"Bonne fille." He grabs my ankle and presses a kiss on it before I feel him crowning my entrance. Rubbing his head against me one final time, he begins pushing in.

Despite how wet and placid I am, the stretch still stings, burning bright. Enough for me to squeeze my eyes shut and whimper. "Jerome."

"Shh, it's going to be okay," Jerome whispers, stroking my hair. "La douleur ne se fera pas sentir longtemps, je te le promets. Reste avec moi, Tate."

His words are like a lifeline, pulling me back from the edge. I focus on his voice, on the feeling of his calloused hands stroking my skin, their roughness contrasting with his gentle touch.

SAINT BRYDE

Inching inside me, Jerome groans above me. He's breathing heavily, hips trembling against mine as he braces himself.

I watch his Adam's apple bob. "Show me what you do to yourself, Tate." His voice is hoarse, thick with need. "Show me how you touch yourself when you're alone."

My face flames at the request, but I can't deny him. Slowly, I hook my heels over Jerome's shoulders, my hands move to my clit, circling it gently at first, then with more pressure as the sensations build. Jerome watches my every move, his hips moving in time with my fingers.

"That's it," he murmurs. "Let me see you fall apart."

I bite my lip, my fingers moving faster as the coil in my belly tightens. My muscles relax around him, and Jerome's thrusting become more instant. The pain fades, replaced by a pressure that's almost – *almost*—pleasurable. His cock slides deep inside me, stretching and filling me. It's overwhelming, the sensation of being so full, of feeling him take me like this. But the more I feel it, the more I like it. My toes curl as I clench around him, milking his cock.

"Fuck, Tate." He groans. Jerome's eyes are dark with desire, his jaw clenched as he pumps into me. "Do you like that?"

I nod, unable to speak, my entire body focused on the feeling of him inside me.

Jerome's fingers dig into my hips, his grip tightening. His movements become rougher, more urgent. I can feel his balls slapping against me with each thrust, the sound of our bodies coming together filling the room. The rough fabric of the couch scrapes against my back. I'm lost in the moment, lost in the pleasure, his name a mantra on my lips.

"Jerome, oh God—Jerome," I chant, my nails digging into couch.

Jerome growls above me, the sound making me quiver. He leans over me, forcing my legs into the air and he shifts deeper inside me, and I moan. He stops thrusting to focus on my breasts, pinching my nipples, rolling them between his fingers. A gasp tears from my throat, and he places a kiss between my breasts. I can feel my orgasm building, a wave of pleasure that threatens to consume me.

But then he draws back oh so slowly, his eyes watching his hard length inching out of me. He leans back so far, I wonder if he's going to pull out completely.

Then Jerome slams back to the hilt, the force of it earth-shattering. I cry out, my body bowing beneath him as he fills me completely, and he doesn't stop. Rutting against me like a bucking bull.

"F-fuckkk," I whine. All I can do is bear the force and let Jerome use me, and it's the best fucking feeling of my life.

He grips my legs to his shoulders again as he readjusts, leaning back till he's shallowly penetrating me. Jerome rocks his hips steady, his cock twitching inside me, the velvet smoothness of his shaft feeling even larger as he hits a sweet spot with each thrust. The coil in my abdomen tightens, an ache building deep within me turns to bursting. It's like nothing I've ever felt before, this intense pressure that demands release.

"I think I'm going to pee." The words rush out of me without a thought.

Jerome grins, tenderness in his eyes. "That's it, baby." His eyes fix on my face. "That's how it's supposed to feel. Come for me."

He hits that sweet spot again and I come undone, a cry escaping my lips as my orgasm crashes over me. Jerome rips his cock from me, and I'm gushing, squirting all over his hips, my thighs trembling and convulsing.

Fuck me.

The shock of it makes me push up onto my elbows, but my head is still reeling, breathing a mile a minute.

Jerome releases a deeply satisfied groan. "Ma belle, I could watch you come apart like this all day." His lips brush over mine in a slow, sweet kiss, fingers brushing through my mussed hair. The soft patter of rain reaches my ears, lightning slicing through the darkness, thunder shaking the windows. The power flickers, plunging the room into brief bouts of darkness.

"Every day," I say, surprising myself.

Jerome perks up at that, and slowly I push him down on the couch. "I want more."

15

JEROME

It's cute Tate thinks I would be done with her. As she settles on top of me, I clutch her waist and give her a crooked grin. "Baby, that was only the beginning."

My cock is pulsing, begging for release, and Tate has yet to make up for being such a naughty girl.

In the heat of the moment, I kick off the rest of my jeans and pull Tate flush against me, kissing her mouth. Our skin is slick and sticky as we slowly rock into each other.

"I want you inside me." Her hair curtains my face when she rises onto her knees, grabs my dick and guides herself back onto it. Her tight heat wraps around me, and my eyes roll to the back of my head, engulfed by her weight on top of me.

Tate makes a sound of surprise. "This feels so much deeper."

Get used to it, sweetheart.

In this position, I'm at perfect eye level with her tits. Lifting my head, I latch my mouth onto one of Tate's breasts, swirling my tongue around the pert peak. Sucking gently, I feel her shiver above me, her breath quickening. I love how responsive Tate is to my every touch, how she loses herself in the pleasure.

Pulling away, I blow a cool stream of air over her sensitive nipple, enjoying the goose bumps that erupt across her skin. She lets out a little gasp, her eyes flashing with a mix of surprise and pleasure. I repeat the action, this time rolling the hardened tip between my teeth.

Tate moans, her body tensing as she grinds on my lap, her fingers digging into my shoulders.

"That's it, baby. Ride me hard." I buck my hips up, slapping her clit with each grind of my pelvis. Her beautiful taut body swivels on top of me, glistening with sweat, her breath hot in my face.

"Yes," she pants, locking eyes with me. "I love the way you feel inside me. Don't stop."

I do as she says, fucking up into her as she bounces on my dick. The more Tate gets used to moving on me, the sounds coming out of her mouth make me teeter closer to the edge.

Tate's breath comes in ragged gasps now, her walls fluttering around me as she gets closer. I smirk, my hands gripping her ass tighter, guiding the pace of her hips.

Her face dips to mine, tongue sweeping into my mouth and I groan. I fucking love kissing, I was angry at Tate before, so I didn't kiss her as much. But now, I latch on to her sweet little mouth like nothing else as I snap my hips up into her.

She moans into my mouth and heat trickles down my spine. "Give me every last drop," she says breathlessly.

Fuck, this is so dirty and reckless of me. It's too late to ask if Tate's on birth control now. I'm so deep inside her, she'll never get me out.

Her cunt contracts, and I grit my teeth with a hiss as heat rushes to my groin. Tate's arms circle tightly around my neck. Without thinking, I roll us over so she's sitting splayed on the couch, hook my arms under her thighs and hoist her up around my hips till I'm standing up. Tate squeals, out of nerves or excitement I don't know, before I'm pistoning into her cunt at the deepest angle possible. The only thing holding her in place are my arms and my cock.

"Yesyesyes." She gasps, clutching on to me for dear life. The slap of our bodies so loud it drowns out the thunder. Tate rocks against me, her body tensing and shuddering, and I know I don't need to hold back anymore.

She cries, reaching release, and her cunt squeezes around me. Blood rushes to my swollen cock, and I grunt, spurting into Tate like a geyser. I stand there, twitching and holding her for what feels like the longest time, before fatigue rushes over me and I drop Tate down on the couch and crumple to my knees.

My head is empty, and I feel boneless.

It feels like minutes pass before I recover, and lift my head to stare at Tate. She gazes down at me through half-moon lids, tendrils of blond hair sticking to her face. Her lips swollen and red from our kissing, her breathing slow and steady. There's a languid ease in her body as she refuses to lift a muscle, and my eyes trail down to her pussy, so red and raw from the beating I just gave it, my cum trickling out of her.

I forgot what it felt like to be crazy over a girl. It doesn't feel real, this contentment. My heart flutters, I kiss the inside of

Tate's knee and she grins at me. I come up and kiss her on the forehead, then the lips.

"You know what, Tate?" I brush my thumb over her cheek. "I think the best thing your mom did was bring me to you."

Even if I can't have her, Tate is a gift all the same.

"Mmmm." She nods, a lazy smile spreading across her face. It's all the response I get from Tate, as she's been thoroughly fucked to drowsiness.

My stamina can still outweigh an eighteen-year old's, at least.

"Come on," I say, pulling her up. "Let's get you cleaned up and into bed."

In the bathroom, I turn on the shower and wet a washcloth, wringing it out before gesturing Tate to get in. She looks at me expectantly under the shower spray, wondering what I'm intending to do.

I step inside and close the glass door, holding the washcloth to her skin. "Let me wash you."

Tate gives me a small smile, and nods. Wiping her down, I watch her face as she slowly comes down from her orgasmic high, her eyes closing as she takes a breath.

"You okay?"

She nods, looking up at me with blown pupils. "Yeah. Wow."

I chuckle, pulling her into a hug. "You sure took your sweet time figuring out this part of adulting."

Tate hides her face in my chest, and I work the washcloth over her neck and shoulders.

"Didn't Leon show you a good time?"

Some tiny part of me—behind the jealously—trusts Leon to show Tate a good time, and there's a weird sense of comfort in that. I don't know why I ask it, but Tate doubles back.

"Leon and I didn't…" She trails off, her cheeks flushing.

I pull away, searching her face.

Tate meets my gaze. "You were my first."

My chest swells with pride, and horror. The reality and consequences of our actions rushing back to me.

"Don't panic," she soothes me, "I enjoyed every second of it. And I'm on birth control; I wouldn't have done it otherwise."

Relief floods me, and I kiss Tate's forehead. I continue to wash her under the hot stream, cleaning between her legs.

Then my mind's back on Leon. On how Tate could never be mine, and I'm not bitter about it now. But I need to set the record straight with her. "I know you like him. It's obvious."

Her mouth falls open, her eyes darting away guiltily before she meets my gaze again.

I shake my head, smiling softly at her. "It's okay, Tate. I get it."

Tate opens her mouth and then closes it, blinking. "But I like you too, Jerome."

I'm not delusional, there's no reality where Tate chooses to be with me. It's not acceptable. Leon, maybe. But not me.

If I can spend time with Tate, for however long it lasts, that's enough. It's our secret.

After wiping her down, she places a kiss on my lips and exits the shower to let me have the water spray. I clean myself, the warm water soothing my languid muscles.

When I make it to my bedroom, refreshed and dry, I find Tate already in my bedsheets. Rain pattering softly on the house.

"Go to your room," I say.

She rolls over, her tone matter-of-fact. "No."

And I don't have the conviction in me to fight her for it.

I slide under the covers, and Tate immediately curls into me like she belongs there. Her body is warm and soft, fitting perfectly against mine. The gentle weight of her head on my chest brings a peace I haven't felt in years.

My fingers trail through her damp hair, still slightly wet from the shower. She makes a contented sound, nuzzling closer. Her breath tickles my skin, slow and steady.

"This feels right," she whispers, her words barely audible.

I kiss the top of her head, breathing in the clean scent of her shampoo. My arms tighten around her instinctively, protective. Something inside me clicks into place—a missing piece I didn't know was gone.

Her leg hooks over mine, and she traces lazy patterns on my chest. The simple intimacy of it makes my heart ache. I've had women in my bed before, but none have made me feel this... whole.

Tate's breathing grows deeper, her movements stilling as sleep takes her. I listen to the soft rhythm, feeling my own exhaustion creep in. The warmth of her body, the weight of her against me, it's like a balm to my soul.

My eyes grow heavy as I hold her, and I drift off with the knowledge that for this moment, everything is perfect.

I wake to a dull gray dawn. The rain has passed, and birdsong is filtering through the open window.

Tate is a warm, soft weight in my arms, her breath gentle against my chest. I bring a hand to her hair, resisting the urge to wake her.

Instead, I take a moment to appreciate her. Her hair, fanned out across my pillows. The rise and fall of her chest as she sleeps. The peaceful expression on her face.

She's like a little wild thing, untamed and restless. And yet, here in my bed, she's found a moment of solace. I know that feeling.

The urge to protect her washes over me, and I tighten my arms around her.

She stirs, a soft sound escaping her lips. I bring my hand to her cheek, gently stroking her skin. Her eyes flutter open, and she blinks up at me, a sleepy smile spreading across her face.

"Hey," she whispers, her voice thick with sleep.

I bring my lips to hers, kissing her softly. "Good morning."

She stretches, her body arching against mine, and I feel a spark of desire amidst the haze of sleep. "What time is it?"

I glance at the clock, my hand still tangled in her hair. "Early. Go back to sleep."

Tate shakes her head, her eyes sparkling with mischief. "I don't want to."

I smile, leaning in to capture her lips again. This kiss is deeper, more demanding. She responds eagerly, her hands twisting in the sheets as she presses herself against me.

My body reacts instantly, desire flaring to life. I pull her closer, my hands roaming over her bare skin. She's soft and warm, her curves fitting perfectly against me.

I break the kiss, trailing my lips down her jaw to the sensitive spot just below her ear. She lets out a soft moan, her head tilting back to give me better access. I take my time, tasting her skin, savoring the feel of her in my arms.

Her fingers tangle in my hair, holding me close. I move lower, nipping at her collarbone, and she arches off the bed, a breathy laugh escaping her. "Jerome."

I look up, my eyes dark with desire. "Hmm?"

"You're going to tire me out before the morning's begun."

I chuckle, my breath tickling her skin. "Then I'll have to carry you."

She smiles, her eyes full of challenge. "Try it."

I shift, rolling her beneath me. She lets out a startled laugh, her legs automatically wrapping around my waist. I lean in, my lips inches from hers.

"I'll take that as a yes."

Tate's response is silenced by my mouth on hers.

The morning passes in a haze of touches and whispered words. Tate's skin glows in the pale sunlight streaming through the windows, her hair a mess from our lovemaking. I can't keep my hands off her—each brush of skin against skin ignites another spark.

Eventually, hunger wins out. I pull on jeans while Tate wraps herself in my discarded shirt, the hem barely covering her thighs. The sight makes my mouth go dry.

"We need furniture for your cabin," I say, forcing myself to focus. "And breakfast."

Tate's eyes light up. "So it's my cabin now?"

I nod, and she smirks. Anything that's mine is hers. She can catch a break from me there, too.

***

The furniture store is quiet this early. Tate bounces from display to display, running her fingers over smooth wood and plush fabrics. Her enthusiasm is infectious. We pick out a bed—my chest tightens at the implications—along with a small sofa and some storage pieces.

Then she stops in the lighting section, in awe at a pair of strung fairy lights coiled with fake vines and budding flowers.

"This needs to go in the movie room," she says, turning to me.

Of course, I buy them.

At the café, Tate demolishes her croissants and café au lait while I watch, amused. Powdered sugar dusts her lips. It's tempting to lean across the table and kiss it away, not caring who sees. But I can only smirk at her.

The drive home is comfortable silence, Tate's hand resting on my thigh. The furniture will be delivered next week, and Tate's got the fairy lights in her lap.

The drive home is comfortable silence, Tate's hand resting on my thigh. The furniture will be delivered next week, and Tate's got the fairy lights in her lap.

We pull up to the house around noon. The sky has cleared to a brilliant blue, but neither of us suggests going outside. Instead, Tate has a gleam in her eye that promises we're not done with our morning activities.

My phone buzzes as I cut the engine.

"Merde," I mutter, reading the message. "The store needs me to come back. Something about the delivery paperwork."

Tate's lips curve into a slight pout. "Now?"

I lean over, pressing a quick kiss to her temple. "I won't be long. Why don't you get started on those fairy lights?"

She nods, gathering the shopping bags. "Don't take too long."

I watch her head inside before backing out of the driveway, already missing her warmth beside me.

16

TATE

I 'm humming softly as I string the fairy lights along the movie room wall, balancing on the stepladder. The soft glow transforms the space, warming the corners in a way that makes me smile. I was right about these lights.

My mind drifts to Jerome, to last night, to this morning. The warmth of his skin against mine, the quiet contentment in his eyes over breakfast. For the first time since Mom left, I feel... happy.

A pang of unease follows the thought. What about Leon? The question I've been pushing away all day surfaces again. I try to imagine his reaction if he found out about last night. Would he be hurt? Angry? Would he even care?

I wonder what Leon will think about the lights. He'll probably tease me about it, but I hope he'll like it too. Maybe we could all watch something in here tonight. The three of us together, comfortable. Safe.

God, who am I kidding? I slept with his father. There's nothing simple about that. But maybe if I just act normal, if I pretend everything is fine, then somehow it will be. The knot in my stomach tightens, but I ignore it, focusing instead on the lights. One problem at a time.

A violent crash from outside breaks my reverie, followed by what sounds like metal hitting concrete. I freeze, lights still dangling from my fingers. Through the small window, I can see the garage door is open.

I shouldn't go look. I know I shouldn't.

But my feet are already moving.

The garage smells of motor oil and metal. Leon's hunched over an engine, his movements sharp and aggressive. A wrench lies on the ground several feet away like it's been thrown. Another tool clatters to the floor as he yanks something free with too much force.

"Leon?"

He doesn't turn around, but his shoulders stiffen. "Go away, Tate." His voice is low, dangerous.

"Are you okay?"

A bitter laugh escapes him. He grabs a rag and wipes his hands with short, angry motions. "La ferme." He finally turns, and the look in his eyes makes me take a step back.

My stomach drops. Somehow, I already know what this is about. The guilt I've been suppressing all day rushes to the surface.

"What happened?" I ask anyway, my voice barely above a whisper.

Leon stares at me, his eyes moving over my face like he's searching for something. Then he slams his palm against the workbench, making tools jump. "Que diable se passe-t-il?" His pupils are blown wide, and a muscle ticks in his jaw. "You want to know what happened? I heard you last night."

The confirmation hits me like a physical blow.

"With him," he continues, his voice dropping to something raw and wounded beneath the anger. He turns back to the engine, grabbing a bolt and twisting it with savage intensity. "I wanted it to be me."

The contentment I've been clinging to all day shatters completely. Guilt rises in my throat, thick and terrible.

"Leon, I—" I start, but the words die in my throat. What could I possibly say?

He throws down the tool, removes his latex gloves and steps toward me, eyes dark with something that's shifted from just anger to something more complicated. More intense. "Tell me," he says, his voice rough. "Tell me you didn't feel anything when we kissed in the truck, in the pool."

My breath catches. "That's not fair."

"None of this is fair." He's closer now, close enough that I can smell the motor oil and sweat on his skin. "You want him? Fine. But don't pretend you don't want me too."

His words hit somewhere deep, somewhere honest. I do want Leon. Differently than I want Jerome, but just as intensely.

"I don't know what I want," I whisper.

Something flashes in his eyes—triumph, maybe, or determination. "I think you do."

His hand comes up to cup my face, gentle despite the tension radiating from him. For a moment, we stand there, breathing the same air, the garage silent except for the distant hum of machinery.

I should step back. I should walk away. But I don't. Instead, I lean forward, closing the distance between us until our lips meet.

The kiss is nothing like the ones we shared in the pool. This is desperate, hungry. His hands tangle in my hair, holding me in place as his tongue demands entrance. I taste anger on his lips, but also need—raw and undeniable.

"I need to know," he murmurs against my mouth, backing me against the workbench. "I need to know it's not just him."

Heat curls low in my belly at his words. My hands find his waist, fingers digging into the firm muscle there. "It's not just him," I breathe, the confession tearing free before I can stop it.

Leon growls, the sound vibrating against my lips as he presses me harder against the workbench. His hands are everywhere—tangling in my hair, gripping my waist, sliding beneath my shirt to find bare skin. Each touch leaves a trail of fire in its wake.

"Show me," he demands, accent thick with desire.

I arch against him, gasping when he grips my thighs and lifts me onto the workbench. Tools clatter to the floor, but neither of us cares. His body pins mine in place, solid and demanding. This isn't the careful tenderness of last night with Jerome. This is something wilder, darker, born of jealousy and need.

"Leon," I gasp as his mouth finds my neck, teeth grazing sensitive skin. My legs wrap around his waist instinctively, pulling him closer. I can feel him hard against me through our clothes, and the realization sends a jolt of electricity straight to my core.

His hands find the button of my jeans, working it free with impatient fingers. "Tell me to stop," he says, voice rough against my ear. "Tell me you don't want this."

But I do want this. Want him. The guilt is still there, but buried beneath a more urgent need. "Don't stop," I whisper, fingers fumbling with his belt.

He groans, forehead pressed against mine as I work his jeans open. His breath is hot against my face, coming in short pants that match my own. When my fingers find him, he hisses through his teeth, hips jerking involuntarily.

"Fuck, Tate," he growls, yanking my jeans down just enough. The cold metal of the workbench against my thighs makes me gasp, but the shock is quickly forgotten as his fingers find me, testing, teasing.

I'm already wet, already desperate for him. The knowledge that this is wrong—that just hours ago I was with his father—only seems to intensify the sensation. Like we're stealing something forbidden, something that belongs only to us.

"Now," I demand, pulling him closer. "Please, Leon."

He doesn't hesitate. In one swift motion, he pushes inside me, filling me completely. We both freeze, panting, adjusting to the sensation. His forehead rests against mine, eyes locked on my face. In this moment of stillness, I see the vulnerability beneath his anger, the fear of rejection lurking behind his bravado.

I touch his face, a tender gesture at odds with the urgency of our position. "I want you," I whisper. "I have since I first saw you."

Something shifts in his expression—relief, triumph, something deeper I can't name. Then he's moving, setting a pace that steals my breath and my thoughts. There's nothing gentle about it, nothing careful. Just raw need and the sound of skin against skin, of harsh breathing and half-swallowed moans.

My back presses against cold metal, my legs tight around his waist as he drives into me again and again. Tools dig into my back, but the discomfort only adds to the desperation of the moment. This isn't about comfort or romance—it's about claiming, about proving something to ourselves and each other.

"Look at me," he demands, one hand gripping my chin. His eyes are dark, pupils blown wide. "See who's inside you now."

The possessiveness in his voice should anger me, but instead it sends me hurtling toward the edge. My nails dig into his shoulders through his shirt, leaving marks I know he'll wear like badges of honor.

"Leon," I gasp, feeling the tension building, coiling tighter with each thrust. "I'm—"

"Yes," he growls, pace increasing. "Let go, Tate. Let go for me."

The orgasm hits me like a tidal wave, unexpected in its intensity. I cry out, back arching off the workbench as pleasure crashes through me. Leon follows moments later, his rhythm faltering as he buries his face in my neck, a string of French curses muffled against my skin.

For a moment, we stay frozen, connected, breathing hard in the quiet aftermath. Reality creeps back slowly—the hard workbench beneath me, the tools scattered around us, the fact that we're both still mostly clothed, that Jerome could have walked in.

Leon pulls back first, eyes searching my face. There's uncertainty there now, the anger temporarily spent. His thumb traces my lower lip, gentle in a way that makes my chest ache.

"This doesn't fix anything," he says quietly, helping me down from the workbench.

I nod, adjusting my clothes with shaking hands. "I know."

The silence stretches between us, heavy with unsaid things. I don't regret what just happened, but I don't know what it means either. For me, for him, for Jerome. For all of us.

Leon turns back to the engine, picking up a wrench from the floor. His shoulders are tense again, but differently now. "You should go," he says, not looking at me. "Before he comes back."

I want to say somethingthat I'm sorry, that I care about him, that I don't know how to navigate any of this. But the words stick in my throat.

Instead, I turn and walk away, leaving him alone with his engine and his thoughts. The fairy lights will have to wait.

I sink down against the closed door of my bedroom, my legs giving out beneath me. The wood is cool against my back as I draw my knees to my chest, trying to process what just happened.

The raw pain in Leon's voice, the desperate way he'd kissed me—it wasn't just about attraction or jealousy. This runs deeper, years deeper.

I think about the way Jerome looks at Leon sometimes, like he's trying to bridge a gap he doesn't know how to cross. The way Leon bristles under his father's attention, yet seems to crave it. Their relationship is a minefield of unspoken hurts and expectations.

And here I am, stumbling right into the middle of it.

My chest aches as I realize—I'm not just some girl caught between two men. I'm the match that lit years of buried tension between father and son. Every smile I share with Jerome, every moment I spend with Leon—it's all feeding into something that started long before I arrived.

I press my palms against my eyes, fighting back tears. I never meant to hurt either of them. My feelings for them both are real, raw, and completely different. Jerome makes me feel safe, seen, understood. Leon challenges me, excites me, pushes me to be bolder.

But my love for them was never meant to be the thing that tears them apart.

I drop my hands, staring at the ceiling. The truth hits me like a physical blow—I need to leave. Not just this house, but their lives. They need to heal their relationship without me complicating things. Without me being the excuse they use to avoid dealing with their real issues.

It doesn't matter that the thought of leaving makes me feel as if I'm being torn in half. It doesn't matter that I have nowhere else to go. I won't be the reason their family falls apart.

And my mom…

I'm done waiting for her.

I push myself up from the floor, my body aching in ways both pleasant and painful. I can still feel Leon on my skin, inside me. Still taste him on my lips. The memory sends a shiver through me—shame and desire tangled so tightly, I can't separate them.

My reflection in the bathroom mirror shows a girl I barely recognize. Flushed cheeks, swollen lips, hair a tangled mess. But it's my eyes that stop me—wild and lost and somehow older than they were this morning.

I lost Mom in fragments. But this? This feels like an explosion. Like a family shattering all at once.

I can't lose them too. Not when they've become my anchor in this storm. Not when they're all I have left.

But as I wash away the evidence of what Leon and I just did, I know that staying might cost them each other. And that's a price I'm not willing to let them pay.

17

JEROME

The house is quiet when I return. Too quiet. I find Tate in the living room, curled up in the window seat. She's staring out at the garage, and I don't need to ask to know what happened.

"Tate?"

She turns to me, and the look in her eyes makes my chest ache. This is the mess I've made—the pain I've caused both of them.

"I'm sorry," I say, though I'm not sure what exactly I'm apologizing for. For this morning? For not being strong enough to resist her? For putting her in this position?

She shakes her head, a sad smile touching her lips. "Me too."

The walk to the garage feels longer than usual, each step weighted with years of things left unsaid. The door is partially open, light spilling onto the gravel. Tools clang against metal—Leon's way of announcing his anger to the world.

I push the door open. Leon doesn't look up from the engine he's dismantling with more force than necessary. His knuckles are raw, a smear of blood mixing with the grease on his hands.

Leon shakes his head. "This is low, even for you, Dad."

"I know." I shut my eyes. "I've fucked up."

"Did she like it?" Leon's eyes are glossed over. "Fucked up and nasty? That's what it sounded like. Didn't expect her to be such a whore."

He's hurting, but the insult makes my hackles rise. Leon can hate me all he wants, but he can't hate Tate—can't be so disrespectful. It makes me want to guard her from him. Which is not what's supposed to happen.

Tate will leave soon to start her own life. What else would she do? Stay here as a side piece?

Or she'd run off with Leon. That feels right to me, but I'd also lose my son. He won't want to see me again. I know I wouldn't if I were in his shoes.

I fucked up.

A little paradise for a little pain.

I wipe my face. "I'm not marrying her, Leon. I know how she feels for you."

He strokes his chin, nonchalant. "Maybe I'll fuck her mom. Maybe, we could fuck Tate together as father and son. What great bonding that would be."

"Don't be stupid." My voice is low, threatening, but Leon just smirks. I can feel my body starting to shake with anger—this isn't the time for him to push my buttons. "I know you're hurting, but you can't say shit like that about her."

Something in his eyes shifts, a flash of shame replacing the anger. He looks away, running a hand through his hair.

"I shouldn't have said that," he admits quietly. "About her."

I nod, some of my own anger dissipating. "This is on me, Leon. Not her. I'm the one who should have known better."

"It's not that simple." He picks up a wrench, turning it over in his hands. "She and I... after I heard you two..."

He doesn't finish the sentence, but he doesn't need to. I see the guilt in his eyes, the confusion. The pieces click into place—Tate's averted gaze when I spoke to her, the scattered tools on the workbench.

"She came to find you after I left," I say, not a question.

Leon nods, not meeting my eyes.

I should feel betrayed, angry. But all I feel is a strange sense of relief. Like something has aligned the way it was always meant to.

"Good," I say simply.

His head snaps up, eyes wide with surprise. "Good? That's all you have to say?"

"What do you want me to say, Leon? That I'm angry? Jealous?" I shake my head. "You're young. You're right for each other."

"So, what was last night? This morning?" he demands, confusion giving way to fresh anger. "Just killing time until someone better came along?"

"No," I say firmly. "It was real. But it was also a mistake. My mistake."

I step closer, wanting him to understand. "I care about her. More than I should. But you two make sense in a way that she and I never could."

He laughs bitterly. "You're unbelievable. You fuck her, then hand her off like she's a gift, and expect me to be grateful?"

"That's not what I'm saying and you know it." I run a hand through my hair, frustrated. "I'm saying I made a selfish choice. And now I have to live with the consequences."

Leon studies me for a long moment. "You really think I'm the better choice for her?"

"I do." The admission costs me, but it's the truth. "You always were."

He's silent for a long moment, staring down at his bloodied knuckles. "I can't compete with you," he finally says. "I never could."

The words knock the air from my lungs. "This isn't a competition, Leon."

"Isn't it?" He looks at me then, and I see the boy beneath the man, the child who never felt good enough. "It's always been a competition. For Mom's attention. For your approval. And now for her."

I step forward, closing the distance between us. "You don't need to compete with me. You never did."

"She chose you first," he says, voice cracking slightly.

"And then she chose you." I reach out, gripping his shoulder. "We've made a mess of things, you and I. But don't blame her for that."

He doesn't pull away from my touch, which feels like its own kind of victory. "What happens now?"

It's a good question—one I don't have an answer for. "I don't know," I admit. "But we need to figure it out. Together."

18

TATE

I never thought I'd feel this way.

I never thought a place like this existed. I wake up every morning and pinch myself because the dreams I'm having are so vivid. I never want to leave. Maybe it's the jet lag, maybe it's the food, or the towering trees, or the way the sun paints everything gold here… Or maybe it's Jerome.

There is something about him. The way he fills up a room, a heady mix of cologne and timber and earth. He is a constant, steady presence. I can't help but be aware of him, every minute of every day. And his son… Leon. What a tangled mess we've become. It's like neither of us can help ourselves.

That's why I think it's time I leave.

When mom told me she was taking me to France, I wasn't happy. Kids are usually grateful when their parents pull them out of school for a holiday, but not me. It was simultaneously the worst and best thing that happened to me.

I hope Mom is ok, but I don't need her anymore. She doesn't get to decide what I'm good for because I'm gonna build the life that I deserve.

I close the embroidered diary, feeling a weight lift off my shoulders. It feels good to get the words out somewhere no one can see them—except me.

Since the fight between Leon and Jerome, I've put some distance between us. The furniture Jerome ordered arrived a few days ago, so I've moved into the cabin. It's nice to see all the work we've done on it, and now it's a liveable space.

I never knew I'd like working on house design this much. When I get back to California and complete my finals, I'll look into interior design. My flights are booked, and I'll be leaving in two days.

I haven't told Jerome or Leon. If I do, I'll get a lecture.

The sound of tires crunching on gravel breaks through my thoughts. Probably Jerome heading out to get supplies—he mentioned something about needing more lumber for a new deck. But then I hear his voice, deep and clear through my open window. There's an edge to it I've never heard before.

I move to the window, but can't see past the oak tree blocking my view. The voices continue, Jerome's tone growing more intense.

My curiosity gets the better of me. I slip on my shoes and head for the cabin door, leaving my half-packed suitcase sprawled across the bed. The afternoon sun hits my face as I step outside.

A black taxi idles in the driveway, its engine humming. I stop dead in my tracks as I see my mom standing there, poised as ever with her large suitcase at her side.

Jerome is rooted to the spot, a statue at the front door. His face is a mask of confusion, his eyes fixed on my mom, taking her in like a puzzle he can't quite solve.

She's come back to make things right, like she always does. But all I can feel is the blood draining from my body, leaving me cold. My mom is covered in bruises and cuts, even a nasty black eye, and I can't feel a lick of sympathy for her. I don't have it in me anymore.

I'm not one for confrontation or fighting. I knew with my mom it was always a losing battle, just like fighting a brick wall.

But with Jerome and Leon at my back… it's a fight I can win.

The thrill of it flares through me like live wire. Mom watches as I approach her, and I can see it in her face she's not happy. It's a look I've seen a thousand times, as if I've done something wrong, and that tips me over the edge.

I hit her square in the jaw.

"You're nothing but a piece of shit." Once I start, I can't stop. All the hurt inside me flows out vicious and true. "Coming back here, showing your face. How dare you think I'd just accept it, you fucking bitch. Go and die in the ditch you crawled out of; everyone would be so much better for it."

It feels too fucking good. Losing my shit instead of bottling it up. If she thinks she's getting her husband back… I'm not losing Jerome to her. Let me have something good—something that's mine. Jerome and Leon are the best thing that ever happened to me. Mom can't take them away. I won't allow it.

"Stop it!" Mom yells, trying to hold my wrists down, her nails sinking into my skin. But I push her down to the gravel before being hoisted back by strong hands.

"Tate, cut it out," Jerome says gruffly.

But I fight his grip.

I growl at him. "Get off me."

When I briefly get free of Jerome, he buckles down and cages his arms around my waist dragging me back to the cabin. I thrash and scream, hating that he's stopping me—that he's helping my mom.

"I hate you," I scream.

He roars at my back, "That's enough, Tate."

"I hate you."

"Leon," he calls out as he stops and forces me to sit on the sofa bed in the cabin, and I hear Leon following close behind.

"I want someone on my side," I choke out as he turns to address Leon.

"Keep her away from Bianca," he orders. At the threshold of the door, he stops and takes a breath. "I am on your side." Unable to face me, I watch his shoulders raise and fall with each breath. His voice breaks apart. "Just—stay here, please."

I curl into myself on the sofa bed, my hands still shaking. The sound of voices filters through the window—Jerome's deep rumble and my mom's shrill tone carrying across the yard. I press my palms against my ears, but fragments of their argument still pierce through.

Leon leans against the doorframe, arms crossed. His jaw clenches each time my mom's voice rises. I catch him stealing glances at me, but I can't meet his eyes.

"She's not worth it." His words slice through the quiet of the cabin.

I wrap my arms tighter around my knees. "I know."

The bruises on her face flash in my mind. Part of me wants to feel bad, wants to run out there and make sure she's okay. But that part is getting smaller every second.

"I shouldn't have hit her." My voice cracks.

Leon pushes off the doorframe and sits beside me, keeping a careful distance. "For the record, I would have let you beat her up."

"You're no better than he is," I accuse, something breaking inside me. Tears spill down my cheeks, hot and unwanted. I don't even know why I'm crying—relief, anger, grief, they all tangle together until I can't tell them apart.

Leon shifts closer, pulling out a blunt. He doesn't try to comfort me with empty words or awkward hugs. He just sits there, solid and real, smoking.

19

JEROME

I can barely breathe as Bianca takes a seat at the kitchen island, adrenaline coursing through me.

I force myself to move, my legs feeling like lead as I walk to the freezer and grab some ice. The fight hangs heavy in the air, filling the room with tension. As much as I want to yell and take it out of Bianca, I will myself to stay calm.

I'm not going to get answers unless I'm reasonable.

I pass her the ice bag, and she presses it to the side of her stomach. There's a fresh split in her bottom lip that wasn't there until Tate had a go at her.

"Here, let me help you with that." I reach for the first aid kit, my hands shaking slightly as I pull out some antiseptic wipes and a cloth.

"It's not necessary, Jerome." Bianca's voice is sharp, but I ignore her, focusing on cleaning the cut on her lip.

"Shh," I murmur, meeting her eyes briefly before looking back down at my task. "I need to make sure you're okay."

When she pulled up in the driveway, Bianca had mentioned running from a cult. But she didn't explain the bruising, where she'd come from, or the reason she ended up in a cult.

But I recall the cryptic text message and the detective's findings, and I can't wait for answers anymore. "You intended to abandon Tate with me. This all wasn't an accident, was it?"

Bianca's eyes flicker with something unreadable. "I needed time to think. I needed space. You know how overwhelming you can be."

Overwhelming? If that was really how she felt, she didn't have to come on a holiday to France. Family functions aren't always a piece of cake, I get it, but the choice was Bianca's all along. I grit my teeth, clenching the wipe tighter. "How is abandoning your daughter anywhere okay? You left her at an airport, Bianca."

She shrugs, wincing as the movement pulls at her lip. "She's almost an adult." She doesn't look remorseful. Instead, there's a defiance in her eyes, as if she's daring me to challenge her.

"Almost an adult?" I laugh, the sound bitter and incredulous. "Bianca, we're talking about leaving your daughter—my stepdaughter—to fend for herself. If I hadn't been there, what then?"

"She would've figured it out. She's a smart girl."

"You're right. She is smart. She's also dealing with the fallout of your neglect and your constant criticism." My voice rises with each word, and I can't stop now.

"How dare you?" Bianca's expression hardens. "You have no idea what it's like to be a mother. To have to carry the weight of another life on your shoulders. You don't know the sacrifices I've made, the things I've given up for her."

Like I don't have a son of my own.

"You act like she's a burden." My voice lowers, and I know I'm bordering on dangerous territory, but I can't stop the words from tumbling out. "You left her, Bianca. You chose to walk away." I sigh heavily, putting the first aid kit back into the cupboard.

"You think I didn't care? I care. I just needed to focus on myself for a change," she says. "I was sick of everything in my life. When I found this health and wellness program online, it made me believe I could get the life I wanted."

She breaks eye contact, and tears well up. "Turned out it was a scam."

I pinch the bridge of my nose, needing a moment before I speak again. Bianca never acted this way around me when we first met, but I suppose I never saw the full picture of her to begin with. "I'm sorry it didn't turn out the way you thought it would. But there are better ways to find help. You know that."

I almost feel sorry for her in this moment as I study her face. Sorry for the way her eyes shine with unshed tears, her defenses crumbling despite her efforts to hold it together. Almost.

"You could've called," I say, my voice steady. I won't let her see how much this hurts me. "You could've told me you were struggling. We could've figured this out together."

She looks up at me, her eyes glittering with a mix of anger and hurt. "You would've tried to talk me out of it. I know how you feel about my life choices."

Every word she speaks is like a knife twisting in my chest. I keep my features carefully schooled, not letting her see the impact of her words.

We were supposed to connect as a blended family on this holiday. I saw the ambition in Bianca's eyes when we were planning everything, the determination to build a new life for herself away from California, and I thought I could be a part of that. Help build it with her.

Now, sitting across from her, seeing the hurt and anger in her eyes, I feel like a fool. She never wanted this life, not really. I was just another stepping stone for her, and when it didn't work out, she ran back to the one place she knew she could get a reaction—the one place she knew I'd be.

"I wanted to support your life choices, Bianca. I just wanted you to be happy." My voice is hoarse, the weight of the truth settling on my shoulders. "But you never gave me a chance to be there for you. You never trusted me enough to let me in."

She opens her mouth to respond, but I hold up a hand to stop her. "No, let me finish. I've kept quiet for too long, hoping that things would change, that you'd include me in your plans. But now I see that you were only ever thinking of yourself."

"That's not true!" she exclaims, her voice rising. "I was thinking of both of us. I wanted to build a future where we could both be happy."

I shake my head, no longer able to hide the disappointment and hurt in my eyes. "A future where I financed your dreams? Where I was just another accessory to your life?" I stand, no longer able to sit across from her. "You used me, Bianca, and I fell for it."

I see the hurt flash in her eyes at my words, and a part of me wants to take them back, to soften the blow. But I can't. Not this time.

"Go rest, I'll bring up your luggage." I turn away, needing to put distance between us.

"I know I messed up. I know I should've handled things differently." She pauses, wetting her lips before continuing. "But I'm here now. Can't we just—"

"No, we can't, Bianca. You can't just waltz back into our lives and expect everything to be okay." I cut her off, my voice cold. "You made your choice. Now, I suggest you go rest. We'll talk about this later."

She needs to understand the gravity of what she's done.

I watch as she nods slowly. Without another word, she turns and walks out of the kitchen.

I'm giving her a week, then she's out of here.

I push myself to go check on Tate. But a twisted feeling in my gut tells me not to. A line has been crossed. I had to manhandle and put Tate in her place today. She was ready to beat the shit out of Bianca.

But I couldn't let that happen.

I hate you!

I stop by the cabin window, and spot her crumpled on the bed. Leon lies beside her, scribbling something in his pocket journal.

Slowly, I open the door and Leon's eyes meet mine.

I point to Tate, and Leon mouths, *Sleeping.*

I step back so he can follow me out the door, and he does for a change.

"She cried herself to sleep," he says, and my heart breaks. "I don't think she's coming back into the house."

"I don't blame her." I sigh. When we reach the front door, I stop, making Leon turn to me. "Thank you for keeping Tate company."

His gaze widens with astonishment, before glazing back over. "No big deal."

"Today was a big deal," I correct him. As angry and jealous as we were over Tate, Leon really had my back today. My mind drifts back to the fight we had, the way I pushed him.

I feel rotten for it.

We're both exhausted after today. I bet Leon doesn't want to stay in the house either. So I wrack my brain, trying to think how I can make everything more comfortable for us. At least for now.

"Do you want to come get pizza with me? I have to go to Marseille."

Leon nods.

***

The drive to Marseille is quiet at first. Leon stares out the window, his profile illuminated by the midday sun. The silence between us isn't hostile anymore, but it's heavy with unspoken words.

"Thanks for coming with me," I say, breaking the silence. It feels strange, this tentative peace between us.

Leon shrugs. "Better than staying at the house."

I nod, understanding completely. After today's chaos, neither of us wants to be under the same roof as Bianca. "I know a good place near the old port. Best pizza outside of Italy."

"Whatever," he says, but there's no bite to it.

I park in a narrow street lined with cafés and restaurants. The Mediterranean air carries the scent of salt and herbs as we walk toward a small pizzeria tucked between two larger establishments. Its red awning flutters in the gentle breeze.

"I used to bring you here when you were little," I say as we approach. "You probably don't remember."

Leon glances at the place, recognition flickering in his eyes. "The one with the football photos on the wall?"

I'm surprised he remembers. "That's the one."

Inside, the restaurant is warm and busy, filled with the clatter of plates and animated conversations. A waiter recognizes me with a smile and leads us to a corner table beneath a signed jersey in a frame.

We order quickly—a margherita for Leon and a quattro formaggi for me, plus two beers. When the waiter leaves, the silence returns, more awkward now that we're facing each other across the small table.

Leon fidgets with his napkin, folding and unfolding its corners. I take a deep breath.

"We need to talk about what happened," I say, meeting his eyes. "Really talk."

He looks up, wary. "About Tate."

"About everything." I lean forward slightly. "When did it happen, Leon? When did we stop being close?"

The question hangs between us. Leon takes a sip of water, buying time.

"I don't know," he finally says. "Gradually, I guess. After I turned sixteen."

I think back to those years. Leon withdrawing, me throwing myself into work. "I was so focused on providing for you that I forgot to be present with you."

The waiter returns with our beers, giving Leon another moment to gather his thoughts. When we're alone again, he speaks.

"You were always working. Building things for other people." His voice is low, almost lost in the restaurant noise. "And when you weren't, you had all these expectations. University, career."

I wince, hearing the truth in his words. "I wanted to give you opportunities."

"But you never asked what I wanted." There's no anger in his voice now, just resigned honesty. "You just... decided."

Our pizzas arrive, steaming and fragrant. Neither of us reaches for a slice yet.

"You're right," I admit. "I thought I knew what was best. I was trying to give you the guidance I never had, but I went too far." I run a hand through my hair, feeling the weight of my mistakes. "I'm sorry for that, Leon. Truly."

He nods slowly, accepting my words. "And I could've tried harder instead of just rebelling. Could've told you how I felt instead of just… pulling away."

We both take slices, the momentary focus on food giving us space to absorb what's been said. The pizza is perfect—thin crust, bubbling cheese, the slight char on the bottom—but I barely taste it.

"What about you?" Leon asks suddenly. "When did you get so angry all the time?"

The question catches me off guard. Have I been angry? I think about my outbursts, my frustrations, the tightness that seems to live in my chest these days.

"I don't know," I answer honestly. "Maybe it started with your mother leaving. Or maybe it's been building for years." I take a swig of beer. "It's no excuse."

Leon takes a thoughtful bite of his pizza.

I set down my slice, needing to focus. "When I saw you with Tate in the pool, it felt like you were taking something from me. Again. But that's not fair to either of you." I pause, choosing my next words carefully. "I care about her. More than I should."

"Yeah, I figured that out." Leon's voice is dry, but not angry. "Me too, though."

And there it is—the elephant in the room, finally acknowledged.

"So what happens now?" he asks.

I look at my son, really look at him. He's not a child anymore, hasn't been for years. He's a young man with his own desires and decisions to make.

"I don't know," I answer truthfully. "It's complicated. She's technically still my stepdaughter, even if Bianca and I are…" I trail off, not wanting to finish that thought yet.

"Getting divorced?" Leon finishes for me, eyebrow raised.

I nod. "I'm filing the papers after this."

He takes this in, chewing thoughtfully. "Good. She's toxic. For you and for Tate."

"The situation with Tate—" I begin, but he cuts me off.

"I know it's messed up. For all of us." He sets down his pizza, meeting my gaze directly. "But whatever happens between any of us, I don't want to lose you, Dad."

Dad. Something about how he says it breaks open inside me, a dam I didn't know was still holding.

"You won't," I promise, my voice rougher than I intend. "No matter what."

We eat in more comfortable silence for a while, the weight between us lightening with each passing minute. The restaurant bustles around us, other families and couples sharing meals and conversations, unaware of our small reconciliation.

"Remember when we used to go fishing?" Leon asks suddenly. "At the lake near Grandma's house?"

I smile at the memory. "You were terrible at it. Never had the patience to wait for the fish."

"Because you kept telling me to be still," he laughs. "I was eight."

"You caught that massive trout, though," I remind him. "On your own."

"Because I ignored your advice and used the lure Grandpa gave me." His smile is genuine now, the kind I haven't seen directed at me in a long time.

"Maybe you were right to ignore me sometimes," I concede.

The conversation flows more easily after that. We reminisce about camping trips and school projects, carefully navigating around the harder years, saving those for another time. It's not perfect—we're both still cautious, finding our way back to each other—but it's a start.

When the bill comes, I reach for it automatically.

"Let me get half," Leon says, pulling out his wallet.

I hesitate, then nod. "Okay."

It's a small thing, but it feels significant—acknowledging him as an equal, not just my son.

Outside, the sun is shining over Marseille. The harbor glimmers in the distance as we walk back to the truck.

"About Tate," Leon says, stopping suddenly. "We need to figure this out. Together."

I turn to face him. "You're right."

"She's been through enough without us making it worse." His expression is serious, mature. "Whatever happens between any of us, she comes first now."

I feel a surge of pride for the man standing before me. "When did you get so wise?"

He shrugs, embarrassed by the compliment. "Probably around the time I started screwing up enough to learn from it."

I laugh, clapping him on the shoulder. "That's how it works for all of us."

As we get into the truck, I feel lighter than I have in years. I'll face the courthouse and the end of my marriage. But today, I've begun rebuilding something far more important.

"One more thing," Leon says as I start the engine. "If you hurt her—even accidentally—I won't just stand by."

I glance at him, seeing both the challenge and the love in his eyes. "Same goes for you."

He nods, accepting the terms. We pull away from the curb, heading to the courthouse to pick up the necessary forms, with a new understanding between us.

Whatever happens next with Bianca, with Tate, with our tangled lives, Leon and I will face it differently now.

Together.

***

Three days later, we're back in Marseille. Leon decides to wait in the truck, while the imposing courthouse looms before me. I grip the envelope containing the divorce papers, the paper crinkling slightly under the pressure of my fingers.

This is it. The severing of a tie that once felt like the next best thing. And yet, amidst the sadness and regret, a flicker of resolve ignites within me. This isn't just an ending; it's a new beginning. A chance to rebuild.

I push open the heavy courthouse doors, the echoing clang resonating through the cavernous hall. The air inside is thick with hushed whispers and the rustling of papers, a symphony of legal proceedings unfolding.

As I approach the clerks counter, I smooth out the wrinkles on the envelope one last time, a small, almost involuntary gesture of respect for what has been, even as I prepare to let it go.

The clerk, a young woman with tired eyes and a neatly pressed suit, looks up as I place the envelope on the counter. "Divorce papers?" she asks, her voice devoid of emotion, a testament to the countless similar transactions she must process.

I nod, my voice barely above a whisper. "Yes."

"Alright, let me take a look."

My heart pounds as she thumbs through the documents, her eyes scanning each page with practiced efficiency. The fluorescent lights overhead cast harsh shadows across her desk.

She pauses on one page, her brow furrowing slightly. "Mr. Beaumont, I notice there's no signature from Mrs. Beaumont on page four."

Of course there isn't. Bianca hasn't left the house since she arrived, refusing to acknowledge the reality of our situation. "She's been served the papers but hasn't signed yet."

"I see." The clerk's expression softens slightly. "Well, we can still process the initial filing without her signature. You'll need to pay the filing fee today, and then we'll schedule a hearing date."

I pull out my wallet, ready to hand over my credit card. The leather feels worn under my fingers, just like my patience with this whole situation. The sooner this is done, the sooner we can all move forward.

"The fee is three hundred and fifty euros," she says, sliding a payment form across the counter.

I fill out the form and the clerk takes it back, her fingers moving efficiently across her keyboard.

"Your case number is BF-2023-4721," she says, printing out a receipt. "Keep this for your records. The court will send notification of the hearing date to both parties."

I fold the receipt and slip it into my wallet.

"Is there anything else you need assistance with today, Mr. Beaumont?"

"No, that's all." My voice comes out steadier than I expect.

She nods and stamps the last page with practiced precision. "The filing is complete. You'll receive all further correspondence by mail."

I thank her and step away from the counter, my footsteps hollow against the marble floor. The afternoon light streams through the high windows, casting long shadows across the courthouse hall.

Leon raises a brow at me as I get into the driver's seat.

"It's done," I say.

Leon pounds my back in celebration. "Fuck yeah!"

ARCADIA

The steering wheel feels solid beneath my hands as I navigate the winding roads back home. My mind drifts to my past romances.

First there was Amelie, Leon's mother. Young love—passionate, wild, and ultimately unsustainable. We were too young, too caught up in the romance of it all to see how incompatible we really were. The pregnancy pushed us together, but we drifted apart like leaves in opposite currents.

After Amelie, there were a few casual encounters. Nothing serious—just brief connections that helped ease the loneliness. I focused on raising Leon, building my business, creating a stable life. Romance took a backseat.

Then came Sophia. She swept into my life like a summer storm—all passion and intensity. We dated for two years, and for a while, I thought she might be the one. But her ambitions lay elsewhere. She wanted to travel, to explore the world, while I needed to stay rooted for Leon. We parted amicably, but it stung.

Then Bianca came along, and I thought I'd finally found what I was looking for. Someone who seemed to understand family, who could balance independence with commitment. How wrong I'd been.

Each one taught me something, shaped me in some way. Amelie taught me about responsibility and growing up too fast. Sophia showed me that passion alone isn't enough. Bianca's helped me understand that compatibility on paper doesn't always translate to real connection.

The road curves sharply, and I grip the steering wheel tighter—maybe I'm just not built for the long haul. The cabin renovations, my work, even raising Leon—I excel at projects with clear beginnings and ends. But relationships? They're meant to be endless, continuous, always growing and changing.

The mountains rise up around me, solid and unchanging. Every woman I've loved has eventually seen through me. The need to move, to build, to change.

Even now, with the divorce papers filed, I feel that familiar itch. The urge to throw myself into work, to lose myself in the tangible satisfaction of creating something with my hands. It's easier than facing the reality that maybe I'm better off alone.

A hawk circles overhead, riding the thermal currents with effortless grace. Free. Unbound. Perhaps that's what I've been fighting all along—my own nature.

I pull up in the driveway, the sound of crunching beneath my tires. The main house stands silent, but I know Bianca is inside. It's time. No more delays.

Leon makes sure to steer clear of the house while I head inside. I find Bianca in the living room, sprawled on the sofa with a glass of wine. She looks up as I enter, her expression unreadable behind large sunglasses.

"Where have you been all day?" she asks, the slight slur in her words telling me it's not her first glass.

I remain standing, unwilling to settle into this moment. "The courthouse."

She stiffens slightly, then takes another sip. "And why would you be there?"

"I filed for divorce, Bianca." My voice is steady, calmer than I expected. "It's done."

The glass pauses halfway to her lips. "You what?"

"You heard me." I pull the receipt from my pocket, placing it on the coffee table between us. "I've started the proceedings. The court will send you the formal papers."

She removes her sunglasses, her eyes narrowed. "Without even discussing it with me? After everything I've been through?"

"We've been 'discussing' it for three days. You've refused to sign the papers I gave you. And yes, after everything—especially after everything you've done to Tate."

"This is about her?" Bianca stands, wine sloshing dangerously close to the rim of her glass. "Of course it is. It's always about her."

"No, it's about us. There is no us, Bianca. There hasn't been for a long time, even before you disappeared. You know that as well as I do."

She laughs, the sound brittle and sharp. "So, you're throwing me out? After I came back injured? After I escaped that place?"

"I'm not throwing you out. But yes, I want you to leave. Today." I keep my voice level, though anger pulses beneath every word. "I've booked you a suite at Le Chalet Provençal in the village. It's comfortable, private. You can stay there until you decide where you want to go next."

"And if I refuse?"

"Then you'll be staying in a house where no one wants you, including your own daughter. Is that really what you want?"

Her expression hardens. "She'll get over it. She always does."

The casualness with which she dismisses Tate's pain ignites something in me. "No, Bianca. She won't 'get over it.' And she shouldn't have to. The way you've treated her—"

"Oh, spare me the parenting lecture," she cuts in, draining her glass. "You've known her, what? Three weeks? I raised her for eighteen years."

"And that's exactly the problem. You never saw what an amazing person she is. All you saw was someone to criticize, someone to mold into whatever you thought she should be."

Bianca sets her glass down with deliberate care. "And you think you know her better? You think playing house with my daughter for a few weeks makes you an expert?"

I clench my jaw, refusing to be baited. "This isn't about me. It's about you leaving. Today. The car will be here at five to take you to the hotel."

"You can't just—"

"I can and I am. The reservation is for two weeks, paid in full. After that, you're on your own."

She studies me, searching for any sign of wavering. Finding none, her shoulders slump slightly. "Fine. I'll go. But don't think this is over, Jerome."

"It is over. That's the whole point." I turn to leave, suddenly exhausted. "I'll help you with your bags."

As I walk toward the stairs, a strange silence settles over the house. I should feel relieved, triumphant even. Instead, there's just a hollow emptiness.

I decide to check on Tate first. She hasn't left the cabin since Bianca showed up three days ago. Leon's been taking her food, but she won't talk to anyone else. Maybe telling her about the divorce will help her understand she's not alone in this mess. That I am on her side.

The cabin door creaks as I push it open. "Tate?"

No answer. The small space feels emptier than usual. Her bed is made—too neat, like no one's slept in it. The few clothes she'd unpacked are gone from the dresser.

My heart speeds up as I scan the room. That's when I spot it—a folded piece of paper on the side table.

I cross the room in two strides, my hands trembling slightly as I pick up the note. The paper is torn from the embroidered journal, her hurried handwriting covering the page:

Jerome and Leon,

I can't stay here anymore. Not with her. I thought I could handle it, but every time I look at that house, I see her face. I see how easily she walked away, and how easily she walked back in.

Please don't look for me. I need to figure this out on my own.
Tate

Returning to the house, my feet pound against the wooden steps as I burst through the door. This can't be happening.

227

"Tate!" My voice echoes through the hallway. I check the kitchen first—empty. The living room—nothing. Taking the stairs two at a time, I race to her former bedroom.

"Tate, are you here?" The door swings open to reveal an untouched bed. The bathroom door stands open, dark inside.

Leon appears at the top of the stairs, concern etched on his face. "What's wrong?"

I thrust the note at him, my hands shaking. He scans it quickly, his face draining of color.

"When did you—"

"Just now. In the cabin." I run my fingers through my hair, trying to think straight. "Check the garage, see if any of the bikes are missing."

Leon's already moving, the note crumpled in his fist as he thunders down the stairs. I hear the front door slam, followed by his voice cutting through the evening air.

"Tate!" His shout echoes across the property. "TATE!"

I follow him outside, watching as he sprints toward the tree line, still calling her name. The sun's starting to set, casting long shadows across the yard. My chest tightens as I think about her out there alone, probably scared, definitely hurting.

Leon's voice grows more desperate with each call, fading as he disappears into the forest behind the house.

20

JEROME

TWO MONTHS LATER

The reservation came through last week. A retired couple from England wanted the "authentic Provence experience." I'd promised them a cozy retreat, but the house and cabin needed a final inspection before their arrival tomorrow.

I push open the French doors, inhaling the crisp autumn air. The guest room looks ready—fresh linens, polished wood, not a speck of dust. The cleaning service have done their job well.

My footsteps echo through the empty hallway as I make my way to the movie room. The leather couch still holds a slight depression where she used to curl up. Where we'd spent those evenings together.

A glint catches my eye—fairy lights tangled in the corner. My throat tightens. Tate had strung them up the afternoon me and Leon fought. It was her idea alone to brighten up the space.

I pick up the lights, the delicate wire cool against my palm. Two months feels like two years. The house is too quiet now, too orderly. I haven't been back up here since Tate left. No more half-empty tea mugs scattered around. No more paint-stained clothes draped over chairs. No more late-night laughter.

The fairy lights kink and twist as I wrap them around my hand. Her scent still lingers here—vanilla and something uniquely her. Or maybe that's just my imagination playing tricks on me.

I sigh, shoving the lights into a drawer. I have guests arriving tomorrow. No time for memories.

But my hand lingers on the drawer handle. In the darkness, I can almost hear her voice: "These will make it cozy, Jerome. Trust me."

I force myself out of the movie room, heading toward the cabin. The gravel crunches under my boots as more memories flood back—showing her the grounds, watching her eyes light up as she sorted through paint colors, feeling her soft touch against my skin…

I shake my head. These thoughts won't help anyone.

The cabin door creaks as I push it open. Morning light streams through the windows, highlighting the fresh paint and restored wooden beams. Everything looks perfect, pristine—exactly what tourists expect from a Provence getaway.

But all I see is her.

The corner where she'd perched on a ladder, biting her lip in concentration as she painted. Where I'd almost kissed her, paint smudged on her cheek.

My phone buzzes—a text from Carson. He wants to catch up for drinks tomorrow night, and I think that's what I need. I haven't seen him since visiting the farm.

I send back a quick text, and I find myself tracing my fingers along the wall she painted. The color we chose still makes my chest ache—Jade Mist, a soft pale green, letting the outside in.

"Get it together, Jerome," I mutter to myself. But the silence that follows only emphasizes how empty this place feels without her.

I pull out my checklist, trying to focus on the practical—inventory supplies, check the water pressure, test the heating. Anything to keep my mind off her. Off us. Off what could have been if Bianca hadn't shown up that day.

Even now, I can feel the ghost of Tate's touch, hear the whisper of her voice, taste the sweetness of her kiss.

"Shit," I whisper into the empty room. Tate made her choice; she left without notice. She was never tied to this place—to us. It's been months, and she's clearly moved on.

She made the right choice for us all. But God, I fucking miss her. How long before these memories stop haunting me?

The taxi drops me off on Rue de la Roquette, and I spot Carson through the window of Le Baron Rouge. His red hair stands out against the worn burgundy walls of the century-old wine bar.

Inside, the scent of oak barrels and aged cheese hits me. Wooden casks line the walls, their brass spigots gleaming in the dim light. The original zinc bar counter, scratched and patinated from decades of use, runs along one wall. Behind it, shelves overflow with dusty wine bottles, their labels faded but still showing prestigious vintages from across France.

Carson waves from a corner table, surrounded by locals perched on rickety stools, sharing plates of charcuterie and arguing politics.

"You look like shit." Carson grins, pulling me into a rough hug. He's already ordered a carafe of house red and two glasses.

I laugh. "Wow, thanks."

I settle onto the wooden stool across from him. The table wobbles slightly—these old bistro tables have seen better days, but that's part of their charm. Above us, vintage posters advertise long-discontinued aperitifs, their colors muted by years of tobacco smoke from before the smoking ban.

"How's the house?" Carson asks.

I pour myself a glass, letting the familiar routine wash over me.

"The house's…" I swirl the wine in my glass. "Empty. Getting my first guests today."

Carson leans back, his weathered hands wrapped around his glass. "Ah, the Airbnb thing. You finally did it."

"Had to. Can't keep living off savings forever."

"And the kid?"

"Leon's good. Got an apartment in Nice, and is working for a mechanic." The wine tastes bitter on my tongue. "He's left the nest."

Carson's eyes narrow. "And what about the girl?"

My fingers tighten around the stem of my glass. "Haven't heard from her since Bianca showed up."

"That woman." Carson shakes his head. "Always knew she was trouble. Remember that time in Marseille when she—"

"Rather not walk down that road." I take another sip. "Two months of radio silence. Tate's probably graduating school."

"You miss her." It's not a question.

I study the deep-red liquid in my glass. "She brought life back to the place. Even Leon was different around her."

"Different how?"

"Happier. More engaged." I pause. "Until everything went to hell."

Carson reaches across the table, clapping my shoulder. "You did right by that girl, Jerome. Gave her a home when she needed one."

"Fat lot of good that did." The words come out sharper than intended. "Sorry. It's just…"

"Just what?"

I drain my glass, the wine doing little to dull the ache in my chest. "I fell for her. Hard. And now she's gone."

"You're both adults," Carson says, refilling our glasses.

"I'm significantly older than her, Carson," I say. "I could be her father."

"But you're not." He states, matter-of-factly.

I run a hand through my hair. "I was supposed to protect her, be someone she could trust. Instead, I…" The memory of her skin against mine, her soft gasps, makes my chest tighten. "I took advantage."

"Bullshit." Carson's voice cuts through my self-loathing. "That girl knew exactly what she wanted. And from what you've told me, she pursued you as much as you pursued her."

"She was vulnerable—"

"She was lonely and scared when she arrived, sure. But by the time anything happened between you two?" He shakes his head. "She'd found her footing. You helped her do that."

The evening crowd starts filtering in, their chatter filling the small space. I reach for the carafe and refill my glass as a waiter squeezes past with a tray of fresh baguettes and pâté.

"You know what your problem is?" Carson leans forward. "You're so busy feeling guilty about wanting her, you've convinced yourself you somehow corrupted her. But Tate's not some delicate flower you deflowered. She's a woman who chose you."

My throat tightens. "And look how well that turned out."

"Life's messy, Jerome. Doesn't mean it wasn't real." He takes a sip of wine. "Question is, what are you going to do about it?"

I stare into my glass, refilling it. "Nothing to do. She's moved on. Best thing for everyone is to let her live her life."

Carson slams his glass down. Wine sloshes over the rim. "For fuck's sake, Jerome. When did you become such a coward?"

"Excuse me?"

"You're sitting here wallowing in self-pity instead of fighting for what you want." He jabs a finger at me. "The Jerome I know wouldn't just roll over and accept defeat."

"It's not that simple—"

"It's exactly that simple. You're just too scared to admit it."

Heat rises to my face. "You don't understand the situation."

"I understand you're being a bloody idiot." Carson's Irish accent thickens with frustration. "But fine, keep torturing yourself. See if I care."

234

The silence stretches between us, broken only by the clink of glasses and murmur of conversation around us. I take a deep breath, forcing down my irritation. Fighting with Carson won't solve anything.

"How's the sanctuary doing?" I ask, desperate to change the subject. Besides working as a farrier, Carson also has a property back in Ireland for rescue animals.

Carson's shoulders relax slightly. "Got three new rescues last week. A pair of abandoned donkeys and a retired circus horse."

"The horse giving you trouble?"

"Nah, she's a sweetheart. Just needs time to remember how to be a horse again." His eyes light up as he talks about his work. "The donkeys though—stubborn little bastards. Remind me of you, actually."

I crack a smile despite myself. "Thanks for that."

"At least donkeys know what they want." Carson winks. "Unlike some people I know."

I roll my eyes, but can't help chuckling. The wine's starting to work its magic, softening the edges of my mood.

"Remember that summer we spent hitchhiking through Spain?" Carson's eyes get that faraway look. "God, we must've been what—twenty-four?"

"Twenty-three." I lean back, memories washing over me. "That piece of shit car that broke down outside Barcelona."

"And that mechanic who tried to charge us triple because we were tourists." Carson grins. "Until you started arguing with him in broken Spanish."

"The look on his face." I shake my head, grinning. "Then he invited us to dinner with his family."

"Maria." Carson sighs dramatically. "His daughter. Now there was a firecracker. She had you wrapped around her finger for what, two weeks?"

"Three days, you ass." The memory makes me laugh. "Then her boyfriend showed up."

"Never seen you run so fast." Carson wipes tears from his eyes. "Though that time in Morocco was a close second."

"We agreed never to speak of Morocco."

"You mean the camel incident?"

"Carson—"

"Or the belly dancing fiasco?"

"I will throw this wine at you."

Carson raises his hands in surrender, but his eyes sparkle with mischief. "Those were the days though, weren't they? Just two idiots with backpacks and no plan."

I smile. Yeah, it's bittersweet. I raise my glass. "The adventures don't end."

"True." Our wine glasses clink. "We're just two older idiots now. You know where we should travel to next?"

Travel is the last thing on my mind. "No?"

"America."

The wine sits heavy in my stomach, and I roll my eyes. "Carson."

Carson's voice softens. "Here's what I know—time is of the essence." He taps his finger on the table between us. "And you'll never get it back."

***

"Watch the corner." I steady the couch as Leon navigates backward through his apartment doorway. "Little to the left."

The leather sectional slides into place against the exposed brick wall. Leon drops onto it, chest heaving. "That's the last piece of furniture."

I survey the industrial-style loft—high ceilings, steel beams, and floor-to-ceiling windows overlooking downtown Nice. Pride swells in my chest. My son's first real apartment, paid for with his own money from apprenticing under a mechanic.

"Beer?" Leon holds up two bottles from the mini fridge— the only appliance he bothered to plug in so far.

I catch the bottle he tosses. "Thanks." The cold glass feels good after hours of moving boxes and furniture. "Kitchen boxes next?"

"No." Leon sprawls deeper into the couch. "I need five minutes to appreciate that we didn't die carrying this thing up four flights of stairs."

I chuckle and sink down next to him. The past few months have smoothed the rough edges between us. The silence between us feels comfortable now—a far cry from the tension-filled void of two months ago. Leon takes a long pull from his beer, his shoulders relaxed.

"The shop's been good," he says. "Marcel wants to give me more responsibility with the classic restorations."

"You've earned it." I think back to the vintage Citroën he rebuilt last week, how his eyes lit up explaining the engine modifications. "Your attention to detail is impressive."

He scratches his neck, a small smile playing at the corner of his mouth. The compliment lands different now—he actually lets it sink in instead of bristling.

Our Sunday dinners have become a highlight too. Last week, he brought fresh bread from a bakery near his work, and we spent hours talking about everything and nothing. No heated arguments, no storming off. Just father and son sharing a meal.

"Thanks for helping with the move." He gestures around the loft. "I know you're busy with the renovation business picking up."

"Always have time for you." The words come easy now. They used to stick in my throat, weighted down by years of miscommunication.

Leon nods, understanding passing between us. The past months have taught us both how to bridge the gap—him learning to open up, me learning to listen better. Sometimes the hardest storms bring the clearest skies.

"Have you heard from her?" Leon's question hangs in the air.

I take a long pull from my beer. "No." The word comes out rougher than intended. "You?"

"Last week. She's graduated and has a job." He picks at the label on his bottle. "She's trying to get into design school or something."

My chest tightens with pride and something else—an ache I can't shake. "Good. That's… good."

"Dad." Leon shifts to face me. "You should get in contact with her."

"That's not a good idea." I set my beer down on the concrete floor. "She needs space to build her own life, without complications from her past."

"Fuck's sake." Leon's voice carries that familiar edge of challenge. "You're just scared."

"Watch it." But the warning lacks heat. He's not entirely wrong.

"Look, I see how you get when someone mentions her name. Hell, you still have that paint swatch she picked for the cabin taped to your fridge."

Heat creeps up my neck. I'd forgotten.

"And every time you walk past that cabin, you look like someone kicked your dog." Leon leans forward, elbows on his knees. "You won't stop missing her until you see her again. Clear the air."

"It's more complicated than that." My fingers trace condensation on the bottle. "The age difference—"

"Didn't matter then, doesn't matter now." He cuts me off. "She's an adult making her own choices. Has been since day one."

The truth of his words hits hard. I've spent months convincing myself I did the right thing letting her go without a word. That the distance was what she needed. But maybe I was just protecting myself, and being a fool.

"I have feelings for her," he continues, voice steady. "So do you. And I think we both know she has feelings for both of us."

I close my eyes, rubbing my temples. "This is a mess."

"Only if we make it one." Leon's voice drops lower. "Dad, we both care about her. And she cares about us both. We shouldn't make her choose."

My eyes snap open. "What are you suggesting?"

"Let Tate decide what she wants. Whether it's you, me, or…" He hesitates. "Or both of us. Just give it a chance."

The implication makes my breath catch. "Leon, that's—"

"Unconventional? Yeah." He shrugs. "But so is everything about this situation. I'm just saying."

I stare at my son, seeing the determined set of his jaw. "You'd be okay with that? Sharing her?"

"If she wants it that way." His gaze doesn't waver. "Would you?"

The question cuts to the heart of it. Would I be willing to let my son love the same woman I love? Could I handle seeing them together? But then, could I handle losing her entirely?

"You're asking if I could handle seeing her with you." I choose my words carefully. "Being intimate with both of us."

Leon nods. "It only works if we're both honest. If we're both all in."

I take a deep breath. "And if she chooses just one of us?"

"Then we respect that. Whatever she decides, we don't let it come between us. We've worked too hard to fix things."

I think about how far we've come. How this conversation would have been impossible months ago.

"I'll think about it," I murmur.

"Good."

I toy with my phone, my heart pounding in my ears. "When did you get so wise about relationships?" I attempt deflection, but there's genuine wonder in my voice.

Leon snorts. "Someone in this family had to figure their shit out." He stands, grabbing our empty bottles.

★★★

The flight back to Paris stretches long and dark. Leon's words echo in my mind, mixing with memories of last summer.

I slam my apartment door behind me, dropping my keys on the counter. The space feels hollow, sterile—nothing like the warmth of my countryside home where Tate once lived.

My chest constricts. The weight of months of denial crashes over me like a tidal wave. I stumble to the couch, gripping the leather as if it could anchor me against the storm of emotion.

"Fuck." The word comes out broken. Hot tears spill down my cheeks for the first time since she left. Since I let her walk away without fighting for what we had.

Every suppressed feeling bursts free—the ache when I wake up alone, the phantom touch of her fingers against my skin, the emptiness in my chest her presence used to fill. I've been going through the motions, convincing myself this was better for her. What a goddamn fool.

My hands shake as I pull out my phone, scrolling through old photos I couldn't bring myself to delete. There she is, paint smeared across her cheek, grinning at the camera. Another of her curled up reading in the window seat, sunlight turning her hair to gold.

The truth hits like a physical blow—I can't do this anymore. Can't pretend I'm fine without her. Can't keep lying to myself that letting her go was noble or right.

I need Tate. Need her quick wit and gentle heart. Need her determination and creativity. Need the way she sees through my gruff exterior to the man beneath.

Tears blur my vision as I scroll through my contacts, finding Leon. He'll know how to reach her.

Because Carson and Leon were right—I've been scared. Scared of judgment, of complications, of loving someone so completely. But I'm more scared of living the rest of my life wondering what could have been.

Jerome:

We talk to Tate together, present this option together. No going behind each other's backs.

Jerome:

What's her Facebook?

Leon:

Fucking finally, it's a deal. I knew you would crack.

21

TATE

ONE WEEK EARLIER

I stand in front of the bathroom mirror, eyes narrowed in concentration as I carefully apply the dye to my roots. The rich, copper color slowly seeps into my blond strands, transforming my look.

I need to look sharp for my shift at Maison & Co. this morning. It's a home décor store. I'm trying to save up money to apply for design school, so unlike every other high school graduate partying right now, I'm paying the bills and keeping busy. As I finish up the last section, I rinse the excess dye from my hair, watching the coppery water swirl down the drain.

Patting my hair dry, I examine the results in the mirror. Not bad, if I do say so myself. The warm hue complements my skin and brings out the green flecks in my hazel eyes. Satisfied, I gather my things and head out of the bathroom, ready to get dressed.

Exiting the bathroom, I nearly collide with my roommate, Jess.

SAINT BRYDE

"Woah, watch it!" she exclaims, steadying me with a hand on my arm. Her eyes light up when she sees my new hair. "Tate, girl, you look amazing! That color is so you."

I can't help but smile at her enthusiasm. "Thanks, Jess. I was going for something different."

"Well, it looks great," she says, giving me a thumbs-up before disappearing into the bathroom.

I hear the water running as I head to my room to get dressed for work.

Slipping on a pair of dark skinny jeans and a flowy blouse, I do a quick once-over in the mirror. The new hair color gives me a boost of confidence.

As I grab my purse and head out the door, I can't help but think about how different my life is now compared to a few months ago. Back then, I was a lost, anxious teenager, abandoned by my own mother. But Jerome and Leon took me in, giving me a sense of stability and belonging that I'd never known.

My mind drifts to the time I spent with them, the growing connection I felt with both men. The way Jerome's green eyes would linger on me, his touch sending sparks through my body. And Leon, with his mischievous smile and the way he'd make my heart race.

I shake my head, trying to push those thoughts aside as I climb into my car. I can't afford to get distracted, not when I'm so close to achieving my goals. Still, a part of me can't help but wonder what might have been if my mom hadn't shown up and ruined everything.

ARCADIA

The drive to work is short, and soon I'm walking through the doors of Maison & Co. My boss, Isabelle, greets me with a warm smile.

"Good morning, Tate. Love the new look!"

I smile. "Thanks, Isabelle."

She nods approvingly. "Let's get you started on that display for the new patio furniture..."

I nod and follow Isabelle to the stockroom, eager to get started. As we unload the boxes, I can't help but feel a twinge of excitement. Decorating and design have become a passion of mine.

"I'll grab the rest of the hardware," Isabelle says, heading back toward the storage area.

I'm arranging the first few pieces when I hear it—that familiar voice that used to make me shrink.

"So, this is where you've been hiding."

My body freezes before I slowly turn around. Standing there in designer sunglasses and a white linen dress that probably cost more than my monthly rent is my mom.

"Mom," I say flatly, straightening my spine. "What are you doing here?"

She pulls off her sunglasses dramatically, eyes scanning the store with thinly veiled contempt. "Is this really what you're doing with your life? Arranging furniture in a little shop?"

The old me would have wilted under her gaze, desperate for any crumb of approval. But something has changed. I feel it in the steadiness of my hands, in the calm of my breathing.

"Yes, it is," I reply, continuing to unpack the box beside me. "I'm good at it, too."

Bianca sighs, moving closer. "Darling, this is beneath you. You know that, right? Come back to—"

"How did you find me?" I interrupt, continuing my work.

"Oh, please. It wasn't that difficult. You still have the same friends on social media, just a different name." Her voice sharpens on the last words. "Which we need to discuss."

"There's nothing to discuss." I finally look up at her. "I legally changed it."

Her perfectly manicured hand clutches at imaginary pearls. "To what? Something ridiculous, I assume."

"Foster," I say simply. "Tate Foster."

"Foster? As in… foster children?" She laughs, the sound like breaking glass. "How delightfully pedestrian."

I don't bother explaining that it means I'm fostering growth and nurturing myself. She wouldn't understand anyway.

"What do you want, Mom?" I ask, my voice steady.

She takes a step closer, lowering her voice. "First you run away, then you change your name to something that practically screams 'neglected child.' I get it, Tate. You're angry at me. Message received."

"This isn't about you," I say, and I'm surprised to realize I mean it. "This is about me building my own life."

"By folding napkins and arranging pillows?" she scoffs.

"By doing something I love while I save for design school," I counter.

Something flickers across her face—surprise? "Design school?"

"Yes. I'm applying next semester."

Bianca studies me for a moment, and I can see the calculations running behind her eyes. "Well, I can help with that. You know I have connections—"

"No," I cut her off. "I don't want your help."

"Don't be stubborn, Tate. This is what mothers do."

A laugh escapes me before I can stop it. "Since when?"

Her mouth tightens. "I've always wanted what's best for you."

"What's best for your image, you mean." I set down the screwdriver I've been holding. "Listen, I don't mind you tracking me down for… whatever this is. But I'm working. I have a life. And it doesn't include you anymore."

"You can't just erase me," she says, and for a second, I glimpse something like hurt in her eyes. "I'm your mother."

"You're right. I can't erase you." I take a deep breath. "But I can choose who I let into my life now. And I'm not choosing you."

She blinks rapidly, caught off guard by my directness. "This is about Jerome, isn't it? And his son? They turned you against me."

"No, Mom. You did that all on your own." I pick up a throw pillow, arranging it on the patio couch I've just assembled. "Years of criticism, neglect, and making me feel like I was never good enough."

"That's not fair—"

"Maybe not. But it's true." I meet her gaze steadily. "I'm done looking for your approval. I'm done trying to be the daughter you wanted. I'm just… done."

Isabelle appears at the end of the aisle, eyeing us curiously. "Everything okay over here, Tate?"

"Yes," I say, not breaking eye contact with my mother. "My visitor was just leaving."

Bianca looks between us, her composure slipping for just a moment before the mask slides back into place. "Fine. Have it your way." She puts her sunglasses back on. "But when this little independence fantasy falls apart, don't come crying to me."

"I won't," I say simply.

She turns on her heel, stalking toward the exit. At the door, she pauses, looking back at me one last time. I expect another cutting remark, but instead, she just stares for a long moment before walking out.

I release a tense breath.

"You okay?" Isabelle asks, coming to stand beside me.

"Yeah," I say, surprised to find it's true. "I am."

"Alright, then let's get these pieces set up. I want it looking fresh and inviting for our customers," Isabelle says, handing me a set of instructions.

I get to work, carefully assembling the sleek, modern pieces. The process is methodical, and I find it soothing. My hands are steady now, steadier than they've ever been before. Soon, the display starts to take shape, the different textures and colors complementing each other perfectly.

"Nicely done!" Isabelle comments as she returns, admiring my handiwork. "I knew I could count on you."

I smile, feeling a sense of pride. "I'm happy to help however I can."

"Well, keep it up and you might just be running this place one day," she teases, giving my shoulder a gentle squeeze before heading back to her office.

The morning rush starts soon after, and I find myself greeting and assisting a steady stream of customers. I'm grateful for the distraction—I hate quiet days, time seems to slow down.

As I help a young couple select throw pillows for their patio, I can't help but imagine what it would be like to have my own outdoor space, one where I could entertain friends or curl up with a good book. The thought fills me with a longing I've been trying to ignore.

"Excuse me, miss?"

I turn to see an older gentleman standing beside me, a polite smile on his face.

"How can I help you today?" I ask, pushing aside my wistful thoughts.

"I'm looking for some new patio furniture. Do you have anything in a more traditional style?"

"Absolutely, let me show you our selection over here." I guide him to the other side of the display, pointing out the classic wrought iron and wicker pieces.

By the time my lunch break rolls around, I feel drained, but also strangely accomplished. This job may not be my ultimate dream, but it's helping me get one step closer. And right now, that's all that matters.

I head to the breakroom, eager to refuel with a quick sandwich. As I settle into one of the chairs, my phone buzzes in my pocket. Pulling it out, I feel my heart skip a beat when I see the name on the screen.

It's Leon. How did he find me? I thought I'd covered my tracks by changing my last name.

Hey, Tate. It's Leon. Saw your new profile pic—looking good.

I bite my lip, unsure how to respond. Part of me wants to ignore it, to pretend I never saw the message. But another part of me is intrigued, curious to know what he wants.

Before I can overthink it, my fingers are flying across the screen.

How did you find me? I type, then pause, deleting the words. That sounds too accusatory. I try again.

Hey Leon, what's up? I send, cringing at how casual I sound.

The response is almost immediate. *Just saw you pop up on my suggested friends. Didn't realize you changed your name.*

I sigh, running a hand through my newly dyed hair. Of course he would see my profile, even with the name change. I should have known better than to think I could hide from him.

Yeah, I, uh, didn't want to be tied to my mom anymore, I reply.

Mom was calling me every week until I finally picked up. It was my graduation day.

You can't ignore me forever, I'm your mother.

To her, this was only a little blip in our relationship. But as soon as I said I changed my last name, I think it finally sank in.

She doesn't call me anymore.

I'm glad you emancipated yourself, he says, and I can practically hear the smirk in his voice. *How have you been?*

I hesitate, wondering if I should be honest or try to downplay everything. In the end, my desire for connection wins out.

Honestly? It's been tough, I admit, my fingers trembling slightly as I type. *But I'm doing okay, all things considered.*

There's a brief pause before his next message. *I'm sorry to hear that. I wish I could do something to help.*

I bite my lip, a flicker of hope stirring in my chest. *Well, maybe you could start by telling me how you're doing?* I suggest, my thumbs flying across the screen.

I'm...alright, I guess. Busy with work in Paris. But I think about you a lot, Tate.

My breath catches in my throat at his words. I can feel the familiar heat rising to my cheeks as I try to compose a response.

I think about you too. I finally admit, my heart pounding in my ears.

Just then, the breakroom door opens and Isabelle pokes her head in. "Tate? Your break's almost up, hon."

I jump, quickly shoving my phone back into my pocket. "Uh, yeah, I'm coming," I call out, giving Isabelle a sheepish smile.

She nods, disappearing back through the doorway. I let out a shaky breath, my mind racing.

Leon... what am I going to do about you?

***

The California heat is suffocating, even with all the windows open in my cramped apartment. I'm sprawled on my second-hand couch, phone in hand, trying to ignore how the fabric scratches against my skin. Nothing like Jerome's buttery leather sofa that I used to sink into after a long day.

Leon's texts have become a lifeline these past few weeks, though each one is both a comfort and a torment. I congratulate him on his apprenticeship at the auto shop, surprised but pleased. He seems happier now, more settled.

My thumb hovers over the screen. The question I really want to ask burns in my throat, but I try to keep it casual. *How's your dad doing?*

My heart pounds in the seconds before his response appears.

He's…managing, I suppose. It's been a tough couple of months for him, working, organizing the Airbnb guests and all.

I curl deeper into the couch, guilt churning in my stomach. The cabin must be finished by now. I wonder if the walls are still that shade of green I picked out that day, when Jerome stood so close behind me, I could feel the heat radiating from his body. Do tourists sleep there now, completely unaware of the stories those walls could tell?

I'm sure it hasn't been easy. I miss him, you know. My fingers tremble as I type the words.

He misses you too, Tate. More than you know.

A sob catches in my throat. I press my face into a throw pillow, breathing in the artificial lavender of cheap fabric softener. Nothing like the rich, earthy scent of Jerome's cologne, or the fresh pine that always clung to his clothes.

I never meant to hurt you both, I type, then pause, tears blurring my vision. *I just…I needed to get away. To clear my head and figure things out.*

I get it. Trust me, I do. He understands, Tate. He's waiting for you to come back home.

Home. The word hits me like a physical blow. Outside my window, palm trees sway in the hot breeze—so different from the sturdy oaks surrounding Jerome's house. A car alarm blares in the distance, nothing like the gentle symphony of crickets and wind in the trees that used to lull me to sleep.

Leon sends another text: *Dad's planning the Christmas decorations already. You should see his sketches for the front porch.*

I close my eyes, imagining Jerome planning out every detail. Would he hang lights along the front of the house? Set up a tree in that corner of the movie room where I used to curl up?

My laptop sits open on the coffee table, browser still showing the Air France website I'd been obsessing over earlier. The prices mock me—three months' worth of money, at least.

I can't afford it, not now, I text back, hating myself for using such a pathetic excuse. The truth is, I'm terrified. Terrified of facing them both again, of dealing with the mess of feelings I have for both father and son. Terrified that maybe I've lost my chance at whatever we could have been.

But God, do I miss home.

22

TATE

23RD OF DECEMBER

T he Christmas music is giving me a migraine. Mariah
Carey's hit song is playing for the forty-seventh time
today, and I swear if I hear "All I Want for Christmas Is You"
one more time, I'm going to snap. At least arranging displays
is better than dealing with customers who insist we must have
more of those silver mercury glass ornaments "in the back."

I smooth the Italian silk duvet over our newest bedroom
display, trying not to think about the imported bedding in
Jerome's guest room—my old room. The fabric beneath my
fingers is butter soft, and probably costs more than my monthly
rent, but it's nothing compared to the memories of those cool
sheets against my skin on warm Provence nights.

I wonder what the south of France looks like in December...
Those sprawling vineyards stripped bare, their gnarled vines
dusted with frost. The lavender fields under a blanket of snow,
just mounds where the fragrant purple blooms will return in
spring. Finally, all those hearths in the house would be put to
use.

ARCADIA

My fingers tremble as I arrange the throw pillows, each one perfectly chopped and positioned just so. The store's Christmas playlist switches to "Last Christmas," and I have to not roll my eyes. Stupid song. Stupid holidays. Stupid homesickness that won't go away no matter how many shifts I pick up or how exhausted I make myself.

"Excuse me..."

That voice. Deep, rich, achingly familiar. My heart stops, then starts again at double speed. No. It can't be. I'm hearing things—it's happened before. Sometimes I think I hear him in crowds, or catch his cologne on a passing stranger. I've learned to ignore it.

"I'll be with you in just a moment," I call out in my best retail voice, not turning around, focusing instead on adjusting the angle of an overpriced decorative pillow.

Then I hear it—that distinctive laugh. Soft, half suppressed, but unmistakable. Leon's laugh.

The pillow slips from my suddenly numb fingers.

I turn, slow motion, like I'm moving underwater. And there they are, standing in the throw pillow section of my overpriced California home goods store: Jerome, devastating in a charcoal wool coat, and Leon, hands stuffed in his brown leather jacket pockets, wearing that crooked smile I see in my dreams.

Jerome's holding one of our handblown glass ornaments, pretending to examine it with scholarly interest, but his green eyes are fixed on me. They're both staring at me like I'm some kind of apparition, while around us, oblivious holiday shoppers browse throw blankets and argue about table runners.

My stupid reindeer antlers—mandatory store Christmas wear—suddenly feel ridiculous.

"Your hair," Jerome says softly. "It's beautiful."

A woman squeezes past them with an oversized shopping basket, complaining loudly about our cushion prices to her friend. The Christmas music switches back to Mariah Carey. And I stand there, frozen, as my carefully constructed California life collapses around me.

I back into the display, sending a pillow tumbling to the floor. The thud is distant, unimportant. All I can focus on is them. Here. In California. While I'm wearing reindeer antlers.

"What..." My voice cracks. I clear my throat and try again. "What are you doing here?"

"Well," Leon says, his smile widening, "someone told me California was beautiful in December." He glances pointedly at the fake snow in our window display. "I'm not convinced."

Jerome sets down the ornament he's been pretending to examine. "We thought perhaps..." He pauses, and I see uncertainty flicker across his face. "You wouldn't want to spend Christmas alone."

Alone. The word echoes through me like a thunderclap. My eyes burn with sudden tears.

"I..." I gesture helplessly at the store around us, at my name tag, at everything. "I have a job, I have..."

"I know, and that's amazing, Tate." Jerome steps closer, and I catch the familiar scent of his cologne. My knees go weak. "But we've been dying to see you—to know you're okay."

I flex my fingers at my sides, unable to jump into his arms and get swept away. It means so much to hear him say that, to see both him and Leon in the flesh.

A customer brushes past us, jingling with shopping bags, and I suddenly remember where we are. My boss could walk by any second. This isn't the place for… whatever this is.

"My shift ends in an hour," I hear myself say.

Jerome's eyes soften. "We'll wait."

"We've got time," Leon adds, and something in his tone makes my heart skip.

The store speakers start playing "I'll Be Home for Christmas," because apparently the universe has a sick sense of humor.

The longest hour of my life. I straighten merchandise with trembling hands, ring up customers on autopilot, all while acutely aware of them browsing nearby. They're trying to be subtle about it, but I feel their eyes on me. Every time I glance their way, one of them is watching me.

Jerome examines our French pottery collection with a slight smirk—probably comparing it to the real stuff he has at home. Leon flips through our coffee table books about Provence, and I want to tell him to stop, because those glossy photos are nothing compared to the real thing…

"Tate?" My manager Sarah appears beside me. "Your shift's over. You can clock out."

I nearly drop the ceramic vase I'm holding. "Right. Thanks."

When I emerge, they're waiting by the front doors. Jerome's holding a small shopping bag.

"You bought something?" I blurt out.

He shrugs. "That ornament. A souvenir of California."

"More like evidence," Leon mutters, and Jerome shoots him a look.

The evening air hits me as we step outside. It's actually cold for once, California's version of winter finally making an appearance. String lights twinkle in the shopping center's trees, and somewhere distant, Christmas music plays—but not Mariah Carey, thank God.

I turn to Jerome, my heart constricting at the sight of him, his broad shoulders tense beneath that damn charcoal coat. I can't believe he's here. It feels like something out of a dream, a wish I'd unconsciously made while staring at the stars from my tiny apartment window.

"Why now?" The words come out more harshly than I intended, but the hurt is still there, a raw wound that hasn't fully healed.

The corners of his mouth turn down, and I see the weight of my question in his eyes. "I wasn't ready before. I needed to sort through my own mess, and I had to be certain that…you were where you wanted to be."

I swallow hard, not trusting myself to speak. The last time I spoke to him, I was screaming *I hate you*. It hadn't been true, but in that moment, his actions felt like the greatest betrayal of my life. Jerome cared about me, and when it came down to it, he chose to aid my mom who never had.

"Every day, I've thought about you," he continues, his voice a low rumble. "I know I messed up, Tate. I should've fought harder for you, but I was afraid. Of losing you, of admitting I needed you..." He reaches out, almost touching my hand before letting his fingers fall back to his side. "Of letting someone in after so long. I was a fool, and I regret every day that I let you go."

The ache in my chest intensifies. I want to tell him that I've thought of him too—that I've lain awake at night wishing I could hear his voice, that I've seen his face in my dreams and woken up with tears on my pillow. But the hurt is still there.

He takes a breath, steeling himself. "Nothing has been the same since you left. The silence is suffocating. Every room echoes with memories of you."

My eyes burn, and I blink rapidly, refusing to cry in the middle of this shopping center.

He steps closer, his eyes searching mine. "I know I don't deserve it, but...if you could find it in your heart to forgive me, I'd spend the rest of my life making it up to you. Every day, I'd prove to you that you're the woman I love, the one I want by my side."

Love. The word hangs between us, heavy with meaning and promise. My heart pounds, and I have to force myself to breathe. "I—"

"No pressure," Leon interrupts, clearing his throat.

I blink between him and Jerome, who has hope and uncertainty in his eyes. "I need..." I begin, my voice shaking. "I need to think."

Jerome's shoulders relax slightly, and he nods. "Take all the time you need, Tate. We're staying at an Airbnb."

I nod, my mind spinning.

I feel like screaming or maybe throwing up. California has been my escape, my refuge since the day I ran away. Running from the pain, the desire, and most of all, running from the impossible choice that's always felt like a mirage: Jerome or Leon? I've spent the past two months convincing myself I'd made my choice, that I was bad to get between them, I'd chosen a new life and a future without either of them in it.

But now they're here. They came for me—for me.

From the beginning, Jerome was the rock I needed desperately. He was steadfast and protective, and of course, I developed a crush. But then he pushed me away. Opening myself up, giving my heart away, to have him throw it back in my face, made me close off that part of myself.

Then Leon kissed me, and everything changed.

I remember that kiss as if it were branded into my memory. The rain, the truck, the noise of the storm drowning out our hungry gasps. I felt like I was on fire, every nerve ending in my body igniting with a new awareness of him. And yet it was more than physical; it rocked me to my core.

Leon had always been there, attractive and infuriating, challenging me at every turn. But when I let myself look past the surface, I saw a different side of him. A vulnerability he kept hidden beneath that brooding, bad-boy act. I wanted to know *that* Leon, to see beneath the walls he'd built up. And being loved by him felt thrilling.

But my heart shies away from that realization, because how can I choose between them? How can I put into words the different kinds of love I feel, knowing it's taboo? That people would judge. There are no labels here, no neat boxes to fit this love into. It's just us, tangled up together in ways society might never accept.

The longing I feel for them both demands to be heard. And I can't suppress it anymore.

And if I can spend my life with them...

Wordlessly, I reach up to Jerome's face, hesitant. It's been so long since I've felt the heat of his skin. His beard has grown like a true mountain man, all woolly and dark. A pulse in his neck is the only movement, he's so still when I touch him.

My eyes flick to Leon, and my other hand cups his freshly shaven cheek. For a moment, he looks so frightened over what I'm about to say. Like us reconnecting and texting each other was some dream that never happened.

Christmas lights twinkle above us. The parking lot is full of families loading presents into their trunks. But in this moment, it's just the three of us. Me and my unconventional family.

"I love both of you," I blurt out, my eyes flicking between them, taking in Jerome's green eyes, the dark hair falling into Leon's face. My cheeks flame. "I've tried to forget, but I can't. I think about you both every day. It's so messed up, but I can't seem to let go of either of you."

Leon's shoulders rise and fall with each breath, barely containing himself. Jerome's gaze locks onto mine, and his hand instinctively goes up to caress the side of my neck.

Leon takes a hesitant step toward me, and his thumb brushes my wrist again. "Tate, we—"

"It's taboo." I interrupt them, needing to get it out. "What we feel for each other. It defies everything. The age gap, the fact that you're…" I gesture between them. "Family. A word people throw around like it's simple, but it's not. You're father and son, the two most important men in my life, and I…" I swallow, my mouth suddenly dry. "I'm in love with you both."

Leon's eyes close briefly, like he's steeling himself, and when they open again, they're intense. "I don't care what anyone else thinks—" He exchanges a glance with Jerome, and adds quickly, "We don't care, Tate. My heart is yours, and so is his."

I stare at him, feeling a warmth spread through my chest. I'm aware of shoppers walking by, of the world moving around us, but in this moment, nothing else matters but crushing my lips against Leon's.

It's as if every part of my body has been waiting for this, longing for the solid reality of Leon against me. I kiss him like I'm trying to convey everything I couldn't say—the nights spent lying awake, staring at my phone, the ache of missing them, the relief of having them here now. His taste, his touch, is like a drug I've been craving, and I can't get enough.

When we finally part, breathless, I step back, my heart hammering against my ribs. Jerome is watching us, an unreadable expression on his face. Leon's thumb brushes my cheek, sending another shiver down my spine, but I long to taste the love I know I'll find in Jerome's kiss.

When Jerome kisses me, it's like coming home. Gentle at first, then deeper, months of longing poured into a single kiss.

Jerome's arms encircle me, pulling me close, and I thread my fingers through his hair.

I can't contain my smile as I break away from him.

The sound of a car honking nearby startles us, and I'm suddenly self-conscious, as a stranger hurries by, offering an apologetic smile.

Jerome's arms are still around me, his breath warm on my cheek. "Let's get out of here," he murmurs, his voice husky.

They've chosen a contemporary beach house for their Airbnb, all clean lines and soaring glass panels that stretch from ground to roof. Through the crystalline barrier, the ocean dances with golden light from the sinking sun. I should be mesmerized by the view, but all I can focus on is the deafening rhythm of my heart and the way my lungs seem to have forgotten how to work.

As the door clicks shut, sealing us in our own private cocoon, I feel like I'm stepping into a new, dark world. Their eyes seem to devour me, and the air thickens with anticipation.

Leon's fingers find mine, his touch hesitant at first, then more confident as he laces our fingers together. I feel reassured by his easy touch, the warmth of his palm against mine.

But my nerves keep persisting. "Are you both sure about this?"

"Dad and I have discussed boundaries, what we're comfortable with, and we don't want you to feel uncomfortable." Leon's thumb grazes the back of my hand, and he glances up at me through thick lashes. "Just tell us if it's too much. Okay?"

Jerome's presence looms behind us, a solid force. I feel his eyes on me, gauging my comfort. He rests a hand on my shoulder, his touch light but grounding. "We want this to work, but do you really want to fuck us both, Tate?" he adds, his voice a low rumble, his eyes fixed on me with an intensity that leaves no doubt about his desire. "Doesn't have to be tonight if you're unsure."

Is he insane? Coming all the way to California and not expecting me to jump into his arms? I laugh a little. The uncertainty in me melts away, the tension finally breaking, and I look at both of them. "Just fuck the nerves out of me, please. It's been a while."

Leon pulls me into his arms, and I breathe in his familiar scent, my worries slipping away. Pressing his mouth to mine in a fevered kiss, his tongue traces the seam of my lips, and I part them willingly, deepening the kiss as our tongues duel. My fingers find their way into his hair, and I pull him closer.

Leon groans into my mouth, one hand sliding up my back to tangle in my hair. His other hand slips lower, cupping my ass and pulling me firmly against him. I gasp at the sudden contact, the evidence of his arousal clear against my stomach.

Jerome's warm breath fans my neck, and I stiffen, my senses flaring at his closeness. His fingers skim my waist, sending goose bumps up my arms. "Leon can't contain himself," he murmurs, then his mouth is on my neck, lips trailing fire across my skin. "I'm making it up to him by letting him have the first turn."

A bolt of heat courses through me at Jerome's words. His lips find the sensitive spot below my ear, and he sucks gently, his beard scratching my skin in the most delicious way. I tilt my head back, offering more of myself to him, my hands gripping Leon's shoulders.

Jerome's hand slides up my side, under my work shirt, his warm palm smoothing over my ribs. I moan at the overwhelming sensation, arching into his touch. But as soon as his fingers barely glide over my bra, he lowers them, stroking, teasing. Leon's mouth leaves mine, and his lips trail down my neck, following Jerome's path, their touches overlapping, igniting my skin.

I'm sinking into the most blissful trance ever pressed between these two men.

Leon kisses my navel, his breath fanning along the exposed skin of my lower stomach where it dips into my pants. My heart flutters, and I find myself reaching for his hands and guiding them under my shirt.

Jerome presses kisses to my hair, steadying me by the hips. I dip my head back against his shoulder, and his lips are on mine, stealing my breath away. The kiss is desperate, hungry, Jerome's tongue sweeping into my mouth like he's claiming me, and maybe he is. I cling to him, my fingers curling into his pants as he deepens the kiss. His hand slides up my back, caressing my whole body.

I break away breathlessly, giggling. "We haven't even made it to the couch. Or the bed."

Leon's fingers push my bra over my breasts, giving them a squeeze that makes me gasp. He snickers. "We'll get there, baby. Couldn't hold back."

"We're taking our sweet time with you tonight," Jerome whispers against my ear.

Just as Leon finishing unzipping my pants, Jerome spins me around to claim my mouth. It's a delicious, momentary distraction as I feel Leons fingertips brush my skin, a whisper-light touch as he pulls my pants down my thighs. His lips trail lower, leaving a scorching path below my spine. Leon pauses when he reaches the curve of my ass, and I feel his open-mouthed kiss there, his teeth grazing my skin. His hands caress my ass, thumbs gliding over my skin in a possessive manner.

"You're ours," he murmurs, his voice thick and filled with desire.

I moan softly as his worship intensifies, teeth gently biting down on the fleshy part of my ass. I'm brought back by Jerome's hands on my breasts, kneading them before reaching around to unclasp my bra. He flings it to the side, and I push my shirt over my chest, and his eyes turn hungry. He leans down, lips brushing gently against my skin, and those calloused hands begin gliding over my body, exploring the soft swell of my breasts.

Liquid heat pools in me, and I'm dying for his mouth on them. I'm barely able to keep my eyes open as I succumb to the sensations.

"Good girl, lose yourself," Jerome purrs, drawing a nipple into his mouth.

Leon's fingers find me, and I gasp, my knees buckling. I'm pressed between Leon's forceful rhythm, and Jerome's towering body, feeling both claimed and cherished. His fingers plunge into me at the perfect angle, and I'm consumed by pleasure. He curls his fingers, hitting that spot that makes me arch my back.

I moan, my head falling forward against Jerome's shoulder. My bones feel like jelly, and my thighs are trembling as they press together in response to the aching fullness. Leon's relentless fingers are pushing me closer, so close...

My release crashes over me, a tidal wave of bliss, and I whimper, my hands grabbing Jerome's shirt. Leon rises, sucking a mark into my shoulder as I come, and it's too much. I can't take any more pleasure; my body feels like an overstrung instrument.

"Fuck, I can't stand anymore," I pant, managing to detach myself from both of them. On wobbly legs, I chuck my shirt to the floor and pull the rest of my pants off.

When I reach the bedroom, I look back at Jerome and Leon expectantly. They look dumbfounded.

"Come on," I urge.

I hear a faint snicker and a *yes ma'am* before I collapse onto the king-sized bed. They pad into the room, following my lead and undressing.

My God, I'm going to sleep with two men...

As my body calms, I find the strength to sit up. Leon stands before me in all his naked glory, holding out his fingers.

"Taste yourself," he commands, and I don't hesitate, sucking his fingers into my mouth. Making sure not to break eye contact.

He grins down at me. "Good girl."

It's almost too much, the two of them standing there, unashamedly wanting. My gaze locks with Jerome's, and with a subtle tilt of his head, he gives me an unspoken command.

Jerome sits at the head of the bed as I crawl to him, I feel Leon's eyes on me as well, a scorching path down my back.

"Climb on," he says, moving me so my back is against his stomach. His hard cock pressing up between my legs, my stomach flutters.

As I settle on his lap, I feel the muscles of his thighs tense beneath me. Jerome's arms band around my waist, possessive, and his lips find my neck, his beard scratching me deliciously.

Leon moves closer, standing before us at the side of the bed, his arousal bobbing stiffly. His eyes are dark with need. He runs a hand through his hair, that frustrated yet amused expression on his face.

"Like this, belle," Jerome teases the head of his cock against my entrance, moving the slickness up and down my folds. "Warm my cock with your pussy, like when you ride it."

Oh. Well, I'm figuring out the sex position as I go, I guess.

I pitch forward and angle myself, then he holds firm against me as I slowly open around him, engulfing his hot length.

I moan, half discomfort, half pleasure. Fuck, it's been too long. I think he won't fit.

"Focus on Leon," Jerome commands, and my eyes snap to Leon now stroking his cock. "And don't look away."

I expect Leon to move closer, but he just stands there, intently watching as his dad fills me up.

"I thought Leon was getting the first turn," I pant, adjusting to the fullness of Jerome inside me. He hooks his hands under my knees, pulling them up to my chest. Leaving my already slick and swollen pussy exposed.

"He'll be the one moving," Jerome grunts. "You warm my cock, and he fucks you."

Both of them are going inside me? But how?

I give out a nervous laugh. "That doesn't seem possible. But I'd like to be proven wrong."

"Don't worry, bébé. If it doesn't feel good, you say," Jerome reassures me.

Leon kneels on the bed, lowering himself to the right height. He rubs the head of his cock against my clit and I jolt at the touch, clenching around Jerome.

"Fuck, this is going to be good," Leon comments. "You look perfect, Tate. So perfect I could eat you up."

Panting, I struggle to keep my bearings as sensations bombard me. Jerome's thickness stretches me open, his girth sparking fires along every nerve ending. The stimulation on my clit sends shockwaves through my body, and I'm teetering on the edge.

"Leon, please," I gasp, my voice cracking with need.

With a mischievous glint in his eye, Leon lowers the head of his cock, teasing my entrance. The pressure builds as he notches himself right at my center, ready to claim me. Then, slowly, he slides in, making space for his cock where there is none. I whimper as he fills me, inch by exquisite inch. His thumb finds my clit, circling it in time with his steady invasion.

"You feel so damn good," he murmurs, his breath hot against my face.

I'm full—so deliciously stuffed. It's not just the physical sensation of taking two men; it's the weight of both of them, surrounding me with their warmth, the overwhelming evidence of their desire... It makes me feel powerful. Leon's body presses closer, and his cock slides deeper, the friction against Jerome's shaft making both of them groan.

Leon's hand reaches out, gripping my shoulder as he finds his balance. Then, with a sharp thrust, he begins to move, his hips snapping as he fucks into the space Jerome's cock creates. My body becomes a playground for their desires, and I revel in it.

All I can do is take it.

My fingers clutch at the bedsheets, the fabric providing some anchor as my body is rocked by Leon's relentless thrusts. Jerome's grip on my thighs tightens, his fingers digging into my skin as his own hips move in shallow undulations, grinding his hardness against my sensitive spot.

My whimpering is swallowed by Leon's mouth, and I'm caught between them, moaning between each kiss and thrust, my voice echoing off the walls.

"You feel incredible," Jerome growls into my hair, his hips stuttering in short, sharp thrusts. "So tight and perfect."

Leon's breathing quickens, his movements becoming more desperate as he chases his release. He fucks me harder, his cock plunging deep, and my own climax begins to coil within me, a tightening spring ready to snap. I grab onto his hips, my nails scratching his skin.

"Tate, I—" Leon's words devolve into a hoarse groan as he loses his battle for control.

"Let go, Tate," Jerome urges, his voice low and commanding. "Come for us."

His words are my undoing. I cry out, my body shuddering as I climax, my pussy clenching rhythmically around both their cocks. White-hot pleasure explodes behind my eyelids, and I'm aware of Leon stiffening, his own release triggered by mine. He empties himself inside me, pulsing.

Jerome's grip tightens almost painfully on my thighs, holding me in place as he continues to grind up into me, prolonging my climax. Then he's spurting into me, and my vision goes dark as I fall into a boneless heap onto the bed, my body still shuddering with aftershocks.

Leon collapses beside us, his face flushed and eyes glazed with satisfaction. He pants, spent, his hair tousled and sexy as hell.

I try to catch my breath, my body buzzing with the aftermath of that mind-blowing orgasm. Their cum gushes out of me, making my thighs sticky. "I can't believe it…" I trail off, unable to find the words.

"Your pussy was made for us, Tate," Leon finishes, his voice hoarse. "I've never felt anything like that."

Jerome snakes an arm around my waist, tugging me back against his chest. I snuggle into him, still not quite believing what just transpired. My whole body pulses with aftershocks, tingling in my limbs.

"It was fucking sublime," Jerome says softly, his lips grazing my temple. He cups my cunt, and more of their cum pools onto his fingers. "You took us both so damn well."

"Wait." I struggle up from his lap and crawl off him. "I don't want to get the bed dirty."

Leon pipes up, his tone amused. "I think it's too late for that now, sweetheart."

"I'm a mess," I say, glancing at the stickiness on my thighs. "I'll be right back."

"Hold up." Leon grabs my hand as I get off the bed, and I turn to face him. He lets me see the full force of his desire, and it makes me weak at the knees. "Don't get any ideas about shutting us out."

"I wasn't—"

"Don't even think about hiding in your room when we're done," Jerome adds. "You're mine and Leon's now, remember?"

I laugh, breathless. Their worry amuses me. "I'm just going to wash myself off. You can join me?"

It's a heady sensation, knowing I possess the power to steal their control, to have them panting and desperate for more. These two strong men, mastered by their lust and love for me. It's intoxicating.

ARCADIA

I'm safe here. With Jerome and Leon. Their love shields me from my fears, and nothing will break us.

23

EPILOGUE

TATE

M y heels echo against the polished concrete as I complete my final walk-through of The Edison. After three years of hustling my ass off, this is it—my first solo project as lead designer, and it's a freaking boutique hotel in Downtown LA. Not too shabby for the girl who was supposed to never make it past the fries.

I run my fingers along the brass light fixture I fought tooth and nail to keep in the budget. The way it catches the late-afternoon sun, throwing honeyed patterns across the concrete—perfection. My phone buzzes in my pocket, and my stomach does that ridiculous flip it still does when I see Jerome's name.

"Just landed." His voice is gruff, probably from the eleven-hour flight. "Ready for two weeks of having me all to yourself?"

I laugh, because he knows damn well Leon's not going anywhere. "You mean besides the part where I share you with my favorite mechanic?"

He chuckles, his voice so velvety and deep, it makes me blush. "Right, speaking of sharing... I'll grab takeout from that Thai place you love."

Hell yes, I've been craving Thai so much. "Perfect. I'm just finishing up here. I'll see you in an hour, babe."

I end the call and slip my phone back into my pocket, trying to focus on my final checks and not on what awaits me at home. Delicious food, and the two men I love. The Edison is my baby, my proof that I've made it. Every detail—from the salvaged industrial windows to the hand-painted tiles in the bathrooms—represents hours of work, countless decisions, and more than a few heated debates with contractors.

But right now, all I can think about is home.

Our house sits on the outskirts of LA, close enough to the city for work but far enough out that Leon has space for his garage. Jerome made it a point to bring a slice of France back to California, and built his own rustic kitchen, Leon's custom metalwork scattered throughout—including the ridiculously oversized shower he built for *practical reasons*—and my designer's touch pulling it all together.

I pull into our driveway just as Jerome's Uber is leaving. He's standing there in his travel clothes, looking deliciously rumpled, a bag of pad Thai in one hand and his carry-on in the other. The sight of him still makes my heart stutter.

"Welcome home," I say, and he drops everything to pull me into a kiss that tastes like airplane coffee and promises. His large hand slides down my waist, settling on the swell of my belly. At five months along, there's no hiding the evidence of our love anymore, especially in a tight dress.

"How's our little Emmanuelle treating you today?" Jerome smiles.

"She's been pretty chill." I lean into Jerome's touch, his warmth seeping through my dress. "Though my groin feels like I've been doing the splits for hours. Doctor says it's normal—something about my pelvis spreading."

Jerome's hand slides lower, massaging the spot where my hip meets my thigh. "You should have called. I would've come home sooner."

"And miss your big presentation in Paris? Please." I grab the takeout bag before he can protest. "Besides, Leon's been hovering enough for both of you."

The mention of Leon makes Jerome's eyes crinkle. Our daughter will have the best of both worlds with two dads. I decided not to find out which of them has fathered her—Leon and Jerome were surprisingly on board with it.

A sharp twinge makes me wince, and Jerome's arm tightens around me. "Let's get you inside, mon coeur. Food first, then a hot bath for those aching muscles."

We barely make it through the door before Leon appears from his garage, grease-stained and grinning in his jeans and tight undershirt.

"About time," he says, kissing me before stealing the bag.

ARCADIA

I kick off my heels while Jerome and Leon head to the kitchen. The familiar domestic scene—Leon plating food while Jerome pours wine—fills me with warmth. It's so different from those tense early days at the house in France, when every glance felt loaded with unspoken words.

We've gotten used to the double takes and whispers when we're out together. Jerome's old-school neighbors back in France nearly had collective heart attacks when they figured out our arrangement. Even here in LA, where people pride themselves on being open-minded, we still get the occasional raised eyebrow or confused "So… who's the actual father?" but we stopped giving a shit about other people's opinions long ago. Our happiness isn't up for public debate.

I notice Jerome pulling out a folder from his carry-on. He spreads some papers out onto the glass dining table and begins signing them methodically.

"What's all that?" I ask, leaning over to peek.

"Just finalizing the rental agreement for Arcadia," Jerome says, his pen moving across the signature line. "The new tenants are moving in next month."

I catch sight of the address at the top of the document. **Arcadia, 8 Impasse des Roches, France.** Something tightens in my chest. That name had never really registered with me back then, too caught up in my own drama to notice the poetry of it.

"It really was Arcadian," I murmur, trailing my fingers over the embossed letterhead.

Jerome glances up, his expression softening. "What was that?"

"The house," I say, smiling at the memories. "Arcadia—a perfect, simple paradise. Ironic considering how complicated everything got."

Leon snorts from across the kitchen. "Perfect? You two were sneaking around behind my back, and I was an asshole."

"And yet," Jerome says, shuffling the papers before putting them back in the folder, "here we are."

Leon hands me a bottle of sparkling water as I sit at the table. He dishes out our food one-by-one. "How's the hotel coming along?"

"Final walk-through today. We open next week." I twirl my fork in the pad Thai, savoring the spicy aroma. "I still can't believe they gave me creative control over the whole project."

"Why not?" Jerome says, his thigh pressing against mine. "You've earned it."

Leon snorts from across the table. "She's fishing for compliments."

"I am not!" But I'm grinning, because this is us—the teasing, the casual touches, the way we orbit each other like planets locked in a perfect gravitational dance.

Jerome's hand finds my knee under the table. "The hotel will be magnificent. Just like everything else you touch."

"Everything?" Leon raises an eyebrow, and heat floods my cheeks at his meaning.

Jerome's fingers tighten on my knee. "Everything."

The air shifts, growing thick with possibility. Leon's eyes darken as he watches Jerome's hand slide higher on my thigh. My breath catches as Jerome leans in, his lips brushing my ear.

"Dinner first," he murmurs. "Then I'll teach Leon how to properly massage your feet in the bath."

Leon's eyes widen before narrowing. "Don't shit on my technique. She likes it."

Jerome's lips press into a line. "That's not what I heard last time, it was *more to the left, no—too soft, harder.*"

Leon's resulting groan and eye roll makes me chuckle. Some things never change—like how these two men still make my heart race, how Jerome's touch still sets my skin on fire, and how Leon's smirk still makes me weak in the knees.

But some things do change—like the nursery upstairs we painted together, the tiny clothes folded in drawers, and the way Jerome and Leon want to build a bigger family with me.

THE END.

KEEP READING FOR A PREVIEW OF BOOK
TWO IN THE STEP DUET

Blackmoor

COMING SPRING 2026

24

BLACKMOOR | CHAPTER 1

INDIANA

It's a four-hour train ride to Blackmoor from London. The only thing I know about Blackmoor is that it sits in the Lake District National Park and contains the country's biggest lake.

"Look at this like it's a holiday." Nikola says as the train rattles on the tracks. "I know it's not what you wanted. But you get to see the English countryside and stay in an old manor."

I appreciate Nikola trying to cheer me up. But being bound to a wheel chair means I can't move around as much as I'd like.

I'm not supposed to be here, I'm supposed to be dancing at the royal ballet theatre. It's the whole reason I moved to the UK in the first place.

"You just reminded me I need to tell him I'm in a wheel-chair." I pull out my phone and quickly text my uncle. I'm assuming my sister Summer told him—as all this was her idea—but I better text just in case.

Nikola leans back in her seat, staring out the window. "Surely they'd have an elevator? An old manor can have one installed."

"I hope he does." But I doubt it.

The rhythmic clattering of wheels against iron rails becomes oddly soothing. I watch the scenery whip past, clusters of houses with their charming brick façades line the tracks. The occasional sheep grazes lazily in the fields, unfazed. Clouds hang heavy overhead, casting shadows that flicker across the landscape.

Just as I find myself drifting off, a flash of doubt stirs within me; will I ever dance again?

I focus on my breathing as Nikola reads aloud from her book, her voice blending into the sound of the train. It's comforting to have her here; she immediately came to my side when I'd landed wrong on stage. And she's going out of her own way to take me to Blackmoor.

After what feels like ages, the train screeches to a halt.

Nikola steers me off the train onto the platform, and we make our way through the small station until we're out the front. Among buses and black cabs, one round man in particular holds a cardboard sign with my name above his head.

"Indie, this is your taxi driver." Nikola mutters to me as she approaches the man. "Hello sir."

"Hello loveys." He beams in a thick Irish accent, he looks down at me and shakes my hand. "It's good to meet you Indiana. You can call me Clint, I'm your uncle's personal cabbie."

"Likewise Clint." I smile.

He then outstretches his hand to Nikola. "And what's your name?"

She shakes his hand. "I'm Indiana's train chauffeur, Nikola."

That makes Clint chuckle.

"Let me help you with your bags." Clint takes my luggage and loads it into his black cab. The trunk slams shut with a metallic thud that echoes across the nearly empty parking lot.

Nikola helps me into the back seat, folding my wheelchair with practiced ease. "Text me when you get there, okay?"

My throat tightens. "Do you really have to leave?"

She gives me a sympathetic look. "Indie, you know I have to get back to London." She squeezes my hand. "I'm only a phone call away."

I wish that comforted me, I'm about to be surrounded by strangers and my head is spiraling. The uncle I've never met. The one who suddenly appeared in my life after my injury, offering his home as a place to recover. I grip Nikola's hand tighter, not wanting to let go of the last person I know.

"Right then." Clint settles into the driver's seat. "It's about an hour's drive to Blackmoor Manor. The roads get a bit windy, so let me know if you need me to slow down."

Nikola gives me one last hug through the window. "Remember what the doctor said. Rest, physio exercises, and no pushing yourself too hard."

I watch her grow smaller in the side mirror as we pull away from the station. The familiar ache in my foot throbs, and I slump back in the seat.

"Your uncle's quite excited to meet you." Clint's voice breaks through my thoughts. "Been talking about nothing else for days."

Interesting. I don't know how to feel about that. "What's he like?" The question slips out before I can stop it.

"Ah, he's a bit of a recluse, truth be told. Keeps to himself mostly, but he's a good man." Clint navigates through the narrow cobblestone streets, the aged stone buildings lining the quiet thoroughfares. "Spends most of his time in his library or the east wing."

The east wing. Like something out of a Gothic novel. "How big is this manor exactly?"

"Three floors, plus the attics and cellars. Though some parts haven't been used in years." He catches my eye in the rearview mirror. "It's rumored to host many spirits."

The buildings thin out as we leave the town behind, replaced by rolling moors and ancient stone walls. The first drops of rain splatter against the windshield, and within seconds, the drizzle transforms into sheets of water, drumming against the roof of the cab. The countryside blurs into a watercolor painting of greens and grays.

"Ah, typical English weather." Clint flicks on the wipers. "You'll get used to it."

I press my forehead against the cool glass, watching rivulets race down the window. The landscape grows wilder with each passing mile. Stone walls give way to untamed hedgerows. Rolling hills morph into brooding mountains that pierce the low-hanging clouds.

I massage my injured foot through my sock, feeling the raised scar tissue beneath the fabric. Six months of my life, gone in an instant. One bad landing. One moment of lost focus.

The cab rounds a bend, and lightning splits the sky. In that brief flash, I glimpse something through the curtain of rain – a tower, maybe? But it vanishes as quickly as it appears.

"Almost there now." Clint slows the cab as we approach a set of imposing iron gates. They swing open silently, revealing a long gravel driveway flanked by towering oak trees.

"Your uncle mentioned you're a dancer?" Clint's voice seems too loud in the enclosed space.

"Yeah." The word tastes bitter. "I hope I'm still a dancer."

Another flash of lightning, and this time I see it clearly. Blackmoor Manor looms ahead. It's massive, a sprawling Victorian mansion with turrets that claw at the storm-ravaged sky.

"Home sweet home." Clint pulls up to the front steps.

The scent of wet earth hits me when Clint opens the cab door, thunder rumbling softly. There's no rest from the bad weather as rain pummels down on the pebbled driveway. But the cab is shielded under a large tree that sits at the front of the house.

"Sit tight, lovey. I'll get your wheelchair and luggage." Clint says in a gruff voice as he hurries to the boot.

I murmur my thanks, and take in the house—which looks nothing like the houses back home. My step-uncle described it as a country house, not a Gothic Victorian mansion. It's three stories high just like Cliff said, with ivy-clad walls made out of natural stone pavers weathered by time, arching neo-gothic windows line the front of the house.

A single light flickers above the grand front door, and three men shielded by umbrellas step out. I can't make out what they look like through the downpour, but then I see them hurriedly place a makeshift ramp down the small front steps before they approach the cab.

"You must be Miss Hart." One of the men says while the other two help Clint. He looks about sixty with his fraying gray hairline, and I note his freshly pressed waistcoat and jacket, suddenly feeling under dressed. But his smile is warm and inviting. "I'm Peter, your uncle's head of staff. He's just inside."

My eyes flick to the front door and my stomach sinks. Heath couldn't even be bothered to step outside his house to get me, that's exactly the kind of rich asshole that makes others do everything for him. This already signifies I'm nothing but a burden. All I want to do is sigh, but I manage a smile and shake Peter's hand. "Nice to meet you."

"All right, lass." Clint comes forward with my wheelchair until it's by the car door, and Peter gestures for my hand. Heat rises to my cheeks, and I see one of the other men trailing my suitcase to the front door while the other opens an umbrella above Peter and I. It feels weird being attended to like this. I take Peter's hand, using my good leg to step down into the wheelchair.

Clint slams the boot and swaggers back around to the drivers side of the cab as he addresses Peter. "Tell that bastard next time he should pick up his injured niece from the train station." My eyes widen at his serious tone, but there's a note of casual teasing behind it, as well as the smug grin stretching his face. "And give him a big hug for me."

Peter snickers, gesturing for the other staff member to hand him something. "He knows that very well, Clint. He sends his best regards."

Clint's face lights up at the bottle of Guinness handed to him. "You beauty." He laughs, before shaking the bottle at the house, as if Heath can hear him. "He also owes me a drink at the pub!"

Peter starts escorting me to the front door. "I'll pass it on. Thank you Clint, and drive safe."

"Thank you for driving me." I shout, as Clint starts the engine and gives us a wave, rolling down the driveway.

The rainfall is nothing but a soft pelt in the foyer as the door seals shut. I have to arch my chin up to get the full scale of the high ceiling. A small chandelier hangs above, and my eyes skim the mahogany wood paneling covering the lower parts of the walls, but the stair case is full wood. A gorgeous iron lamp post adorns the handrail at the landing.

And that's when I spot him.

I don't know what I was expecting Heath Stoker to look like, since there's no blood relation between him and my dad. Heath doesn't have the rich brown hair or the sun bronzed skin of my dad's side. Instead, his complexion is so pale the dark hollows under his eyes stand out. His slight salt and pepper beard makes him look rugged, and cold blue eyes stare back at me under a furrowed brow.

"Uncle Heath?" I say because I don't like the prolonged silence. He mustn't be happy that I'm here.

"Yes," he blinks, his taunt hand letting go of the lamp. He descends the last few steps and outstretches his hand to me. "Sorry, I'm a bit delirious after my late flight. It's nice to finally put a name to a face, Indiana."

I feel like I should be hugging Heath since we're family, but that would be no less awkward than this handshake. His grip is firm, and I give him a tight lipped smile.

We stay there for a moment until one of the staff members begins dragging my suitcase up the stairs.

How the hell am I getting to the second floor?

"Sir, we'll get a ramp." Peter appears at Heath's side, then he looks to me. "I apologize for being unprepared. We didn't know you were in a wheelchair."

As annoying as it is, I can't blame them if they didn't know. "That's all right. Is there a bedroom on the ground floor?"

"No." Heath's voice is stern. "And don't worry about the ramp for now, Peter. We'll have to make a custom one for these stairs. I'll carry you up."

I'd rather sleep in the kitchen then have Heath carry me. My heart races, and suddenly I don't want to be here. It'd be easier if I just stayed at the hospital in London. But since Heath's offered, I feel like I can't refuse. It'd be rude, and I'm tired as it is. "Okay."

None of the staff argue against Heath's idea. I try not to look affected as he gets close, but his scent washes over me. Cedar wood and bergamot, right on the flesh of his neck. Or it's in the mousse in his hair.

I curl my arm over his shoulder, and he's gathering my legs and hoisting me up before I know it. His breath fans across my face as he carries me up the stairs, a triumphant sound escaping his throat.

The cold wet weather that had soaked into me feels like a distant memory as Heath's body heat transfers to me. I keep my eyes focused on the railing as we ascend.

"You're light as a feather." He comments.

"I'm a ballerina." I don't mean to say I'm underweight—a common issue in the ballet world—but my ballet partners need to be able to lift me up like it's nothing.

He quirks a brow. "You're used to being lifted up then."

I nod. It's more than that. It's the lack of physical boundaries. Putting all my trust in the person that's going to lift me, hold me, or touch me.

My heart shouldn't be racing over being this close to Heath. I'm used to it, and yet I can't look him in the eye.

We reach the second floor, and two men haul my wheelchair up the stairs. Heath carefully places me down into the wheelchair. Without missing a beat, he takes a right, steering me down what appears to be a hallway running through open rooms.

They're nothing short of breathtaking—more ornate plasterwork and crystal chandeliers that catch the light. Richly polished wooden floors stretch beneath antique Persian rugs in deep burgundies and blues. Floor-to-ceiling windows draped in heavy velvet allow filtered light to illuminate oil paintings in gilded frames. Each room flows into the next through arched doorways, creating a sense of endlessness.

"How many rooms are there?" I ask in awe.

Heath thinks for a moment. "There are twenty rooms."

That's insane, and I almost smile. "Isn't it just you and your son?"

Heath chuckles. "Some are secret rooms."

So, what? There's extra empty space? "Seems like overkill."

"You have to think about how the Victorian's lived. They had subordinates working under them who lived in these rooms—primarily on the ground floor—as well as secret passage ways. My Great grandfather liked hosting parties too, so certain entertainments needed separate rooms." He elaborates as we turn into a room. "But I'll give you a tour of the full property tomorrow."

I'm immediately struck by a gentle fragrance as we enter – aged wood mingling with fresh lavender. It's both nostalgic and welcoming, like stepping into a cherished memory.

A large four poster bed catches my eye, taking up the space. It's draped in soft gauzy curtains. Original wood paneling lines the walls, and above the wainscoting, emerald wallpaper adorned with golden accents catches the light. I lean forward in my chair, fascinated by the intricate details – delicate golden birds perched among blossoming flowers and twisting vines.

"This is your room." Heath announces.

I nod my head, still taking everything in. In the corner, I notice the staff member who carried my suitcase earlier. He methodically unpacks my belongings, arranging them with practiced efficiency in the antique dresser. Our eyes meet briefly, and he gives a respectful nod before continuing his work. I shift uncomfortably in my chair, watching a stranger handle my intimate belongings. My cheeks warm with embarrassment as I spot him carefully placing my underwear in a drawer.

My attention shifts to a stunning bay window with its generous window seat, overlooking a massive lake in the distance from the manor. A small collection of books sits invitingly on the cushioned bench, their spines showing the gentle wear of frequent reading.

"This is beautiful," I breathe, unable to hide my awe. Despite my initial reservations about coming here, this room feels like it could become a sanctuary.

Heath moves toward the antique desk in the corner, where I notice an older laptop and what looks like a small wireless hotspot device. He picks it up, turning it over in his hands.

"I've set this up for you," he says, placing the hotspot on the nightstand. "Internet connection can be... challenging out here in the countryside. The manor's stone walls don't help matters." His tone is casual but authoritative. "I had to set up special equipment in my study downstairs for my university lectures. This should give you basic access, though I'm afraid the bandwidth is quite limited."

He taps the small display on the device. "You'll have enough for some things. Heavy streaming would overload our system out here." He offers a thin smile that doesn't quite reach his eyes. "My study has the strongest connection, of course. You're welcome to use it when I'm not teaching, if you need anything more substantial."

"Thank you." The words come out softer than I intend. "For everything. The room, letting me stay here..."

"It's the least I can do for family." Heath's eyes lock onto mine, and something in his gaze makes my breath catch. There's an intensity there that seems at odds with his casual tone. "Though I must admit, when your father contacted me about your situation, I was... intrigued."

"You've never met my dad before?"

"No." Heath moves to the window, his reflection ghosting across the rain-streaked glass. "Your father and I have only corresponded through email since he married my step-sister." He turns back to me, and raindrops cast shifting shadows across his face. "But I've always believed in helping family, even those I haven't met."

Thunder rumbles outside, and I jump slightly in my chair. Heath notices, his lips curving into what might be amusement.

"You'll get used to the storms. This house lacks proper soundproofing." He steps closer, and I catch that cedar scent again. "Did Clint tell you the spooky stories?"

I shrug. "He made it sound that way."

He laughs, but it's not entirely warm. "Don't worry. You might hear some strange noises at night," his hand brushes my shoulder as he moves past. "But it's the old pipes, mostly. Or the rats."

The staff member finishes with my unpacking and quietly exits before Heath continues.

"Rats?"

"In the attic. Little buggers won't die." he sighs in frustration, before moving towards the door. "I should let you rest. Peter will see you shortly. Do you need anything else to make yourself comfortable?" His eyes sweep over me in question.

For a moment, I contemplate. "I need duck tape and a plastic bag to keep my foot dry when I shower."

"Right, I'll let Peter know." He smiles. "Dinner is at seven."

The door closes behind him with a soft click, and I release a breath I didn't realize I was holding.

I wheel myself to the window seat, watching raindrops race down the glass. The lake in the distance is a steel-gray mirror, reflecting the turbulent sky.

My phone buzzes in my pocket. A text from Nikola: "Made it back to London. How's the manor?"

I start typing "It's creepy" but delete it. Because it is creepy, in the most fascinating way. And Heath... there's something about him that sets me on edge, makes my skin prickle with awareness. Like he's watching me even when he's not in the room.

As I wheel myself back from the window, my chair bumps the dresser. A picture frame wobbles, then crashes to the floor with a sharp sound that makes me flinch.

"Damn it." I glance toward the door, hoping no one heard. The last thing I need is for Heath to think I'm already destroying his property.

I lean down carefully, stretching as far as I can without falling out of my chair. My fingers graze the edge of the ornate silver frame. The glass is cracked, spider-webbing across the black and white landscape photo. When I lift it, the backing shifts loose in my hand.

Something slips out from behind the photograph—a small square of paper that flutters to the floor just within my reach. I pick it up, expecting to find a note or perhaps an older photo.

It's a sonogram.

I stare at the grainy black and white image, immediately recognizing the unmistakable outline of not one, but two tiny forms. Twins, nestled together in the womb. The date printed along the border is faded, unreadable.

A chill runs through me despite the room's warmth. Why would someone hide this? And in my room of all places?

I turn the sonogram over, looking for a name, but find nothing. Just two unborn babies and a date, hidden away behind a picture as if someone wanted to forget they existed.

Or as if someone wanted to forget that one of them existed.

The realization settles over me like a shadow. Heath mentioned he had a son, but only one. What happened to the other baby in this picture?

ACKNOWLEDGEMENTS

It takes a tribe to publish a book, even if it's self-published. So I want to thank manyyy people. Thank you to Hannah from English Proper Editing Services. Thank you Ritika and Maddi for beta reading. Oopsie Daisy Edits for copyediting. You guys sorted out the rough parts of this story, and I truly appreciate your skill, feedback, and enthusiasm for Tate, Leon and Jerome's story.

To all the online readers who read this story before I published it. You help me see this story to end.

To all the ARC readers, I'm so happy you gave my book a chance, your reviews helped finalize the story you're seeing now.

My family, I know you won't read this (unless you're lucky and I let you) but thanks for always supporting my creative endeavors.

FROM THE AUTHOR

I didn't write *Arcadia* to be safe.

I wrote it because I couldn't stop thinking about that feeling, when something shifts and you know you should pull back... but you don't.

When attention lingers a little too long.
When someone sees you in a way you didn't expect.
When you realize you want something that doesn't fit into the version of yourself you thought you were.

Tate's story came from that space.

Not just desire, but confusion. Loneliness. The kind of curiosity that doesn't feel dangerous at first... until it is.

I think a lot of us have had moments like that. Wanting something and questioning yourself for it at the same time.

This book doesn't try to clean that up or make it easy.

It just sits in it.

If you've ever felt pulled in two directions at once—between what you want and what you think you should want—you'll probably understand her more than you expect to.

And if you don't... you might want to ask yourself what you're avoiding.

ARCADIA

—Saint

ABOUT THE AUTHOR

Saint Bryde writes romance that doesn't behave.

Her stories explore what happens when boundaries blur and desire stops asking for permission. She's drawn to complicated dynamics, morally messy characters, and the kind of chemistry that builds slowly, until it can't be ignored.

Her work leans into tension over spectacle. Into restraint before release. Into the moments where characters understand exactly what they're doing… and do it anyway.

Set against immersive backdrops—from isolated countryside homes to places where no one is watching—her books focus on proximity, pressure, and the emotional consequences of getting too close.

Readers who enjoy taboo tension, slow-building obsession, and emotionally charged relationships will feel right at home.

When she's not writing, she works with animals and spends her time in quiet spaces that tend to inspire her most intense stories.

To get a deleted Chapter 1 from Jerome's POV, sign up for Saint's newsletter!

You can also follow Saint on her socials.

ALSO BY

STEP DUET

Arcadia: A Spicy Forbidden Romance
Blackmoor (Coming soon)

***

STANDALONES

Bound to the Jinni
Filthy Punk

PLAYLIST

- SAY YES TO HEAVEN BY LANA DEL REY
- GUILTY AS SIN BY TAYLOR SWIFT
- LEAD POISONING BY ETHEL CAIN
- À QUOI ÇA SERT? BY FRANÇOISE HARDY
- WILDEST DREAMS BY TAYLOR SWIFT
- 2 HANDS BY TATE MCRAE
- GOOD LUCK BABE BY CHAPPEL ROAN
- CALIFORNIA BY CHAPPEL ROAN